"Flick this noise." Two-Bit lunged at Nova.

She pushed him back with her mind, sending him head over heels to the back of the lobby.

"Stay down." She was practically pleading now. "If you don't get up, I won't hurt you."

Poppo, realizing that there was no way for him to win this, dropped his weapon and held up his arms. "Yeah, okay. Crap, Fagin ain't payin' me 'nough for this."

Two-Bit wasn't as bright as Poppo, and couldn't see past the fact that a teenaged curve knocked him on his ass without even touching him. He got to his feet and charged again.

Nova knocked Poppo into him and they both fell to the floor.

His anger now palpable, Two-Bit whipped out his P100 and placed the muzzle right in Poppo's ear. "You flickin' with me, stud? Huh?"

"I didn't do nothin', I swear, Two-Bit, that curve did it, I'm tellin' you, I—"

"Don't do it!" Nova cried, realizing that Two-Bit intended to pull the trigger.

She wasn't fast enough to stop it.

NOVA

KEITH R.A. DeCANDIDO

POCKET **STAR** BOOKS
New York   London   Toronto   Syndey   Tarsonis

An *Original* Publication of POCKET BOOKS

 A Pocket Star Book published by
POCKET BOOKS, a division of Simon & Schuster, Inc.
1230 Avenue of the Americas, New York, NY 10020

This book is a work of fiction. Names, characters, places and incidents are products of the author's imagination or are used fictitiously. Any resemblance to actual events or locales or persons, living or dead, is entirely coincidental.

ISBN-13: 978-0-7434-7134-3
ISBN-10:   0-7434-7134-2

This Pocket Star Books paperback edition December 2006

10   9   8   7   6   5   4   3   2

POCKET STAR BOOKS and colophon are registered trademarks of Simon & Schuster, Inc.

Cover art by Glenn Rane

Manufactured in the United States of America

For information regarding special discounts for bulk purchases, please contact Simon & Schuster Special Sales at 1-800-456-6798 or business@simonandschuster.com.

INTRODUCTION

I'm very proud of this book. I'm especially proud of what it represents. Sometimes, amidst the general insanity of the video game business, you just have to latch on to a good idea and follow it wherever it leads.

The game *StarCraft: Ghost*, on hiatus as of the time of this writing, has been in development for almost as long as the PS2 and other console platforms have been on store shelves. Designing and building this game was a pretty crazy process. While there were many reasons for the game's development taking as long as it did, one key design element always stood out and gave us inspiration to keep pushing onward:

Ghosts are very, very cool.

These nearly superhuman agents who stalk unseen across raging battlefields were a major component of the *StarCraft* mythos. Not only were these units fun to play with, but they seemed to have a certain mystique that made them stand out amidst all the other (bigger and more colorful) units in the game—*I personally think it was the stunning voice-work*. While we knew that a Ghost would make the perfect focal point for a console game, we were faced with a lot of options about how to bring our new Ghost character to life.

A lot of folks thought it would have been cool to use Sarah Kerrigan, arguably *StarCraft*'s most famous Ghost, and have the game focus on her origins. While that could have been a killer direction (pardon the pun), we all know how Kerrigan's story ends. Ultimately, we decided to create a new character whose origins—and more importantly, whose destiny—wasn't yet set in stone.

Thus, young Nova was born. Her personality and visual design were the result of a lot of hard work by a talented group of people. The spunky, lethal Nova was one of the first characters we had ever created that would take center stage in her own game and really anchor *StarCraft: Ghost* as a new part of the *StarCraft* setting. Needless to say, we were immensely proud of how she turned out.

I'm very pleased that we're finally able to tell her story and show the world just who this enigmatic young character is—and what events molded her into one of the most dangerous assassins in the universe.

Of course, this take would not have been possible without the amazing talents of Keith DeCandido. Keith seemed to have a deep affinity for this character, and he not only brought out all the dark, disturbing nuances of Nova's past—but provided a fresh new look at the gritty underbelly of the *StarCraft* setting as well. I can't imagine this story in anyone else's hands.

So, while we might not be seeing *StarCraft: Ghost* as a video game anytime soon, we will definitely be following Nova's continued adventures through novels just like this one.

Enjoy! I hope y'all dig it!

Chris Metzen
Vice President, Creative Development
Blizzard Entertainment
May 2006

To the staff of the
No. 1 Merrion Street Pub
in Dublin, Ireland,
who kept the pints coming
when I needed them . . .

ACKNOWLEDGMENTS

As with my *Warcraft* novel *Cycle of Hatred*, the most thanks have to go to Chris Metzen of Blizzard Games. I've worked with dozens of licensors in my career, and none of them can match Chris's enthusiasm, energy, and creativity. The usual thanks also to editor Marco Palmieri, publisher Scott Shannon, agent Lucienne Diver, and GraceAnne Andreassi DeCandido, my ever-reliable first reader.

A lot of what is done with telepathy in this novel is influenced by two seminal works of my misspent youth: *X-Men* comics, which were a constant companion throughout my teen years, and the novel *The Demolished Man*, which I read as a seventeen-year-old, and which blew my brain out one ear and stuffed it back in through my nostrils. So a big tip of the ol' fedora must go to Chris Claremont and the late Alfred Bester. Thanks also to fellow *StarCraft* novelist Jeff Grubb, from whose *Liberty's Crusade* I, uh, borrowed the news report in Chapter 3.

Also thanks to the various locales in three different

countries where this book was written, including the
Corus Hotel in Glasgow, Scotland; the No. 1 Merrion
Street Pub and the Mont Clare Hotel in Dublin, Ireland;
the Duane/Morwood estate in Grangecon, Ireland; the
Hyatt Regency Atlanta in Georgia; assorted planes,
trains, stations, and airports to and from those places;
and the usual café and Starbucks in New York City, two
locales where a great deal of my writing gets done these
days.

The usual thanks must go to the Forebearance (for
perpetual encouragement), the Geek Patrol (for the
usual goofiness), the noble folk of CGAG (for helpful
critique), *Kyoshi* Paul and everyone at the dojo (for
beating my body and spirit into shape), and the
Malibu gang, the Elitist Bastards, the Inkwell After
Hours folks, and the Novelscribes loonies (for all the
wonderful online conversations).

And finally thanks to them that live with me, both
human and feline, for constant encouragement.

HISTORIAN'S NOTE

This novel takes place in the three years leading up to the *StarCraft: Ghost* game. Much of it is roughly simultaneous with the novel *StarCraft: Liberty's Crusade* by Jeff Grubb.

PROLOGUE

And what rough beast, its hour come round at last,
Slouches towards Bethlehem to be born?
—William Butler Yeats, "The Second Coming"

AS SOON AS SHE FELT CLIFF NADANER'S MIND,
Nova knew that she could destroy her family's murderer with but a thought.

She'd spent days working her way through the
humid jungles of the smallest of the ten continents of
Tyrador VIII. *Funny how I tried so hard to avoid this*
planet's twin, and now I wind up here, she had thought
when the drop-pod left her smack in the middle of the
densest part of the jungle—before the rebels had a
chance to lock onto the tiny pod, or so her superiors
on the ship in high orbit insisted. The eighth planet in
orbit of Tyrador was locked in a gravitational dance
with the ninth planet, similar to that of a regular
planet and a moon, but both worlds were of sufficient
size to sustain life. They also both had absurd
extremes of climate, thanks to their proximity to each
other—if Nova were to travel only a few kilometers
south, farther from Tyrador VIII's equator, the temperature would lower thirty degrees, the humidity

would all but disappear, and she'd need to adjust her suit's temperature control in the other direction.

For now, though, the formfitting white-with-navy-blue-trim suit—issued by Director Bick at the Ghost Academy when her training period had come to an end—was set to keep her cool, which it did, up to a point. The suit covered every inch of her flesh save her head. The circuitry woven throughout the suit's fabric might interfere with Nova's telepathy, and since her telepathy was pretty much the entire reason *why* she was training to become a Ghost, it wouldn't do to interfere with *that*. This suit wasn't quite the complete model she would be using when she finished this final assignment and officially became a Ghost—for one thing, the circuitry that allowed the suit to go into stealth mode had yet to be installed. Once that happened, Nova would be able to move about virtually undetected—certainly invisible to plain sight and most passive scans.

But she wasn't ready for that yet. First she had to accomplish this mission.

The suit's design meant that sweat dripped into her eyes and plastered the bangs of her blond hair to her forehead. The ponytail she kept the rest of her hair in tugged on her skull like a heavy damp rope hanging off the back of her head. *At least the rest of my body is comfortable.*

The suit's stealth mode would probably have been redundant in this jungle in any case. The flora of Tyrador VIII was so thick, and the humid air so hazy, she only knew what was a meter in front of her from the sensor display on the suit's wrist unit.

Intelligence Section had told her that Cliff Nadaner was headquartered somewhere in the jungle on this planet. They weren't completely sure where—Nova had already learned that the first half of IS's designation was a misnomer—but they had intercepted several communiqués that their cryptographers insisted used the code tagged for Nadaner.

In the waning days of the Confederacy, Nadaner was one of many agitators who spoke out against the Old Families and the Council and the Confederacy in general. He was far from the only one who did so. The most successful, of course, was the leader of the Sons of Korhal, Arcturus Mengsk—in fact, he was so successful that he actually did overthrow the Confederacy of Man and replaced it with the Terran Dominion, of which he was now the emperor and supreme leader. Nadaner did somewhat more poorly in the field of achieving political change, though he was very skilled at causing trouble and killing people.

Days of plowing through the jungle had revealed nothing. All Nova was picking up was random background radiation, plus signals from the various satellites in orbit of the planet, holographic signals from various wild animals that scientists had tagged for study in their natural habitat, and faint electromagnetic signatures from the outer reaches of this continent or one of the other nine more densely populated ones. All of it matched existing Tyrador VIII records and therefore could be discarded as not belonging to the rebels. And now she was reading a completely dead zone about half a kilometer ahead, at the extreme range of the sensors in her suit. *This is starting to get frustrating.*

She had completely lost track of time. Had it been four days? Five? Impossible to tell, since this planet's fast orbit gave it a shorter day than what she was accustomed to on Tarsonis, with its twenty-seven-hour day. She supposed she could have checked the computer built into her suit, but for some reason she thought that would be cheating.

Let's see, I've been eating pretty steadily, more or less on track for three meals a day, and I've gone through fourteen of the ninety ration packs they gave me, so that makes—

Then, suddenly, it hit her. *A dead zone.*

She adjusted the sensors from passive scan to active scan. Sure enough, they didn't pick up a thing—nothing from the satellites, nothing from the animal tags, nothing from the cities farther south.

Nothing at all.

Nova smiled. She cast her mind outward gently and surgically—not forcefully and sloppily, the way she always had back in the Gutter—and sought out the mind of the man who ordered the death of her family.

Nadaner had not actually committed the murder himself. That was done by a man named Gustavo McBain, a former welder who was working a construction contract on Mar Sara when the Confederates

ordered the destruction of Korhal IV—an action that
killed McBain's entire family, including his pregnant
wife Daniella, their daughter Natasha, and their
unborn son. McBain had sworn that the Confederacy
of Man would pay for that action. However, instead of
joining Mengsk—himself the child of a victim of
Korhal IV's bombardment with nuclear weapons—he
hooked up with Cliff Nadaner's merry band of agitators.

Nova learned all that when she killed McBain.
Telepathy made it impossible for a killer not to know
her victim intimately. McBain's last thoughts were of
Daniella, Natasha, and his never-named son.

Now, three years later, having come to the end of
her Ghost training, her "graduation" assignment,
which came from Emperor Mengsk himself, was to be
dropped in the middle of Tyrador VIII's jungle and to
seek, locate, and destroy the rest of Nadaner's group.
Mengsk had even less patience for rebel groups than
the government his own rebel group had overthrown.

Within five minutes, she found the thoughts she
was looking for. It wasn't hard, once she had a general
location to focus on, especially since they were the
first higher-order thoughts she'd come across since
the drop-pod opened up and disintegrated. (Couldn't
risk Dominion tech getting into the wrong hands,
after all. If she completed her mission, they'd send a
ship to extract her, since then they could land a ship
without risk, as Nadaner's people would be dead. If
she didn't complete it, she'd be dead, and her suit was

designed to do to her what was done to the drop-pod if her lifesigns ceased. Couldn't risk Dominion telepaths getting into the wrong hands, either, dead or alive.)

It was Nadaner and a dozen of his associates, but their thoughts were focused on Nadaner—those that were focused at all. The man himself was chanting something. No, singing. He was singing a song, and half his people were drunk, no doubt secure in the knowledge that no one would find them in their jungle location, with its dampening field blocking any signals. It probably never occurred to them that an absence of signals would be just as big a signpost.

Complacent people are easier to kill, she thought, parrotting back one of Sergeant Hartley's innumerable one-sentence life lessons.

She was to kill them from a distance, using telepathy. Yes, her training was complete, and she should have been able to take down Nadaner and his people physically with little difficulty—especially since half of them were three sheets to the wind—but that wasn't her assignment.

The mission was to get close enough to feel their minds clearly and then kill them psionically.

For the next two hours, Nova ran through the jungle, getting closer to her goal. After her "graduation," the suit would be able to increase her speed, allowing her to run this same distance in a quarter of the time, but that circuitry hadn't been installed, either.

The hell with the mission. That slike ordered McBain and

the rest of his little gang of killers to murder my family. I want to see his face when I kill him.

Soon, she reached the dead zone. She could hear Nadaner's thoughts as clearly as if he'd been whispering in her ear. He'd finished singing and was now telling a story of one of his exploits in the Confederate Marines before he got fed up, quit, and started his revolution, a story that Nova knew was about ninety percent fabrication. He had been in the Marines, and he had been on Antiga Prime once, but that was where his story's intersection with reality ended.

With just one thought, she could kill him. End him right there. *You don't need to see his face, you can feel his mind! You'll know he's dead with far more surety than if you just saw him, his eyes rolling up in his head, blood leaking out of his eyes and ears and nose from the brain hemorrhaging. And it's not like you haven't done it before. Kill him now.*

Suddenly, she realized what day it was. *Fourteen packs, which means the better part of three days.*

Which means today's my eighteenth birthday.

It's been three years to the day since Daddy told me I was coming to this very star system.

She shook her head, even as Nadaner finished this story and started another one, which held even less truth than the first. A tear ran slowly down Nova's cheek.

It was such a good party, too. . . .

PART ONE

Things fall apart; the centre cannot hold;
Mere anarchy is loosed upon the world.
—William Butler Yeats, "The Second Coming"

CHAPTER 1

CONSTANTINO TERRA HAD LONG SINCE GIVEN UP
throwing surprise parties for his daughter. She always
knew they were coming and ruined the surprise. *In
retrospect*, he thought, *that should've been the first clue*.
But other evidence had also presented itself, and soon
Constantino realized that his darling Nova was a
telepath.

Were he someone else, Constantino would have
been forced to give in to the inevitable and turn his
daughter over to the military for proper training. But
the Terras were one of the Old Families, descended
from the commanders of the original colony ships that
had brought humanity to this part of space from Earth
generations ago. The Old Families did not turn their
daughters over to anyone they didn't want to.

Her mother agreed. There was little else that
Constantino and Annabella Terra agreed upon, not
that they needed to agree on anything save that they
remain married. Like most Old Family marriages,

theirs was based on financial expediency, a union of two fortunes that would work better together than apart, and would also produce worthy heirs. Those heirs were created by an injection of Constantino's seed into Bella's body, thus saving him the distasteful task of sleeping with the wretched woman. He had his mistress for that, just as she had her jig, as was proper. Constantino had heard whispers among the servants that Bella was growing tired of her jig and seeking out other household employees for her sexual sport. But then, he'd also gotten word of similar rumors regarding him and his beloved Eleftheria, and he would never betray her trust. The mistress-husband bond—and the jig-wife bond, for that matter—was far too strong and important to the household for him to consider sundering it.

Instead of his daughter's spending her fifteenth birthday in some government facility being trained to use her psionic talents as a tool against the alien threats the Confederacy now faced, she was instead being thrown the finest party since . . . well, since the last time one of the Old Families' children had a birthday. It was a competition, in many ways, with each family throwing a more and more outlandish celebration to prove that they loved their children the most.

As a result, the domed roof of the penthouse atop the Terra Skyscraper was decked out as never before. The dome had been polarized to provide an optimum view of the city of Tarsonis without interference from the sun. (The Terra family's building was one of the few that had a virtually unobstructed view, matched only by that of Kusinis Tower and, of course, the Universal News Network Building.) A massive chandelier, six meters wide, hung in midair atop the dome, supported by state-of-the-art antigrav units guaranteed not to fail. (The guarantee was that Constantino would drive the manufacturer to complete ruin if it did fail.) Food from all across the Confederacy was laid out, as expected, but he actually managed to get his hands on Antigan buffalo meat and a limited supply of Saran pepper slices. The price for the latter two items was higher than the aggregate salaries of any ten of Constantino's employees, but it was worth it for his little girl.

All the important people were there—at least three representatives from each Old Family on Tarsonis, and a few from offworld—and UNN had dutifully sent all its gossip reporters, and even one of its news reporters, a woman named Mara Greskin. Constantino smiled at her presence. *She must have cracked off somebody to get assigned to cover a birthday party.* Usually such occasions were fodder only for gossip columns; news reporters considererd such assignments beneath them, which was why Greskin simply had to have annoyed somebody important—or gotten in UNN editor-in-chief Handy Anderson's doghouse.

Then again, if they're covering this, it means one less paranoid story about how aliens are going to wipe us out. It seemed all UNN was talking about these days were the horrors in the Sara system and the emergence of a strange alien threat. Constantino knew more than UNN did, of course—for example, that there were, in fact, *two* alien species fighting a war that the human race got caught in the middle of—which only made him worry more, especially since Arcturus Mengsk and his band of butchers in the Sons of Korhal were using the invasion as a propaganda tool to stir uprisings on planets from here to Antiga Prime.

In the face of all this, Constantino threw a party. It was, after all, his daughter's birthday, and he was damned if he'd let Mengsk or alien scum distract him from *that*.

Nova was becoming a woman. According to the girl's nurse, she had started what the nurse insisted on calling "her monthly time"—as if Constantino wasn't familiar with the female anatomy and its functions—and she had started to develop a woman's chest. Soon, the prepubescent disdain for the opposite sex would give way to hormonal imperatives. *Which means an endless array of unsuitable suitors for my little girl.*

In truth, Constantino was looking forward to it. There was nothing quite so satisfying as watching a young man trying desperately to impress one of the most powerful men in the Confederacy and failing miserably, that failure compounded by Constantino's holding him to an impossible standard. He'd already gone through it with Nova's older sister, Clara—now engaged to young Milo Kusinis—and was looking forward to it again with Nova.

Now, Nova stood in the center of the domed space,

wearing a beautiful pink dress that had a ruffled neck,
the white ruffles opening like a flower beneath her
chin, a formfitting top, and a huge hoopskirt that
extended outward half a meter in all directions and
came to the floor. She walked with such grace and
ease that the skirt's hiding of her feet made it seem as
if she were floating when she walked. (Other girls
achieved the same effect by attaching gliders to their
shoes, unseen under the skirt's voluminous mass, but
Nova, the darling girl, had always felt that to be cheating.) She wore very little makeup, simply enough to
highlight her green eyes; her smooth skin needed no
cosmetic enhancements, and so far the ravages of
adolescence had not blemished her visage.

Her normally straight blond hair had been curled
for the occasion and piled atop her head elegantly.
Constantino made a mental note to apologize to
Rebeka. He had doubted the hairdresser's word when
she said Nova would look marvelous with curls; he
should have known better after all these years. After
all, Rebeka had made even Bella look presentable on
more than one occasion.

All around them, the partygoers were partaking of
the food on the tables, the servants ably refilling any
plates that were in danger of emptying. The punch
bowl remained three-quarters full no matter how
much of it was imbibed—and, it seemed, old Garth
Duke was determined to imbibe most of it himself;
Constantino made a mental note to have Boris keep
an eye on him in case he started undressing again—

and the empty glasses and plates were whisked away. As ever, Constantino had the most efficient servants. If he ever had an inefficient one, he didn't have one for long.

There were those who expressed confusion at his employing of human servants—most of whom were members of the younger, newer rich, the so-called bootstrappers who had made their fortune during the boom a decade earlier. Robots, they pointed out, were more efficient, and you only had to pay for them once. Constantino generally just smiled and said he was old-fashioned, but the truth was, he owned Servo Servants, the largest robotics company in Confederate space, and he knew that you paid for them a lot more than once. Planned obsolescence and sufficiently inefficient mechanisms that required regular repairs were what kept SS in business.

Besides, he preferred to keep people employed. The more he employed, the fewer were infesting the bowels of the Gutter.

Nova glided over to him. "Daddy, you're always going on about how wonderful the servants are—but you never let them partake."

"I beg your pardon?" Naturally, if he was thinking about the servants, Nova would know that, even if only subconsciously.

"They're people too, Daddy—and they work *so* hard. Don't you think they deserve some of this fantastic Antigan buffalo a lot more than, say, *him*?"

She pointed over at Garth Duke, who had apparently decided that the punch bowl was a wading pool, and was taking off his boots. Constantino looked around, but Boris was already making a beeline before Garth could make a scene. *Or, rather, more of one.*

"Well?"

Turning back to look at his daughter, he found himself unable to resist her pleading green eyes. It wasn't the first time she had begged an indulgence for the servants, and she usually got what she asked for— a weakness of her father's that she hadn't taken nearly as much advantage of as she might have. Eleftheria said once that her telepathy probably allowed her to think of the servants as *people* rather than servants, since they had thoughts just like everyone else.

Nova herself didn't know this, of course. She simply imagined herself to be a very perceptive young woman.

He reached across to cup her cheek in his hand. "My darling girl—you know I can deny you nothing." He turned around and activated the mic built into the top button of his suit jacket.

Amplifiers placed discreetly throughout the room carried his voice over the partygoing din. "May I have everyone's attention, please?" As the room started to slowly quiet down, he grabbed two glasses of wine off the tray of a passing server and handed one to his daughter. "Today is the fifteenth birthday of my beautiful daughter, November Annabella Terra. She is the last of our children to reach that age, and indeed the last of our children." He tipped his glass toward where Bella stood, her arm in that of her jig, and she was kind enough to return the gesture and provide an almost-genuine smile. "But being younger than her sister Clara or her brother Zebediah does not make her inferior or any less loved. Indeed, the day she was born was one of the four happiest days of my life, the other three being when her siblings were born—and, of course, when Continental went out of business, granting me a monopoly on holocams."

Ripples of laughter at the admittedly mediocre joke spread throughout the room. Nova just glared at her father, apparently not appreciating the humor. Or maybe she just didn't like it when Constantino used her full name.

"In any case, because that day made me so happy, it pleases me more than I can say that all you good people are here today to celebrate that day's anniversary. So I ask you all to raise your glasses and wish my darling Nova a happy birthday."

Everyone in the room did so, and the words were spoken raggedly throughout. Nova smiled and her cheeks flushed.

After everyone had drunk, Nova looked at Constantino and said, "*Dad*dy!"

"Of course, my dear. And now, I'd like to ask everyone to please step back from the food and drink tables for a time. My household servants have worked hard for weeks to get this party ready, and have worked even harder to keep things running smoothly now that it's begun. So as a reward and to show my great appreciation, I invite all the servants to come forward and partake of this magnificent spread."

Several chuckles spread throughout, and a smattering of applause. Constantino noticed that most of the patrons were less amused. In particular, Bella looked like someone had poisoned her drink. And many of the patrons looked unhappy at having to move aside for servants.

Nova, however, beamed at him with a radiant smile. Turning around, he saw that Eleftheria was favoring him with a similar smile. Those were the only two reactions Constantino cared about.

A moment later, Zeb came sidling up to his father. "Dad, did you *have* to use my full name?"

Nova rolled her eyes. "Don't be such a baby, Zeb."

"Oh, that's funny. I suppose you liked him calling you 'November,' huh, *little* sister?"

"I'm fifteen years old, and I'm taller than you."

Constantino chuckled again. "He's got you there, son." Nova was already taller than both her siblings, and almost as tall as her father, and he doubted she was done growing yet.

Zeb shrugged it off. "That's just the clothes."

"You just keep telling yourself that, 'big' brother."

"Mr. Terra!"

Constantino whirled around to see Lia Emmanuel. Constantino himself was the president of every one of Terra's business ventures, with the individual day-today left to assorted vice presidents. Lia was the vice president in charge of the vice presidents, as it were, and Constantino counted on her as his right hand in all matters relating to his many and varied businesses.

She was dressed in the same suit she always wore. Lia had twelve identical suits, and wore a different one each day, laundering them when time permitted or when twelve days passed, whichever came first. Constantino doubted she owned any other clothes— which was a pity, as she was the only one in the room in business attire. Everyone else was wearing a much more celebratory brand of formalwear.

Moving away from the sibling argument—which would probably keep going for at least another five to ten minutes—Constantino approached his vice president. "Lia—haven't seen you all night. Where've you—?"

"Sir, I'm sorry, we need to talk." Lia stared at him intently with her piercing brown eyes. Her curly brown hair was tied sloppily atop her head, as if she just wanted to get it out of her way as quickly as possible. "In private."

Constantino sighed. "Why didn't you simply call me?"

Lia's stare intensified into a glare. "Because you turned your fone off and left it in your bedroom, sir."

"Imagine that," Constantino said dryly. "You'd think I was throwing a party that I didn't want interrupted by business."

Now Lia winced. "I'm sorry, sir, truly, and I wouldn't have interrupted Nova's party normally, but—"

Again, Constantino sighed. It was true, Lia would never have been so gauche as to have business intrude upon family like this unless it was urgent. "All right, all right, what is it?"

"Rebels, sir. They've attacked and destroyed the plant in Palombo Valley."

Constantino blinked. "Destroyed? The *entire* plant?"

"Effectively, sir. I believe some of the structure is still intact, but the plant is functionally useless at present. This will set back production of the 878 and 901 hovercars and especially the 428 hoverbikes by—"

Waving it off, Constantino said, "I don't care about that right now, Lia—how many people—?"

"The entire night shift, sir. The ID tag scans of the wreckage matches all but three of the night-shift employees, and of those three, one was on vacation and the other two called in sick. Everyone else is dead. DNA verification will take another hour, but we're pretty sure—"

"I want all three of them investigated—find out if they're collaborators." Constantino let out a breath through his teeth, trying to rein in his temper. It wouldn't do to cause a scene here, especially with so much of his competition present.

"That's already under way, sir. The attack was such that it *had* to be an inside job. The bombs used were very specifically targeted to the areas of the plant that either would be most densely populated during the night shift or would have the equipment that would be most expensive to replace."

Knowing this was a stupid question—who else would do this sort of thing, after all?—Constantino nonetheless had to ask, "We're sure it's rebels?"

Lia nodded. "Completely sure, sir. Mengsk did one of his pirate broadcasts at the same time as the attack, condemning the Old Families in general and you in particular as symptomatic of the decay that has gripped—"

Again, he interrupted, not caring about Mengsk's propaganda. "All right, fine. Keep on it, and prepare a full report. I'll read it when the party's over." He sighed. "Dammit. This was a good evening, too."

"Sir, the news gets worse. I've run the financials and—well, you can either rebuild the plant or you can give bereavement pay to the families of the victims. You can't do both."

"Then we'll put off rebuilding the plant," Constantino said without hesitation, "we—"

"Sir, we were counting on that plant to produce enough vehicles, especially the 428s, to counteract last year's falloff."

Sales of most Terra products had flattened out of late, due in part to an economic downturn, in part to fear of rebel and/or alien attacks driving down consumer spending. The one exception to this was the 428 model of hoverbike, which was incredibly popular among both children and younger adults.

Lia continued: "We can stave off maybe a few months, but we *have* to get that plant back up and running right away. Mengsk didn't choose it randomly—

he knew that without that plant, our ability to get back into the black will be next to impossible without—"

"Without screwing over the families of the victims of his attack." Constantino shook his head. "That slike. If we don't rebuild, we start falling apart. If we do rebuild, we give him more fodder for his crap about how we exploit the workers." He had to resist the urge to spit. "Dammit. All right, Lia, thanks."

"Sir, I'm afraid—"

"I'm not going to make a decision about that now."

"Sir, that's not what I need to tell you about. There's more bad news—the Protoss have wiped out Mar Sara. The Confederacy managed to pull back, but I'm not sure how many got out alive."

Constantino shook his head. He knew the experiments being done on the Zerg they'd captured in the Sara system would come back to haunt them all. They'd already wiped out Chau Sara, and now Mar Sara had gone the same way. And who knew where these Protoss slikes would stop?

"Thank you, Lia. We'll talk after the party, all right?"

"Yes, sir." She turned on her heel and headed for the lift.

Looking down at his left hand, Constantino saw that he still had the glass of wine in it. Aside from the sip he took for Nova's toast, he hadn't touched it. Now he swallowed it all in one gulp.

Eleftheria intercepted him on his way back to Nova and Zeb. As was often the case with mistresses, Eleftheria was the opposite of Constantino's wife.

Where Bella was a short, stout brunette with olive skin and an hourglass figure, Eleftheria was a tall, slim, willowy redhead with pale skin.

"That was Lia. She came late, talked to you for two seconds, then immediately left. That usually adds up to bad news."

"No flies on you, m'dear." He chuckled without mirth. Eleftheria had always been observant. He told her only about what happened to the Palombo plant; he couldn't tell her about the Protoss. That was something she wasn't cleared to be aware of, much as it pained him to keep anything from her.

Eleftheria's already-pale face grew paler. "My God, that's awful. How could they *do* that?"

"Apparently, we *all* have to pay for the sins of the Council's idiotic decisions." Constantino had been the loudest among those arguing furiously against the bombing of Korhal IV as too extreme a solution, but many of the Old Families took the Council's side—as well as that of the military—in believing that extreme problems *demanded* extreme solutions.

Except that Constantino and his allies had been correct. Korhal IV had backfired rather spectacularly, turning public opinion further away from the Confederacy. And the bombing gave rise to Mengsk and his band of butchers, not to mention dozens of other smaller rebellious groups who didn't have Mengsk's profile, but were irritants just the same.

He looked over at Nova and Zeb, now talking more

civilly to each other. *Lia said it was an inside job. Maybe one of the three who were out. Maybe one of the corpses in the plant, willing to be a martyr for Mengsk's cause.*

"What are you thinking?" Eleftheria asked.

"That we're going ahead with the plan." He put down the empty wineglass and grabbed a full one from a passing server.

His mistress's eyes went wide. "I thought you said—"

"I said I was considering abandoning it, but this attack makes it imperative." *Not to mention what just happened in the Sara system.* "If they can get someone inside the plant, they can get someone inside this household." He smiled grimly. "Security's a lot more stringent for my businesses than it is for my home, I'm afraid." He took a sip of the wine. This was an inferior vintage to the previous one. *We must have run out of the '09. This tastes like the '07.* As he recalled, the grape crop on Halcyon was awful that year. He made a mental note to ask the wine steward why they had any of that vintage in the wine rack at all.

Eleftheria asked, "But if one of the household staff was untrustworthy, Nova would know, wouldn't she?"

"Not necessarily. She's not trained, she doesn't know what to look for." *And whose fault is that?* a little voice in his head asked, but Constantino tamped it down. The only way to get that training was to lose his daughter altogether, and that he *would* not do—

not to the very same imbeciles who nuked Korhal IV and started this entire nonsense.

"When are you going to tell her?" Eleftheria asked.

"After the party. Let her have a good time tonight—then I'll tell her that she's going to have to go offworld for a while."

CHAPTER 2

NOVA DIDN'T REALIZE THAT SHE HAD BEEN ignoring Zeb for several seconds until her older brother asked, "Uh, Sis, you okay?"

"Hm?" Nova turned toward her brother, who somehow managed to look rumpled and disheveled in an immaculately pressed tuxedo, despite the fact that it was cut to his measurements down to the millimeter. He held a plateful of Antigan buffalo in one hand while shoveling said meat into his mouth with the other. "Sorry, Zeb, I was just worried about Daddy. He's upset."

"How can he be upset?" Zeb asked through a full mouth and while chewing, a thoroughly revolting sight. "It's a great party."

"Don't talk with your mouth full," Nova said automatically, knowing it was a lost cause. Zeb could speak as properly as the next scion of the Old Families, could hold his own in a conversation about business with Daddy—good thing, since he was in line to take over the Terra businesses after Daddy retired or passed on—and could perfectly dance every step he was likely to have to know at any social function, but he was constitutionally incapable of eating neatly or of refraining from speaking while doing so.

Zeb swallowed and turned to follow Nova's gaze. "Yeah, he does look kinda off."

Nova hadn't noticed how he looked, really. She could just *feel* that Daddy was annoyed about something. For as long as Nova could remember, she'd always had a gift for knowing how people around her were feeling. In fact, it had come as something of a shock to her when she was seven years old and was told by her mother that other people weren't as empathic as she—which was also when she learned the word "empathic." Mommy always said that it was because she was such a sensitive child, and that it meant she would make an excellent mother someday. That always made Nova happy to hear; she loved both her parents more than anything in the world, and she hoped to be half as good at parenting as they.

She walked over to her father, Zeb trailing behind, stuffing the last of the meat into his mouth. Now that she looked at him as he chatted with Eleftheria, Nova could see how even Zeb would notice he was upset. Daddy's broad shoulders were slumped, his sandy hair was slightly mussed from running his hand through it—which he did unconsciously, and only when he was distressed—and he periodically tugged on the edges of his thick mustache.

Nova asked, "What's wrong, Daddy?"

Her father put a smile on his face, but Nova could still feel the worry emanating from him, and Eleftheria as well. "Nothing you need to worry about, my darling girl. Just some business problem."

Now Nova glared at him. "*Dad*dy, you promised you wouldn't have any business at this party!"

"It was brief, my dear, and unintentional."

Eleftheria added, "And the nasty young woman who brought it in here has been summarily dismissed so we can get on with your party."

"Good." Zeb seemed to think that was that.

But Nova knew better. "Daddy, what is it?"

"It's nothing that can't wait until after the party, Nova. Now, you enjoy yourself, and we'll talk later, all right?"

"What's all this rubbish about servants eating the food? A damned nuisance, if you ask me."

Nova whirled around to see a sea of patrons parting to allow the hoverchair containing the one-hundred-and-fifty-year-old Andrea Tygore to approach the food tables. Andrea was the matriarch of the Tygore family, and the most formidable presence among the Old Families, a group laden with formidable presences. She had probably just arrived, and therefore missed Daddy's toast. Andrea was often late to such occasions, as she preferred to make a grand entrance when everyone else was already present. Nova had always gotten along with Andrea better than the other children, probably because Nova was the only one who wasn't afraid of her.

"Excuse me, my darling girl," Daddy said. "I had best pay my respects to Andrea." He spoke the words with a dread finality.

"Don't worry, Daddy," she whispered, then spoke aloud to the old woman: "The servants are eating from the food at my request, Ms. Tygore. After all the work they've done, I feel it's a just reward, don't you?"

"Balderdash. They're servants—work is what they're *supposed* to do." She looked up at Daddy. "Honestly, Tino, what are you *teaching* this girl?"

Wincing at the use of the nickname—which only she could get away with using—Daddy said, "My youngest daughter has a mind of her own, Andrea—a trait I would think you'd appreciate."

"To a degree, I suppose." She looked back at Nova. "You're growing into a fine young woman, November."

She was also the only person outside her family who ever called Nova by her full first name, which she hated—though she deflected Zeb's comment earlier, she hated her full name as much as her brother did his—but she could no more correct Andrea than Daddy could. "Thank you, ma'am."

"But be careful. Your lessers are just that—your lessers. You treat them with anything other than the contempt they so richly deserve, and they'll turn on you. How do you think those awful rebels have gotten so pervasive? Nonsense like that, it'll be the death of us all." She looked back at Daddy. "I understand they attacked one of your hoverbike plants tonight."

Nova turned and looked in shock at Daddy. "Is that true?"

Letting out a long sigh, Daddy glared at Andrea. "I'm afraid so."

"Filthy rebels." Andrea shook her head. "We should find them and bomb them, like we did on Korhal."

"But isn't that what caused the rebels to start up in the first place?" Zeb asked.

Andrea made a *tch* noise. "Don't be an idiot, boy—it was that Mengsk person that started up the rebels. Korhal's just an excuse for the likes of him. Tino, fetch me some of that buffalo meat."

Daddy raised an eyebrow. "Are you sure you should be—"

Waggling a finger at him, Andrea said, "Don't go lecturing me, Tino. Bad enough I have to listen to that garbage from my doctors. I'm a hundred and fifty years old—I can eat what I damn well please, and if it kills me, fine. A life without buffalo meat isn't a life worth living, if you ask me. Now fetch me some, then follow me. There's someone I want you to meet."

Nova couldn't help but smile at the helpless look on her father's face as he let Andrea lead him on. She looked around for Eleftheria, but she had wandered off without Nova's noticing, distracted as she was by Andrea. Nova was disappointed, as she had wanted to talk to Eleftheria a bit about what was bothering her father. One of the many advantages to there being a jig and a mistress was that one could speak to them as both parent and confidant—they were especially good for gauging the moods of the parents, while acting as a sounding board for the child. *Maybe I can talk to her later, before Daddy has the talk he promised.*

"Hi, Nova."

Nova turned around to see Morgan Calabas walking up to her. He was wearing a tuxedo of the same design as Zeb's, but on him it fit perfectly. His dark hair was neatly slicked back, and the money his parents had spent on skin modification had paid off, as he no longer showed any signs of the acne that had plagued him a year earlier.

"I just wanted to wish you a happy birthday." He raised a wineglass to her.

Ever polite, Nova said, "Thank you, Morgan."

"I was wondering—the d'Arbanvilles are having their ball next month, and I was wondering if I could escort you there."

Not if we were the last two humans in the Confederacy. However, her training kept her from saying it aloud, and she substituted instead the words, "I'm honored by the offer, Morgan, truly—I will consider it and get back to you."

Morgan flushed with enjoyment, but Nova knew that his interest was not in her company—especially given that his eyes strayed more toward her chest than her face. "Thank you, Nova. I hope you consider me a suitable escort."

Under no circumstances. "You're welcome, Morgan."

And then she heard him say, *I'll get under that skirt in no time flat.*

Nova went pale. She'd *heard* Morgan say the words, as clearly as he'd said he hoped she'd consent to be his escort, but his lips hadn't moved.

Morgan walked away before she could respond.

Zeb snorted. "You shouldn't lead him on like that."

"Hm?" She turned to look at Zeb. "What do you mean?" She hadn't been paying attention to her brother, as she was far more worried about what had just happened. Being sensitive to how others felt was one thing, but she'd never been able to hear what someone was *thinking* before.

"Please, Sis, you can't stand that guy. And I don't blame you—nobody can stand him. If he wasn't Arturro Calabas's oldest son, nobody'd give him the time of day." Zeb grinned as he grabbed a small plate of fish bits off a passing steward's tray. "I heard he may not even be at that ball anyhow—Charlie Quinn says Old Man Calabas is sending Morgan off to Tyrador IX."

That surprised Nova. "What for?"

"Well, Charlie said he thinks it's to some kinda reeducation camp, and that some other people are sending their kids there, but I'm not sure I believe that."

"Why not?"

Zeb grinned. " 'Cause Charlie said it. Charlie usually hears all the good gossip, but he always gets stuff wrong." He popped a fish slice into his mouth, then asked, "So who *are* you going to the ball with?"

Too embarrassed to say that no one was, she instead asked, "Who're *you* going with?"

Nova immediately knew Zeb was lying when he said, "I haven't decided yet."

"You mean you haven't worked up the courage to ask Thérèse yet."

Gently hitting her on the arm, he said, "That's a dirty lie!"

Nova just stared at him.

"Yeah, okay, I haven't asked her yet."

"If you wait too long, somebody else will."

Zeb chuckled. "Maybe Morgan will."

Sighing, Nova said, "I should be so lucky. He's only interested in the fact that my chest is twice the size it was six months ago and in getting under my skirt."

"Maybe you should stop stuffing balloons under your blouse."

Now it was her turn to hit him. "Take that back!"

"Actually," Zeb said as he stuffed more fish in his mouth and talked over it, "Charlie said that Amelie Tygore *did* do that."

Nova's eyes widened. "Really?"

"Well, it likely wasn't balloons—she probably just programmed her tailor to make the chest extra big or something."

Shaking her head, Nova said, "Well, she always complained that the boys never noticed her. Maybe she got tired of waiting."

Suddenly, as it had during the toast, her father's voice rang out over the speakers. "Ladies and gentlemen—the dessert!"

Three of the servants then brought in a huge cake. Nova couldn't help but grin. She had spent an hour with Mommy and the cook going over precisely what she wanted in a cake. It had to have a lot of chocolate, and framberries from Halcyon, and ice cream, and frosting from Olaf's in downtown Tarsonis.

Based on the huge four-layer confection that took three servants to wheel in, the kitchen staff had succeeded in bringing these elements together—a feeling that was confirmed when Mommy and her jig, Edward, came over.

"It's just what you asked for, precious," Mommy said.

"Even the framberries?" Nova remembered Mr. Sim, the kitchen staff supervisor, blanching when she mentioned framberries, which wouldn't be in season for another nine months.

Mommy smiled. "Even the framberries."

Nova put aside her distress about what was happening with Daddy, her revulsion at Morgan, and her confusion at hearing Morgan's thoughts, and followed the cart to the dessert table, where she would receive the honor of being served the first piece of the birthday cake she had designed.

CHAPTER 3

BELLA TERRA WENT STORMING TOWARD HER husband's bedroom. It had been a long time since she had been this angry, and to have it happen tonight made it all the more galling.

Being married to that overbearing ass had been agonizing enough, but at least he was usually good enough to stick to his proper duties. *This*, however, was beyond the pale.

The door recognized her and slid open to allow her ingress. Bella was grateful that he hadn't put a privacy seal on the door, which would have ruined Bella's grand entrance—though it also meant she wasn't interrupting a private moment between Constantino and Eleftheria, something she always derived sadistic pleasure out of, mainly because of the irritated look he got on his face. (It never seemed to bother Eleftheria, who was actually much easier to deal with than most mistresses. Bella got along with her better than she did her own jig, truth be told, as Edward was something of a cold fish much of the time.)

At first, when she entered, she thought Constantino had company, but then she realized that the second person in the room besides its primary occupant was the holographically projected body of a UNN reporter whose name Bella couldn't remember; behind him was a panoramic, if generic-looking, view of Antiga Prime. Mercifully, Eleftheria was nowhere to be found. While Bella generally liked her husband's mistress, she often tried to mediate between them, and Bella simply wasn't in the mood for that right now. She just wanted to yell at Constantino directly.

The holograph was in mid-sentence: "—earned that Mengsk and the Sons of Korhal are in control of powerful mind-control drugs, which they have been using freely on the populace. Hundreds have died as a result of interdimensional spraying, which can only be described as chemical attacks against innocent citizens. Others have been warped into strange mutagenic shapes as a result of the side effects of these drugs. Mengsk sent a sabo—"

Noticing Bella's entrance, Constantino touched a button on the nightstand, which paused the reporter, leaving him with his eyes closed and his lips comically pursed. Bella thought he came across more intelligent this way.

"Bella—what can I do for you?" Constantino asked. He was in the process of removing his tuxedo.

"What in the hell are you playing at?"

His nostrils flared, making him look like a particularly idiotic horse. "I beg your pardon?"

"Beg all you want, you won't get it. How *dare* you?"

"Bella, I haven't the foggiest idea what you're carrying on about, but—"

"Nova just came crying to my room, you jackass. I don't ever remember *seeing* her cry before—or at least not since she was an infant—but I can't blame her for doing it now. She's a fifteen-year-old *girl* who just got told by her father that she's being sent for reeducation on some godforsaken rock in Tyrador!"

Constantino's green eyes—which he had passed on to his daughter—widened and his mouth hung agape, making him look like an especially confused fish. She wondered if he'd work his way through the entire animal kingdom before this conversation ended. "Reeducation? That's the most ridiculous thing I ever heard."

That brought Bella up short. "You mean you're *not* sending her to Tyrador?"

"Of course I am, but it has nothing to do with any kind of reeducation. Where could she have gotten such a notion?"

Bella's fury returned a hundredfold. She couldn't believe he'd spoiled what had been a glorious evening for Nova like this. "And when were you planning to inform me of this momentous decision regarding my daughter, precisely?"

"She's my daughter too, Bella, and—"

"You didn't sneak off and get a sex change behind my back, did you? I only ask because you may have mistaken your role for that of the head of the household. Besides, it's an honest mistake to make, since you seem to have lost your testicular fortitude."

Now Constantino rolled his eyes. "Very droll, my dear, very droll, but this is a necessary step. It's not safe on Tarsonis. The hovercraft plant was attacked last night."

Again, Bella found herself brought up short. "Rebels?" she asked in a much quieter tone.

"Yes."

"How many—how many died?"

"Almost the entire night shift."

For what seemed like the millionth time, she cursed Arcturus Mengsk and his band of murdering scum. She swore that if she ever saw him . . . well, if they were ever in the same room, he'd probably have her shot, but she'd do her best to try to kill him first. A forlorn hope, but one she had kept burning in her gut ever since that rabble-rouser first started causing his unrest.

"And then there's the aliens."

Bella rolled her eyes. "Please *don't* tell me you believe that nonsense on UNN. Mind-control drugs?"

Constantino smiled wryly. "Oh, UNN's reports bear only a passing resemblance to reality." He touched the control on the end table, and the reporter started up again.

"*—teur aboard the* Norad II *and exposed the crew to a*

virulent toxin. The result was the recent crash of that ship. Agents of the Sons of Korhal captured those affected by the mind-control drugs, and left the rest to die at the hands of their Zerg allies. I believe that General Edmund Duke, scion of the Duke Family of Tarsonis, has fallen prey to these mind-control devices, and now has been reduced to a mentally reprogrammed zombie in the service of the terr—"

He paused the playback again. "The best lies contain a kernel of truth." He walked up to Bella, looking down at her and putting his hands on her shoulders. "Bella, I'm not supposed to tell you this, but— An alien race called the Protoss destroyed Chau Sara and Mar Sara."

"D—destroyed?" Bella couldn't believe it. Planets weren't just *destroyed*—well, except for Korhal. . . . "That can't be right."

"I'm afraid it is. And those Zerg that they're talking about on UNN? They're real, too—but they're not allied with Mengsk or anyone else. They are enemies of the Protoss, though, and I suspect that our fate is to be caught in the middle of their war. That's why a number of us have agreed to get some of our children off Tarsonis. And Duke *has* turned—but not because of any drugs. Mengsk has convinced him to join his side."

Bella felt as if she'd been slapped with a metal plate. "That's insane." She wasn't even sure which of the revelations her husband had dropped on her fit that bill best—though the fact that Edmund Duke had gone rogue was no real surprise. The man was always an idiot, and an embarrassment. *If he had been mentally reprogrammed into a zombie, nobody would know the difference.* Then again, recalling Garth's antics at the party, she thought that perhaps that whole family had gone mad.

"This wasn't my idea originally, to be honest, it was Arturro Calabas's. Morgan Calabas, Antonia Tygore, and several others are going to a resort on Tyrador IX, just in case the Protoss or the Zerg target us next. Besides, in a world where a Duke joins the Sons of Korhal, we can't trust *anyone*."

A resort at least sounded better than a reeducation camp. *Where do these children get these insane notions?* "You still haven't answered my question," she said testily.

"Which question is that?" He removed his hands from her shoulders and pulled out his loosened tie from the collar.

"When were you going to tell *me*? The children are part of the *household*, and that is *my* responsibility!"

"Yes, along with choosing the wine. What were you *thinking* using the '07?"

"I *like* the '07. And so does everyone else." She sighed. "You never had any taste for good wine, Constantino, I don't know why you insist on bringing it up every time a vintage doesn't strike your fancy. And you're changing the subject. The disposition of the children—"

He took off his jacket as he spoke. "It's a security matter, Bella, which *does* fall under my purview—and to be honest, I wasn't going to send her at first. When Arturro told me about his plan, I thought it too panicky. But when Lia told me about the plant and about Sara, I . . ." He trailed off.

"What about Clara and Zeb?"

"I need Zeb here. Besides, he's a man now; it's time he started acting like it. As for Clara . . ." He sat down on the edge of the bed and sighed. "Milo refuses to go, so she's staying as well." Looking up, he added, "Besides, we can't appear to be abandoning Tarsonis altogether—it's a show of weakness we can ill afford, especially now. To all outward appearances, it will just be some of the children going on an outing to the resort on Tyrador."

She sat down next to him and put a hand on his thigh. Normally, she'd never think of being that affectionate, but if what he was saying was really true . . . "Do you really think they'll attack *us*?"

"I don't know. A year ago, if you'd told me that there *were* aliens, I'd have laughed at you. But now?" He put his hand on hers. It felt cold and clammy. "I don't know what's likely anymore. And I don't know if this will really do any good. But I'll feel better if I know Nova's safe on Tyrador. It's for the best, Bella, truly."

"You're right, it probably is." She hadn't had cause to say those first two words to her husband in many years. "But you had *no* business making this decision without consulting me. I'm your *wife*, Constantino, and Nova is *my* daughter. If you *ever* make this kind of decision without me again, I will flay you alive, you understand?"

He looked over at her, staring at him with those damn green eyes. "You're right, Bella, I'm sorry. I guess we've been working so independently of each other that it never occurred to me to—"

"Save it." She stood up. "Don't make excuses. You shouldn't be cutting me out of family business. That's grounds for divorce—and no," she said quickly, holding up a hand, "I'm not threatening that, merely trying to make you realize the gravity of what you've done."

He shook his head and chuckled, looking up at her. "You're right. As usual, I suppose. I really don't give you enough credit, Bella—and for that, I truly do apologize."

Biting back a snotty retort, Bella decided to accept what Constantino offered. "Apology accepted."

"Thank you. I promise you, I won't cut you out of such decisions again, my dear—all right?"

"See that you don't." Turning on her heel, she stomped out of the bedroom. *What a jackass.* Yet she had to admit, the plan was a sensible one. If he had come to her when Arturro proposed it, she probably would have been more enthusiastic about the notion than he was. Her only objection to the plan itself was that Clara and Zeb weren't going. She could accept Zeb's remaining—now that he was all grown, it was a business matter, and therefore in Constantino's purview—and Clara was her own woman now. *But dammit, she's also my daughter, and I want her to be as safe as her sister.*

As she headed to the door, Constantino restarted the news report. "—*orists. In this way, Mengsk and his inhuman allies hope to confuse the brave warriors of the Confederacy and cause them to lose faith in their leaders. Only by eternal vigilance can we root out such terorrists as Mengsk and his mind-controlled minions. As I speak, a massive Confederate blockade is surrounding Antiga Prime, and the terrorist should be destroyed within a few days. This is Michael Daniel Liberty for UNN."*

Bella departed, thinking, *Liberty, that's his name. What a stupid name for a reporter.*

She stomped toward her bedroom, hoping for his sake that Edward was still up. If he wasn't, he would be soon. She needed some serious comforting, and he wasn't going to get away with pleading exhaustion tonight. . . .

The seats in the puddle-jumper were quite comfortable. But then, Nova always got to travel first class.

The puddle-jumpers were small, thirty-passenger transports that took one from Giddings Station on Tarsonis to Osborne Port in orbit. This particular puddle-jumper's entire first-class section was occupied by scions of the Old Families who were going to be taken in the Calabases' yacht, the *Padraig*, to Tyrador IX.

Nova didn't want to go.

She had cried in her room for hours after Daddy

told her she was going. Her anguish only abated mildly when, later on, Daddy assured her that she wasn't going to be reeducated along with Morgan Calabas, but was simply being taken somewhere where she'd be safe from the rebels and the aliens. Nova's first instinct was to dismiss his paranoia, but she knew as soon as he said it that his fear was very genuine, that there really were aliens out there who had killed humans and would likely do so again.

But she still didn't want to go.

To make matters worse, she was sitting next to Morgan on the puddle-jumper, and he would not shut up.

"This is smart," he was saying. "This way, if something terrible happens to our families, the best and the brightest will still be safe. Plus, have you *been* to the resort on Tyrador? It's *amazing*. Beautiful countryside, state-of-the-art padball courts—maybe we could play?"

Stunned that he gave her an opening to speak, Nova said, "I don't know how to play padball." Even as she spoke the words, she realized that it wouldn't help.

"I can teach you, then. I'm a master padball player."

In fact, Nova knew that he was a dreadful player, and was only not cut from the school padball team last year because his father was the one who paid for the school's courts. Nobody had ever told her this— mainly because she never cared enough to ask—but she simply *knew* it now.

Nova leaned forward and punched up the menu on the food unit. To her great disappointment, they didn't have any framberry juice. She settled for tangerine juice, which was dispensed in a plastic bottle through the slot a moment later.

Morgan was still droning on, but she'd stopped paying attention.

For three days, she'd tried to convince her parents not to make her go. Mommy and Daddy were both insistent. Eleftheria was less sure, but supported Daddy. The only one who argued against her going was Edward, which surprised Nova. Edward was always hard for her to figure out; it was as if his mind was closed off. Zeb joked once that it was because he was so boring, that there was nothing there for her empathy to pick up. So she was surprised to see him argue for letting her stay.

But no amount of cajoling would work, especially after the reports of rebel attacks on Antiga Prime came in. Whatever doubt was in her parents' minds were gone after that. They were adamant that she go to Tyrador—at least for a few months, until the current unrest died down.

If it died down. If they weren't overrun by aliens.

"Of course, I had my choice of women to escort, but I chose you for a reason."

Nova realized that Morgan was talking about her. "Oh?" she said noncommittally. It wasn't as if her participation were necessary; Morgan simply adored the sound of his own voice.

"That's right. But you're special, Nova. I don't know what it is, but there's something about you that stands out from all the other girls." As he said those words, he was staring right at her chest.

Then she again heard Morgan speak without his speaking: *I can't wait to see what she looks like naked.*

And she heard something else. Something that spoke in her father's voice. *What the hell are you doing?*

Then biting pain, as if someone had punched her in the face.

Without knowing how, she simply *knew* that someone had just hit her father.

At the same time, a computerized voice sounded over the speakers. *"Attention, passengers. We will be taking off in ten minutes. Please activate your restraints in preparation for takeoff."*

Morgan immediately pressed the button that activated the padded restraints that combined with the seats—which would blow up into huge balloonlike cushions before takeoff—to protect the passengers from the intense G-forces of escape velocity.

Nova, however, did not. Something was wrong. She didn't know what it was, but she suddenly, with crystal clarity, *knew* that her family was in trouble.

She got up from the seat. "I have to go."

Morgan looked boggled as she climbed over his seat to the aisle. "What? Nova, what're you—?"

Ignoring him, and thrilled at the prospect of not having to listen to him prattle about padball and think about her body all the way to Tyrador, Nova moved toward the exit.

A steward blocked her path. "Ma'am, I'm sorry, but—"

Drawing herself to her full height—which was considerable for a girl her age—and using the same overbearing tone she'd been hearing from Andrea Tygore all her life, she said, "I am November Terra, daughter of Constantino and Annabella Terra, and you *will* let me disembark this vessel *now!*"

The steward swallowed once, considered responding, then decided that it was best to accede to her request. The Terra name was not one to be trifled with.

Several people behind her asked her where she was going, but she ignored them as she left the puddle-jumper, then jogged across the catwalk to the gate, and then ran through the corridors of Giddings Station to the cab stand.

Bypassing the queue for hovercabs, she went straight to the dispatcher and informed him of her name and family in the same tone she used on the steward. He got her a cab forthwith, leaving several disgruntled people in her wake.

The feeling grew worse, if less well defined. Somehow, someway, she could feel that her parents, her brother, Eleftheria, the servants—they were all in trouble.

All except Edward, for some reason.

Oh, no. No, no, no.

She cast her mind back to her conversation with Daddy two nights ago, before the attack on Antiga Prime made him cease all discussion. "My darling girl, you don't understand. The reason why the attack on the plant worked so well is because Mengsk had people there, working undercover. If he could infiltrate the plant, he might be able to infiltrate this house. I can't take the chance that you'll be hurt, so you *have* to go."

Although she still didn't understand how she could possibly know this, she was sure now that Edward was a rebel, that he had been suborned to the cause after years of dissatisfaction as the jig to a woman he couldn't stand, and that he had now betrayed the Terra family.

That was why he wanted me to stay.

The cab pulled up in front of the Terra Skyscraper. Throwing all the bills she had on her into the slot in the wall that separated driver from passenger and hoping it was enough, she ran into the building, past the public lobby, and to the entry to the private lobby, to which she gained ingress via retinal scan.

As soon as the door opened to admit her, she knew something was wrong. Something smelled funny, and she knew that Bryan, the daytime lobby guard, wasn't there.

No, he was there. Or at least his body was.

Nova had never seen a dead body before. She had been to funerals, of course, but one never looked upon the dead at such occasions—it was sacrilegious.

Even when she was a little kid, she had refused to look at the body of her grandmother, though Zeb tried to get her to sneak into the back room of the funeral parlor with her to take a look.

Dead bodies, she realized, felt empty. A big nothing. And they smelled.

Bryan's uniform was stained with something red that she realized was blood.

If they killed Bryan, they're already here. I'm too late!

Tears streaming down her cheeks, she ran to the elevator and gave another retinal scan. The lift came immediately, of course—she was a Terra, after all, and they always got what they wanted.

As the elevator shot up the hundred stories to the penthouse where Nova had lived her entire life, she found herself overwhelmed by hatred and pain, neither of them her own. Strange thoughts intruded upon her. *What's happening to me?*

Edward, you slike, how dare you!

That was Mommy. She could *feel* Mommy, as if she were right there next to her.

Dammit, look at me! How could you—

Then she didn't feel Mommy anymore. Mommy was ripped from her, like the wings Zeb used to pull off insects when they were little.

"Mom—mommy?"

You'll pay for this, you hear me? You won't get away with this—

That was Daddy. He didn't get to finish his sentence either.

She collapsed, even as the elevator door opened on the top floor.

"Daddy? Oh God, Daddy, please, don't be dead, please!" She managed to clamber out into the domed space, but she couldn't make her legs work right, and she collapsed again to the floor.

Three days ago, this had been the site of her fifteenth birthday party. Now it was full of men and women dressed in all-black clothing, holding weapons of various types. She saw a goodly number of the serving staff lined up against the wall—and a few more of them among those in the black clothes. All the people in black wanted nothing less than to wipe out the Old Families—she could suddenly feel that overwhelming imperative in their minds. But they weren't associated with the Sons of Korhal, the group that was all over the news, the ones who attacked Antiga Prime—no, these were just agitators who had no plan beyond making sure the Old Families all died.

Edward was standing over three corpses. Two of them were her parents; the other was Eleftheria. Next to Edward was a man named Gustavo McBain, who was aiming a pistol at Zeb. Her brother was on his knees, his hands behind his head.

"Y'know," Zeb was saying, "you always were an asshole, Eddie."

"Takes one to know one, kid," Edward said. Then he looked at Gustavo. "Do it."

Gustavo fired the pistol. The bullet slammed into

Zeb's head, causing it to snap back, his blood and brains splattering on the wall behind him.

"Zeb?"

Nova had felt her mother and father die. Now she had felt *and* seen her brother die.

"No."

Edward turned to look at her and smiled. "Well, well, well. After all that, you come home anyhow."

"No."

He walked over to her and raised a pistol of his own. Edward was a tall, skinny man with curly black hair and a black beard, though both hair and beard were flecked with gray. She had never seen him smile quite the way he was smiling now. He had never killed anyone before, and she knew that he was afraid to kill someone now—that was why he had had Gustavo do it, because Gustavo hated the Old Families even more than he did, and would enjoy the killing. Edward wouldn't enjoy it.

But he was going to do it anyhow.

"No."

Aiming the pistol's muzzle at her head, just as Gustavo had done to Zeb, Edward said, "Say good night, Nova."

"Nooooooooooooooooo!"

CHAPTER 4

ONCE, MALCOLM KELERCHIAN WAS THE FINEST investigator in the Tarsonis Police Force's Detective Squad. But the TPF didn't keep good investigators for very long—they were often snapped up by the military or the government, deemed far too useful to be wasted on mere local policing.

That was a pity, as far as Mal was concerned. He liked being a detective. His clearance rate was three times that of any other detective in the squad. Admittedly, this wasn't a difficult feat to accomplish. The TPF was primarily made up of thugs and bruisers who mostly just made sure that the interests of the rich were protected. The few who had at least a modicum of brains generally got promoted over to the Detective Squad, but even then, if the crime didn't involve somebody who made more money than the chief of police, it wasn't worth a detective's time. Everyone in the squad perfected the "Well, you know, it's really hard to track down criminals in these cases" speech, which invariably was given to the middle- and lower-class victims of robberies, assaults, and the like. The only crimes that were solved were the ones whose perpetrators were so completely brain-dead as to be impossible *not* to catch.

At least, until Mal joined the squad. He actually made use of the TPF's resources, and used surveillance sensors employed by the Traffic Control Department to regulate those who abused the hover laws (who were legion and whose fines helped pay the TPF's salaries) to identify criminals—a technique that was heralded as revolutionary by the bosses, but which in fact dated back over two hundred years to Old Earth. He also actually made use of the technological identification tools available to him to track down criminals.

This was all well and good, and did wonders for the public image of the TPF—right up until the Rample murder. Two children of a semiprominent shop owner were viciously murdered and left in an alley in the Gutter. What at first seemed to be a typical Gutter "dead drop" quickly became a huge case once the bodies were identified. The chief put Mal on the case right away, assuring the public through numerous press conferences on UNN that their best detective was on it and the butchers responsible for this reprehensible crime would be prosecuted to the full extent of Confederate law. Mal used every means at his disposal to find the killer—

—who turned out to be Emmett Tygore, a scion of one of the oldest of the Old Families.

Suddenly, other cases became more interesting. The unknown perpetrator of what UNN called the "gore in the Gutter," who was referred to in editorials as a "butcher" and a "deviant," was now a "victim of his own psychosis" and someone who "snapped under the pressure." Rather than being prosecuted to the full extent of Confederate law, he was sent to a rehabilitation facility on Halcyon where the Tygores hoped he would be forgotten.

And he was. The press coverage moved on to other things—there were always new scandals, new attacks, new crimes to cover—leaving only a prominent shop owner to wonder why.

The only person left to speak for the victims was Mal, who objected vociferously every time his attempts to properly prosecute Emmett Tygore were stymied. The chief was caught between a rock and a hard place—Mal was a fairly well-regarded detective, probably the first in TPF history, and his successes had meant budget increases, ones the Council only approved because of the force's improved clearance rate. But the Tygores were calling for the head of this presumptuous detective who dared to sully their good name.

Finally, the military came to the chief's rescue. Someone in the Ghost Program found a notation in Mal's file that he had a Psi Index of 3.5—the average person was a PI2 or lower, with actual telepaths being PI5 or higher. A 3.5 meant that he was sensitive to telepathy, albeit with no telepathic skills of his own.

Which would make him an ideal Wrangler.

When Mal was told he was being transferred over to the military to become a Wrangler, the first thing he said was, "What the *hell*'s a Wrangler?"

In truth, Mal knew the answer—Wranglers were the ones who hunted down telepaths and brought them to the Ghost Program, or wherever else the military thought teeps would be useful—but he was too cracked off to admit it.

Mal had been a detective long enough to understand the politics involved. It got rid of a problem for the chief, and covered his ass with both the Council and the public by looking like it was the military's fault for taking Mal away from him.

That transfer had happened a year ago. The first six months were spent in training—one month of it in using the equipment, the other five in honing his ability to detect telepaths into something useful. Sadly, the latter five months didn't really do any good. Prior to being recruited, Mal always got a headache when he was around a telepath. Twenty-five weeks of brain probes, mental exercises, meditation, and increased focus resulted in his always getting a headache when he was around a telepath.

My tax dollars at work, he had thought bitterly at the time.

Still, at least he had some fun new toys to play with.

Those toys were mostly embedded in the formfitting suit he was forced to wear. Years of eating food that was bad for him and drinking more than was good for him (particularly in the last year) resulted in a form that wasn't really suited to being so closely conformed to by his clothes, so he tended to wear a leather duster over it. The holographic badge identifying him as a Wrangler was affixed to the lapel of the duster.

Now, on the six-month anniversary of the completion of his training, and his identification offically changing from Detective Malcolm Kelerchian, Detective Squad, Tarsonis Police Force to Agent Malcolm Kelerchian, Wrangler, Ghost Program, he found himself standing in the charnel house that the Terra Skyscraper had become.

Even before he got the call to go to the location in question, he had been drawn here by the mother of all migraines. He had been sitting at his desk catching up on some long-overdue paperwork when all of a sudden someone drove a spike through his head.

Moments later, he was told to report to the Terra Skyscraper, but he didn't even let the dispatcher finish the instruction. A telepath had done some major psionic mojo at the Terra Skyscraper, and a damn powerful one at that.

The TPF had already cordoned off a four-block radius surrounding the skyscraper. When Mal went through the cordon, he saw why: There were bodies everywhere. Not a single sign of trauma on any of them. Also damage consistent with a major explosion, but without any of the signs. No burn marks, no scorching, no evidence of any kind of explosive agent. Plenty of broken glass, metal, plastic, and wood, though.

What was of special note was that the damage was the same regardless of the tensile strength of the material in question. To Mal's now-trained eye that could only mean one thing: telekinesis.

Which meant this telepath was on a level greater than anything Mal had encountered. Meant a Psi Index of at least eight or higher. Any lower, and you just had telepathy; adding the ability to move things with your mind put you in a class all your own.

Mal had encountered only one PI8 in his six months on the job. That person was currently locked away in the basement of a government building, drooling uncontrollably and unable to form words.

As for the bodies, there was, in fact, *one* sign of trauma: bleeding through the nose, ears, mouth, and eyes. It was that fourth thing in particular that indicated the likely cause of death to be a psionic attack.

Which meant that Mal would be seeking himself another telepath, who was also telekinetic. Teep/teeks were always nightmares to deal with. *Joy of joys*.

He entered the skyscraper to find more of the same. The only variation here was a dead body whose COD was different from everyone else's: a gunshot wound to the chest. The DB in question was wearing the uniform of a skyscraper guard. That added a whole new wrinkle to the equation.

When Mal stepped off the elevator to the roof of

the skyscraper, his headache intensified almost to the same point it had when the attack first happened—which meant that he was now at ground zero of this psionic attack. The first thing he had to do upon entering the room was touch the control on his belt that would deliver four doses of an analgesic into his bloodstream. The headache was getting in the way of his ability to think.

Thanks to good old-fashioned Confederate know-how, the analgesic took effect almost immediately, which let Mal do the second thing he had to do, the thing he always did better than his fellow detectives: investigate.

All around him were several more DBs, about half of them wearing all black and armed, the other half dressed in either the expensive stylings of the ultra-rich or the just-as-expensive outfits of the servants to the ultrarich.

Just like the Tygores. Only a pity it wasn't them.

Mal's boots crunched as he walked. He double-checked his computer, and was reminded that the Terra Skyscraper's roof was usually covered by a steel-glass dome—which meant the telekinetic attack destroyed the dome, something that was only physically possible with a nuclear weapon. *Mentally possible, though—that covers a much bigger range.*

Either the place had been decorated by a paranoid schizophrenic or the attack had tossed the furniture around pretty thoroughly. Just on first glance, Mal saw a table up against a wall, a chair embedded in the

chandelier—itself lying on the floor at an odd angle—
and a sofa split in twain.

Also present in the space were various TPF techs—
the ones who could never be bothered to make it to a
crime scene in the Gutter were out in force here—and
one of Mal's former colleagues in the Detective Squad.

"My my my," Mal muttered as he wandered
through the sea of corpses, "what a mess."

He noted that the DBs here were also bleeding out
the eyes—with four exceptions. Like the guard downstairs, there were four people dead from bullet
wounds.

"Well, well, look who's gracing us with his presence."

Mal looked up to see Detective Jack Pembleton
smiling at him insincerely from behind the mirrorshades he always insisted on wearing. Today, at least,
he had an excuse, as the mid-afternoon sun was shin-
ing down on the roof, and with the dome shattered,
there'd be no polarizing it.

"What brings you to my crime scene, Mal?" Jack
asked.

Mal touched another control on his belt, and a
holograph projected out from the buckle. "Not your
crime scene anymore, Jack. It's gone confederal. This
is a signed and sealed order of the Council officially
putting this case under the jurisdiction of the Confederate Military, and putting me in charge."

Jack didn't bother reading the holograph, especially since it contained many words that Jack didn't

know, but instead glared at Mal through his shades. "You gotta be kidding me."

"Nope. This is mostly a psionic murder, so it's us Wranglers who get to deal with it."

Shaking his head, Jack said, "Crap. I was hopin' to keep this. We got somethin' like three hundred bodies here, between everyone in the building and the people on the street around it. You know what three hundred closed murders'd mean for my promotion chances?"

"As it happens, bupkus." Patting Jack on the shoulder, Mal insincerely said, "Sorry."

"Yeah—especially since I got more wormfood than everyone else."

Mal frowned. "Anyone else?"

"Yeah, we got something like seven attacks on Old Families today. But this is the only one that has a real body count. Couple of geezers bought it, and some kids, but mostly security forces did their jobs. Not here, though."

That explains why Jack's here alone, Mal thought. Normally, a murder of this magnitude, they'd send the entire Detective Squad to cover it. It would be what they used to call a "red ball" back on Old Earth. But attempts on the lives of the Old Families meant a whole lot of red balls. . . .

"Hey," Jack said suddenly, "whaddaya mean 'mostly'? Lookit, all these stiffs are bleedin' out the eyes. That means teep, right?"

Amused at Jack's slow thought process, Mal indicated the four corpses. "These four died from gunshot wounds, right at the center of the head. Two men, two women, and one of the men looks a helluva lot like that photo of Constantino Terra that's in the lobby, which means the other man's probably his son, and the two women are some combination of his wife, mistress, and/or two daughters. There's another one downstairs, one of the guards, shot in the heart."

"Huh." That was about all Jack was likely to be capable of.

"These people were executed. And the guy downstairs was shot to stop him sounding an alarm." He turned to Philbert, who was the only tech who had anything like a brain. "Hey, Philbert."

"Detective Kelerchian, long time no see! Oh yeah, it's 'Agent' now, yeah?"

"I need you to ID these two women quickly."

"I can tell you now, the brunette's Bella Terra, the redhead's Constantino's mistress."

Mal nodded. Then he activated the computer in his suit, asked it for a location on Clara Terra and Nova Terra and for the identification of Bella Terra's jig, the only other member of the family unaccounted for.

"Talkin' to yourself again, Mal?"

"Yeah, it's my only way to get intelligent conversation." He gave the computer its instructions by subvocalizing, so it sounded to Jack like he was muttering to himself.

The computer gave back the results into his earpiece: Clara Terra was last known to be home with her fiancé, and Nova Terra was scheduled to depart that very morning on a private yacht from Osborne Station to Tyrador IX. Ms. Terra's jig was named Edward Peters, and he was supposed to be in the tower somewhere. Sadly, he had no image on file, so he'd have to be identified retinally—or, if the blood in the eyes made that difficult, by DNA.

"We need to account for the two daughters. Jack, can you send a patrol to the home of Milo Kusinis and make sure Clara Terra's there?"

Jack nodded. "Whoever's there's gotta tell her her parents've croaked, right?"

"Yeah."

Grinning, Jack said, "I'll send Grabowski."

Mal sighed. Jack had hated Grabowski ever since he married the woman Jack claimed to be in love with, so naturally he would saddle him with the onerous duty of telling a scion of the Old Families that she was one of the only members of her family left alive.

He then asked the computer which yacht Nova Terra was supposed to depart on, but was told that that information wasn't available, thanks to a privacy seal.

Damn Old Families . . . They and the Council were the only ones who could put such information under a privacy seal, and it was probably the Terra family or one of their cronies.

Mal put a call through to his boss.

There were many reasons why Mal hated talking to Director Ilsa Killiany, primary among them being that she was the one who found out that he was a PI3.5, which was what led to his being exiled to the Wranglers in the first place. But mostly he hated talking to her because she was a royal pain in the ass.

However, that was what he needed right now. Not that Mal wasn't capable of causing distress to a person's backside all on his own, but Killiany had more authority to throw around.

While he waited for Killiany to be able to spare a second to talk, Philbert walked up to him. "Uh, Agent Kelerchian? We got the scan results, and the bullets that killed these four people?" He pointed at the Terra family corpses. "They all came from *that* gun." He pointed now at the weapon that was under the hand of one of the black-clad corpses.

Mal wondered how Jack could be so surprised that the quartet were executed and not killed by the telepath when Philbert already knew they were killed by bullets—then remembered that he *knew* Jack. "Good job, Philbert. I want an ID on that man, *now*."

"You got it."

At the same time Philbert said those three words, Director Killiany's voice sounded in his earpiece. *"What the hell is it, Kelerchian?"* she asked in a tone that made it abundantly clear that "it" had better be damn good or she'd be filleting him with a rusty butter knife.

"Ma'am, I've got four dead members of the Terra family, with three more unaccounted for. I'm tracking down two of them, but the third, Nova Terra, is supposed to be on a ride out of Osborne."

"So what's the problem?" It sounded like she was rummaging through her desk for the knife.

"Computer won't spit out the name of that ride, ma'am. It's under privacy seal."

There was a pause. Then: *"Give me five minutes."*

As soon as Killiany signed off, a thought occurred to him, and he queried the computer for passenger manifests for all puddle-jumpers going from Giddings to Osborne today.

Sure enough, one first-class passenger turned up: Nova Terra.

Except there was a notation on her reservation, that she had left prior to takeoff. This sort of thing had to get noted, as it changed the weight of the craft, which had an effect on takeoff procedure.

Philbert came back over. "Sir, I haven't ID'd the shooter yet, but I just got a pos back on one of the other bad guys here, and you're not gonna believe it."

"Try me," Mal said dryly.

"It's Edward Peters—the Terra lady's jig."

Mal nodded. "Yeah, that makes sense."

Jack stared at him through his shades. "Makes sense? How, exactly?"

Ignoring both of them, Mal put another call in to Director Killiany. *"Dammit, Kelerchian, I'm in the middle of—"*

"Forget the privacy seal, ma'am, it doesn't matter. Nova Terra never made it up to Osborne. She's our killer, ma'am."

"What?"

"She left the puddle-jumper before it could take off. She probably came back home, saw a bunch of people killing her family, maybe even saw one or two of 'em get shot. She also saw that one of the people doing the killing was her mother's own jig. So she's seen her family slaughtered, she's been betrayed by someone who's as close to her as her father, and she loses it. We're standing right where she did it—I've got a four-dose headache right now, and that's a couple hours after it happened."

"How can Nova Terra be a teep and we don't know about it?" Killiany asked.

"Old Family, ma'am, how the hell do you think?" Mal knew firsthand how much power the very rich wielded in the Confederacy.

"Yeah. All right, we need to find this girl. If she's powerful enough to wipe out a whole building plus, not to mention going all these years without training, we need to find her, pronto." He heard Killiany inputting something into her computer. *"Kelerchian, you're off the murder."*

"What?" Mal couldn't believe it. He finally had a chance to investigate a crime again, and she was taking it away from him.

"I'll have Fiorello handle it. The most important thing right now is to make sure that girl gets found. So move your ass."

Mal sighed. "Moving my ass, ma'am." *Dammit.*

All right, Nova, looks like you need finding. First thing I'm gonna need to do is refill the analgesic supply. . . .

PART TWO

The blood-dimmed tide is loosed, and everywhere
The ceremony of innocence is drowned. . . .
—William Butler Yeats, "The Second Coming"

CHAPTER 5

YOU REALIZE THAT (AND THEN THE GUY JUST sticks it) this is crap, right? I'm not trying to (in his pocket!) fog you, I'm just (Don't you dare walk) sayin', this is total crap, and (out on me, or I) I can't take it. (swear, I'll blow your flickin' brains) I'm tellin' you, this (all over the floor, you scan me,) is the best you've ever had, trust (you stupid habhead?) me. She did (Why won't he do this for) that? I mean, she really (me? I'm not asking) did that? Why didn't he just shoot (much at all, dammit) her? Come on, just a (This outfit makes me) little bit, you can (look stupid.) spare it! I promise, you'll (Can't the Council do something) get it back next (about all these habheads?) week—at the latest! I haven't eaten (They're disgusting!) for so long, I've (Why won't he talk) forgotten what food tastes (to me anymore?) like. Don't you ever do (Hab here, hab here) that again! (getcher hab here. . . .)

Silence.

Somehow, Nova had managed to quiet—or at least dim—the voices in her head.

She didn't know how she had done it—nor did she know where she was. The last thing she remembered was . . .

I don't remember anything. She blinked. *You have a name—what is it?*

But she couldn't recall.

"Excuse me, but you are interfering with my normal operation, and I must ask you to stop."

Looking up, she saw an AAI—advertising artificial intelligence. *Okay, I know what that is, so why can't I remember that my name is—*

"Nova." It came to her suddenly. Her name was Nova. Short for . . . something.

Still, that's a start.

"You are interfering with my normal operation, and I must again ask you to stop."

At last, Nova realized that she was curled up on a filthy patch of pavement, at the feet of the AAI. At the moment it was in its standby mode, between advertisements.

Nova sat upright. All around her were buildings crammed together, with small lines of pavement between them. It was still daytime, she could tell that much, as the artificial lighting was minimal, but no sunlight made it this far. The paved section she was in was a cul-de-sac. On three sides were different buildings, none of which had any windows or doors—no, wait, one of them had a door, but it was closed and barricaded with a maglock, which meant the entrance was long abandoned. She looked up, but couldn't clearly see the tops of any of the three buildings. It was like they went on forever.

At the mouth of the cul-de-sac was a crossroads of two more strips of pavement.

Realization dawned. *I'm in the Gutter.* The poor, the dispossessed, the people who couldn't find work, or who could find only the worst work, what little there was, were all here. Crime was, she knew, rampant in the Gutter.

She'd never set foot here, of course; her kind didn't belong. Scions of the Old Families never came down here. She probably ran on instinct, coming into this abandoned alleyway because there were no people— aside from an AAI, here to remind anyone who accidentally wandered this way that there were still products to be bought.

This area beneath the city of Tarsonis was where people were crammed together in substandard housing in tall buildings—none as tall as her father's skyscraper, of course, but—

Daddy! Oh no!

Unbidden, it all came back to her.

Her family was dead.

She saw Edward, her mother's jig, a man she had always thought to be family, give the order to kill her brother and mother and father. The order had gone to Gustavo McBain, a man whose entire family was killed at Korhal IV. When Mommy was killed, she was filled with fury at Edward for betraying her. When Zeb—poor Zeb; she *saw* him get shot as well as felt it—died, he was thinking about how he'd never get to ask Thérèse to the d'Arbanvilles' ball.

When Daddy was killed, he was grateful that Nova, at least, was safely en route to Tyrador IX.

Poor Daddy. He died thinking she was off Tarsonis. Instead, she had come back to their home and—

The voices.

The voices would not stop.

She heard Edward gloating over how he had fooled the Terra family. She heard McBain's glee at avenging the death of his family, even though Nova's family had nothing to do with it—indeed, Daddy had urged the Council *not* to bomb Korhal IV. She heard one servant, Maia, wonder if dying would hurt. Another, Natale, hated that he'd never see his mother again. One of the killers, Adam, didn't care about the revolutionary sentiments of Cliff Nadaner, the man who'd ordered them to do this horrible thing; he just enjoyed killing people. Another one, named Tisch, was looking forward to living in a world where all the Old Families were dead so the common folk could rule the world like it was supposed to be. A third, Geoffrey, was scared that they'd be caught and put in jail, a concept that frightened Geoffrey to his very core. A fourth, Paul, was aggravated that they were killing pointless rich people, when what he *really* wanted to be doing was killing the Council.

Nova couldn't stand it anymore. Too many voices, too many *thoughts*, all in her head at once.

She made them stop.

But all that did was surround her with more dead bodies. So she ran—but that only made things worse. The farther away she ran, the worse the voices got.

At least, until now. When she came to the AAI, the voices quieted. Perhaps because the only "person" around was an artificial intelligence that didn't have any thoughts.

Because that's what I'm hearing. Thoughts. Like with Morgan. Maybe like it's been all along. I can feel what people think.

I'm a freak.

She was also a murderer.

"You are interfering with my normal operation. If you do not cease, I will be forced to contact the Tarsonis Police Force."

Realizing that the AAI was going to get her in trouble, she clambered to her feet.

Then she laughed bitterly. *Trouble, right. Like interfering with an AAI matters when I just killed hundreds of people.*

With a shock, she realized that she wasn't exaggerating. She knew what each person was thinking when he or she died, whether it was Edward or one of his fellow cronies of this Cliff Nadaner person on the roof, one of the servants they had captured, or someone else in the skyscraper or nearby who simply had the misfortune to be in the wrong place. The woman who was worried about her daughter's grades in school. The man who was afraid his wife would find about about the affair he was having with her brother. The child who was on his way via hoverbike to meet his parents on their lunch break. The—

"Do you want to sail through the air faster than anyone else?" The AAI looked different now—like a kid wearing hoverbike gear. The holographic projectors had changed its shape.

Now the AAI's mouth moved and the voice changed to that of a little kid. "You bet!"

The AAI now appeared to be on a hoverbike, riding over terrain that was suddenly projected behind it. "The new 428 hoverbike. Get yours today."

Nova fell to her knees. She felt pain in her kneecaps from the action, but it barely registered.

The 428s were the ones Daddy's company made.

Daddy was dead.

In fifteen years of life, Nova Terra had never cried. Her life had been a happy one, with nothing that would give her reason to be so sad that she'd be brought to tears.

Now, on a street somewhere in the Gutter, with only an AAI—which was now hawking a soft drink—for company, Nova felt tears stream down her cheeks for the fourth time since she turned fifteen. *Happy birthday to me*, she thought bitterly.

Lookit (Hey, Freddie!) here, it's (What've we got here, then?) a curve!

The thoughts slammed into her brain, denying her the peace that the AAI had given her.

"Hey, Freddie! What've we got here, then?"

"Looks like a curve to me, Billy."

"I believe you're right, Freddie."

She looked up and saw, through tear-streaked eyes, two boys who weren't much older than her. They wore clothes that were too big for them, and smelled like they hadn't been introduced to the concept of bathing. They were standing between her and the mouth of the cul-de-sac.

When she'd heard Morgan's thoughts involving her for the first time, she'd thought them kind of disgusting, but she was so overwhelmed by the fact that she heard them at all that she hadn't given much thought to their content.

What she heard from Freddie and Billy was far far cruder. And far far scarier. Had Morgan acted on his thoughts, he would likely have been clumsy. If these two did, it would be violent.

"Get away from me." Her voice was hoarse and barely audible.

Freddie feigned surprise at her tone. "What's this, Billy?"

Billy did likewise. "I think she don't like us, Freddie."

"We should show her what good sods we are, Billy."

"I agree, Freddie." He started to move toward her. His thoughts became, amazingly, more violent.

"Don't come any closer." If anything, Nova's voice was more ragged. She clambered backward, trying to move away even as they approached. Her stomach twisted with nausea. With a thud, she crashed back into the AAI.

"You have interfered with an official advertising artificial intelligence. This is a misdemeanor punishable by a fine. The Tarsonis Police Force has been contacted and will be here shortly."

Freddie and Billy both laughed. They knew that the TPF didn't come to the Gutter to hand out fines. It was an impressive day if they came to make an arrest. Usually they just beat folks up, but Billy and Freddie were both paid in full for the month, so no cops would touch them.

Under other circumstances, Nova might have been disgusted at this revelation of graft in the TPF, but she was too busy quaking in fear.

Not of Billy and Freddie, however. Rather, she was afraid of what she might do to them if they tried to do what they intended.

"Now now, little curve, don't you worry your pretty little head. We'll take right good care o' you, won't we, Billy?"

"That's right, Freddie."

Freddie was now imagining the very specific things he was going to do to the area between her legs. Nova tried to clear her throat and said, "I'm warning you!"

Billy laughed. "Oh, that's solid, isn't it, Freddie? *She's* warning *us*."

Shaking his head, Freddie said, "Don't no cops come down this way, curve. And even if they did, they wouldn't be doin' nothin' to *us*. So you can scream all you like." Nova knew that Freddie, in fact, wanted her to scream, as that would give him more enjoyment.

At first, Nova did nothing. She couldn't. It was one thing a minute ago—she wasn't thinking. But now she *knew* what would happen if she cut loose.

So when Freddie grabbed her by the blouse, she did nothing. (Only now did she even notice the blood all over her blouse, and the rips that, she now remembered, came when the dome collapsed on top of her. Some of the blood might even have been hers. . . .) When Billy grabbed at the waistband of her pants, she did nothing.

Then she saw what Billy intended to do.

"Get *off* of me!"

A second later, they did. Both Freddie and Billy were lying on the far end of the cul-de-sac. Billy felt a sharp pain in his chest, and Freddie was dizzy and couldn't focus his eyes.

Nova stumbled to her feet. Her first attempt to stand up straight failed, and she almost fell to the pavement again, but she managed to keep her balance, thrusting her arms out to steady herself. Then, finally, she stood up straight.

A spark from behind her drew her attention. She turned around to see that the AAI was so much metal and electronic slag. She was sorry to see that—the AAI had been a refuge of sorts. *It doesn't have any thoughts—it's quiet. Not something I'd ever think about an ad. Maybe I can find another one.*

She turned back around to face her attackers. Neither showed any sign of getting up anytime soon.

Walking over to them, she cleared her throat again. "I warned you. Stay away from me. Or next time it'll be worse."

Freddie was too focused on his inability to focus to truly respond. But Billy's brain went into a red haze of rage. "Flickin' curve! I'll kill you!"

Billy jumped at her clumsily—he was coming straight up from a bent-over position—and pulled a pistol of some kind out of his oversized shirt. Billy himself had no idea what kind of gun it was, so neither did Nova—she knew only that he got it from someone named Grabien, and that he'd always sold Billy good weapons in the past.

He aimed the pistol right at Nova, and she lashed out. The pistol exploded a second later, sending Nova flying backward, pain slicing into her forehead.

This time when she fell to the pavement, she registered the landing quite well. Her own thoughts were now as unfocused as Freddie's, and she felt her grip on reality loosen.

Maybe now I'm *dying, too.* She found this to be a happy thought, and she embraced the darkness that overwhelmed her.

CHAPTER 6

"SO LET ME SEE IF I UNDERSTAND THIS RIGHT, okay? You been selling hab in O'Callaghan for the last two months. Now that's prime territory, okay? My kids, they don't give that to just anyone. You sell in a place like O'Callaghan—or Kitsios or Stephens or somewhere like that—well, then you can carry yourself some *weight*, okay? That's *good*. That's someone who knows how to grab the yous and make 'em take what they know ain't good for 'em. O'Callaghan, that's like a *reward*, okay?"

He paused, then. Over the years, he'd learned that such pauses were useful, in part for the rhetorical effect, but also because silence engendered fear. He liked to soliloquize, it was true, but there were times when not saying anything was the scariest thing.

Right now, he was going for scary, at least to a degree.

He had been born with the name Julius Antoine Dale, but nobody called him that anymore. Most people didn't know his real name, which was how he preferred it. There were some who knew him from his younger days as a pavement wrestler, and then later as a bruiser, who called him "Jules," but only a few of them were still alive.

These days, he was known to almost everyone in the Gutter as "Fagin." It was more title than name, though most people didn't differentiate much. They just called him that because they knew better than to think about calling him anything else.

The object of Fagin's diatribe was a young man named Ian. He was in no position to criticize Fagin's delivery, nor his choice in dramatic pauses, seeing as how Ian was, at the moment, strung up by his ankles, dangling from one of the creakier ceiling beams, while two of Fagin's kids—Sam and Dani—each had a P220 trained on an ear. (Fagin's kids only used P220s. The P180s were always misfiring, and anything else wasn't suitable for the work he needed. His kids needed the best if they was to stay on top, and Fagin intended to stay on top till he died.)

"So after you get this reward, what do you do? You start *skimming*. Now, it's not like you don't get a good wage here, okay? You deal O'Callaghan, that means you're takin' twenty percent—that's better than any other flicker in the Gutter's gonna give you, okay? Which makes me wonder, where do you get off thinking you can *get away* with that?"

Still, Ian said nothing. That was wise, as far as Fagin was concerned, since he had told Dani and Sam that they were to fire their P220s if Ian so much as uttered a peep.

"Some people would say I should make an example of you. That would be the thing to do, okay? Everyone does that. All the time. Someone does that, all right then, let's make an example of the little flicker. Show him who's boss." Fagin let out a very long breath. "Except for one little problem: That never works. Seriously, when has killing someone *ever* been a deterrent? The death penalty has never stopped capital crimes. In fact, capital crimes usually go *up* whenever there's a death penalty."

Ian still said nothing, though Fagin noted that there was more sweat on his brow, no doubt due to the topic of his imminent demise now being the subject of Fagin's monologue.

"So, really, what would I gain? All right, yeah, I'd get the satisfaction of watching as the bullet from a P220 tears a massive hole in your skull and splatters brain matter, blood, and bone all over the back wall. But then I'd have to get the wall cleaned, okay? That's annoying. And besides, I've seen brains a hella lot smarter than yours splattered on walls before." Another long breath. "So that leaves me with punishment. See, those same studies I was talking about? The ones that show that capital crimes go up when there's a death penalty, okay? There's a flip side to that nobody doesn't talk about. See, if it goes up when there's a death penalty, it goes down when there isn't. When there's actual *punishment*, then people aren't likely to do it no more."

For the first time since his monologue started, Fagin actually looked at Ian. The amount of sweat on Ian's forehead increased even more.

"You started out as a runner, okay? Just a little acnoid, beggin' for work 'cause your parents were too poor to give you an allowance. That's how they all start, okay? Doin' whatever everybody else tells 'em to do. And the ones that don't get out, or that don't get killed, or that don't get brain-panned, they move up in my little world, okay? Like you did."

He smiled. When he was a wrestler, Jules had had all his teeth filed down to points in order to intimidate his opponents. Because of that, he didn't smile very often now, saving it for when he really wanted to scare people like he did back then.

Ian was now gushing sweat.

"Only now you're moving down, okay? You're a runner again, Ian, and you're the lowest of them. Some ten-year-old acnoid we just picked up yesterday? He's got more clout than you, okay? You scan me?"

Now Ian nodded quite emphatically.

To Dani and Sam, he said, "Lower your guns and cut him down."

Sam did so right away; Dani looked disappointed for a second, then helped Sam cut Ian down.

Ian fell to the floor with what Fagin imagined was a hollow thud.

Fagin turned around to face Evan, the one who handled Cramville, which was the neighborhood farthest away from Fagin's HQ here in Duckworth.

Duckworth was the closest the Gutter had to a nice neighborhood—which, in real terms, meant that some of the living spaces were more than four hundred square feet. "Put him to work, okay?"

Evan nodded and walked over to Ian, yanking him to his feet. "Move your ass," Evan said. Ian stumbled more than walked toward the door, Evan on his heels.

Fagin then turned to Manfred, who ran O'Callaghan. "Nice job bringin' that to my attention."

Manfred nodded. "Thanks."

Then Fagin took out his own P220 and shot Manfred four times in the chest.

To Sam and Dani, he said, "Call Wolfgang, have him clean that crap up. And somebody get Tenilee up here. She's runnin' O'Callaghan now."

The other area-runners were either looking agape at Manfred's bloody corpse or staring blankly at Fagin. One of them, Francee, who ran Kitsios, said, "The hell happened t'all that crap 'bout the death penalty not deterrin' nothin'?"

"I said it wasn't no deterrent, okay? Didn't say it wasn't useful. See, Ian, he'll learn. He's just a typical panbrain that got too greedy for his own good when we put him in charge of a street. Went to his head. That won't happen again, and by the time he works himself back up there, he won't be stupid." Fagin pointed down at Manfred's corpse. "Now Manfred— Ian pulled that crap for weeks before Manfred figured it out. Or Manfred knew about it and didn't tell me. Means either he's stupid or ain't loyal. Since I took his territory from him, I figure it's disloyal. 'Sides, he's too smart, and too solid to learn nothin'. So he's gone."

Francee just shook her head.

"Anything else? 'Cause I got an appointment I'm *real* late for, okay?" Fagin had postponed a rendezvous with one of the twelve people he kept around for his personal pleasure. He was actually starting to get bored with Number Five—he never knew their names, as he wasn't interested in them for who they were but for what they looked like—so he was thinking he might have to replace him, maybe with someone a little older, more experienced. But tonight was his current favorite, Number Eleven, and Fagin was eager to get in her pants, as it were.

Markus, who was in charge of Pyke Lane, which was the neighborhood geographically closest to the snooty part of the city, stepped forward. "I got somethin', Fagin. I think it's legit, too."

"What?" Fagin asked, hoping this would be brief.

"Freddie and Billy found—"

Holding up a hand, Fagin said, "Stop right there. The last time Billy and Freddie found something, it was an AAI that could spy on TPF HQ, okay? And that's because they were high and hallucinating. So—"

"They ain't foggin' with this one, Fagin, honest," Markus said, insistently. "They found a curve down in Hunter Alley—she's a teek and a teep."

Fagin rolled his eyes. "Teeks're a myth, okay? If you said she was just a teep, I might've—"

"She broke Billy's ribs, Fagin—and Freddie's got a

concussion—and then she blew up Billy's gun. She's just a *girl*, Fagin—little taller'n most, but still a girl. No way she could take out Billy or Freddie for nothin'. I ain't foggin' you, Fagin, I think this curve's legit."

"You sure they didn't beat each other up and then Billy's gun misfired?" Sam asked. " 'Cause Billy's always buyin' substandard crap."

Turning to Sam, Markus said, "He was holdin' a T20—they don't blow up."

Fagin had to allow as how that was true. T20s jammed up *all* the time, but they never blew up. If Billy was still holding his old TX2, that'd be one thing, but if he had a T20 . . .

Markus looked back at Fagin. "I think you should meet her. At the very least—" He hesitated.

"What?" Fagin asked, thinking that he was going to have to wake Number Eleven out of a sound sleep by the time he got to her at this rate.

"She's definitely a teep. She—she *knows* things."

Francee chuckled. "Crap, Markus, if she knew about what happened in the Firefly Club, we *all* know about that."

Markus's dark skin went darker with a blush. "Not that—she knows *other* stuff. Stuff I ain't told *no one*."

Favoring Markus with his sharp-toothed smile, Fagin asked, "Like what?"

"I—I don't wanna say, Fagin. Trust me, though, don't nobody know this."

Fagin sighed. "All right. Bring her by tomorrow."

"Fagin, I—"

Raising his P220 and aiming it at the same spot on Markus's chest where he'd hit Manfred, Fagin said, "Tomorrow."

Quickly, Markus said, "Yeah, yeah, okay, I scan, no problem, tomorrow."

Fagin lowered his P220 and put it back in his jacket. "I'll see you all in the morning."

Then he retreated through the back door that led to his private chambers. Two of his bodyguards—he didn't know their names, as the names of his guards were as irrelevant as those of his sex partners— stepped in front of the doorway to keep any potential intruders out. They were supplements, and less important ones, really. He mostly kept them around for the symbolic value of having two very large men with no necks standing in front of his private chambers. His real security, however, came from touching the control on his belt buckle that sealed the room with a force field that couldn't be broken down by anything short of a large explosive device, and not necessarily then.

Number Eleven hadn't gone to sleep. She also had gone to the effort of removing her clothing, which disappointed Fagin. "Put your clothes back on, okay?" he said sharply. He wanted to be the one to undress her.

A teep-teek, huh? he thought as he removed his clothes as a prelude to removing hers. *This could be interesting.*

CHAPTER 7

MARKUS RALIAN REALLY DIDN'T WANT THAT girl around any longer than he had to. But when Fagin went and pointed a gun at your chest two seconds after he shot up Manfred for no good reason, well, crap, Markus wasn't no panbrain.

So when Fagin's little object lesson was done, Markus went back to his square in Pyke Lane to see what he could do with the girl.

Markus grew up in Pyke Lane—actually on the lane that the neighborhood took its name from—and he knew early on that he wasn't goin' nowhere legit-like. His dad was a musician who couldn't get work; his mom worked as a cook at a diner down in Kitsios, which paid for crap. Mom kept hoping that Markus would get himself a scholarship, go to one of the good schools in Tarsonis City, but they kept turning down his applications. Never gave a reason, just turned them down.

Being no kind of panbrain, Markus didn't waste no

time. If the world outside the Gutter didn't care about him, he wasn't gonna care about it, neither. If he couldn't make it up to their world, he'd do the best he could in this one. That meant drugs.

Again, Markus was no kind of panbrain. Everyone around him, including his dad and both his siblings, did crab, snoke, turk, and especially hab, so he saw what it did to them. Dad was a great sax player—when he wasn't high on hab. Problem was, those times weren't very often, which was why he got kicked out of the Trank Club, and hadn't had steady work since.

No, the people who made it weren't the habheads. The people who made it were the ones who sold it.

Like everyone else, Markus started out as a runner for the local dealer. In his case, it was Orphy Jones, back when he ran Pyke Lane. By the time Markus worked his way up to being a barker, Orphy got his head blown off by a rival dealer, the guy everyone called Grin, on account of how he didn't never smile. Grin's main lieutenant was a fast-loader named Jules.

Wasn't long before Markus saw the words on the screen: Jules was the brains. Grin was just muscle, and wasn't much longer before a bullet from Jules's T20—this was before the P220s came out—was in Grin's skull and Jules started callin' himself "Fagin" for some reason and started taking territory.

Nowadays, nobody who made money on drugs or sex or booze did it without Fagin getting himself a cut.

As for Markus, he just made sure he was loyal to whoever was in charge. Didn't matter if it was Orphy or Grin or Fagin, if he said "Jump," Markus asked, "How high?"

That was how you survived.

Worked, too. His square had a living room bigger than the place he grew up in. Markus's brother and sister both worked for Fagin, too, and he'd gotten at least Geena off of crab. Gary, though, he kept saying he'd given it up, and then Markus'd find him with a hab booster on his arm.

So when Fagin said he'd look at the teep curve tomorrow, that meant that all Markus could do was figure out what the flick to do with her for the night. Normally, he wouldn't have even questioned Fagin, but after that curve started talking about what Dad did. . . .

Markus shuddered. He hadn't even thought about it. Markus himself had just been an infant when it happened, before Geena or Gary was born, and it wasn't something he wanted to remember. Most times, he didn't have to—but then that curve started talking. . . .

He came into his square to see Geena sitting in the living room, counting the day's take, with Tyrus standing over her polishing his T20. Geena looked as pretty as always, especially after she'd had her nose redone for her eighteenth birthday—a present from Markus, who knew that was all she wanted. The op was pretty straightforward, but until Markus started dealing, the Ralians could never afford even that simple an op.

As for Tyrus, he was supposed to be in the spare bedroom with the teep girl. *So what the hell's he doing out here?*

Shaking his head, Markus asked, "What the flick you doin' out here, Ty?" Years ago, Markus never would've shot off at someone like Tyrus, who was at least twice his size, and who could crush Markus's head with one outsized hand.

But Markus was the head of the neighborhood now. He could boss people like that around. It felt good.

Tyrus shrugged his massive shoulders. "Girl ain't doin' nothin', 'cept mutterin' stuff."

"I *told* you to keep an eye on her."

Geena repeated Tyrus's words. "She ain't doin' nothin', Markus. Just lyin' there all curled up. Ain't like she can go nowhere."

"I don't care, I don't want that girl to be alone."

"Markus, she can't go nowhere without us seein'—"

"She's a *teep*. She can leave without us knowin'!"

Tyrus shuddered. "Got *that* right." At Markus's look, he said, "She was goin' on about my sister. I didn't want to be hearin' that, so I came out here."

Markus sighed. Tyrus's sister had worked as a sex dancer to pay for her hab, and died when one of her regular customers got annoyed when she wouldn't go home with him. Because Fagin was the type to reward loyalty, and because Tyrus had been a good soldier, Fagin had made sure that the customer in question died very slowly and very painfully, but that didn't bring Tyrus's sister back. It was the only thing that ever made the big man get emotional, so Markus could understand why he wouldn't want to be in a room with someone reminding him of it.

That didn't make the situation no better, though. Glaring at his sister, he said, "Then you shoulda got someone else. That girl's dangerous, and Fagin wants to see her in the morning."

"Crap," Tyrus said, "we gotta be keepin' her for the whole *night*? You *see* what she did to Billy and Freddie?"

"Yeah, and that's why Fagin wants to see her—but not till tomorrow." Turning to Geena, he said, "Get some people over here. I want three people in the room with her all the time, and two more out here. She even twitches, she gets shot, you scan me?"

"That's what you told us before you left," Geena said testily as she grabbed a fone.

"Yeah, and that worked *real* good." Markus shook his head, pulled out his own P220, which Fagin had given him when he gave him the Pyke Lane neighborhood to run, and walked into the spare bedroom, from which Markus had had all the furniture removed after the girl threw her first temper tantrum and almost broke his favorite chair. It was an interior room with no windows to the outside—in fact, the entire apartment only had one room with windows, and Markus took that one for himself. Geena had been right, in theory—the girl shouldn't have been able to leave without someone in the living room knowing it, since the spare bedroom's only way out was into that room. Still, with a teep, Markus wasn't taking any chances.

He closed the door behind him, cutting off Geena's summoning some more muscle. Markus knew she'd find someone. The Yorod was closed for renovations for the next week, so that was at least four bruisers who probably were at loose ends for a while, plus they'd settled their little problem with the turk supplier—all, Markus was proud to say, without having to involve Fagin, which made the boss very happy—so Zelik and Marina would be free.

It took Markus a second to find the girl—which was surprising, since the room was just a square space of about fifty square feet with nothing in it but the girl.

She was curled up in a corner, her knees tucked into her chest, her hands up, covering her face.

"Go away." Markus could barely hear her speak through the mask of her forearms.

"Can't do that, curve."

"I can't stop it if you're in here." Her voice was a mild whimper. "If you're in here, I know *all* of it! I know about what your father did—"

Markus held up the P220. "Shut *up*! Don't be talkin' about—"

The curve sat up. "Then *leave!*"

She had a pretty face, the curve did. Even with the tears running down her cheeks and the puffy eyes, Markus could see she was pretty. And it was a natural pretty, the kind that happened from good luck, not from a surgeon's laser the way it did for most of the curves in the Yorod.

Which was why Markus made sure to hold up the P220. Pretty faces made studs do some *stupid* crap, and Markus prided himself on not being stupid.

"Nobody's leavin', curve. Fagin wants to see you in the morning, and that means—"

She put her head back behind her arms. "I can't *stop* it if you're here! I can't stop your brother from drugging himself into a fog, I can't stop your sister from selling her body, I can't stop your cat from dying, I can't stop Orphy from not listening to you and getting his head shot off, I can't stop you from singing at the Firefly Club, I can't stop your father from killing your mother, I can't stop—"

"*Shut up!*" Markus screamed, thumbing the safety on his P220. "I swear I will shoot you in the *face* if you don't shut *up!*"

"Then get *out!*" she screamed right back. "I know how much you hate Jules, how much you want to kill him, I know how much you want your father to die, too, and—"

Markus fired a shot over her head.

She didn't even flinch.

Whimpering again, she said, "You really think that's gonna scare me? Don't you get it?" She looked out from behind her arms again. Her green eyes were bloodshot. "*I want to die!*"

"Well, too bad, curve," Markus said, trying and failing to keep his voice from shaking. "Fagin wants to see you in the morning, and that means you don't move, you scan me?"

Without waiting for an answer, he turned around and left the spare bedroom as fast as he could.

"Damn, Markus," Geena said. "You ain't looked like that since the cat died."

Markus snarled at his sister, but didn't say anything.

Tyrus said, "I *told* you, Markus. That curve ain't uploadin' right, you scan me?"

Nodding, Markus said, "Yeah. When the others get here—tell them to stay outside the door. Don't nobody talk to her for *nothin'*." He shuddered. "That curve'll be Fagin's problem tomorrow morning. Till then, we keep her locked up."

"No problem," Tyrus said emphatically.

Markus then went straight for his bedroom. He had a private stash of whiskey in there, and he intended to drink all of it before he went to sleep tonight.

Malcolm Kelerchian was getting entirely the wrong kind of headache.

He'd spent the past three days talking to everyone who knew Nova Terra, both on Tarsonis and off. He'd spent the better part of yesterday talking to the people who were now on the *Padraig*, still en route to

Tyrador IX despite the tragedy that befell several of their families—supposedly it would be safer there. At least Mal had been able to talk to them, and only then by throwing his Wrangler credentials around. Certainly he wouldn't have been able to swing talking to the passengers on an Old Family yacht when he was a mere detective, which marked the first reason he'd had in a year to be grateful for his transfer.

Sadly, those interviews did very little good. Nobody knew anything about Nova beyond the fact that she left the puddle-jumper suddenly for no good reason, and that she had always been a rather empathetic girl, always given to caring about other people's feelings.

Mal's impressions upon hearing that from most of the younger scions of the Old Families was that such was a concept wholly foreign to them.

Talking to her acquaintances on Tarsonis proved equally useless, mostly because they were only acquaintances. They knew who Nova was, they knew she was Constantino Terra's youngest child, they knew she had blond hair, and they knew damn little else.

Now Mal was in the home of Clara Terra and her fiancé, Milo Kusinis, a lavish suite on the upper floors of Kusinis Tower, one of the few buildings taller than Terra Skyscraper. Clara was seated on a wooden chair that was, Mal knew, a reproduction of a French chair from the nineteenth century on Old Earth, and which also cost more than Mal's annual salary. Clara had her mother's brown hair and full figure, and she had also done considerable work to make her face perfectly proportioned. She was holding an embroidered handkerchief to her face and dabbing her eyes, though Mal could find no evidence of crying. The surgeon's laser may have prevented that from showing, of course—with the Old Families, there were lots of ways to buy your way out of feeling emotions, after all.

Mal was seated on a chair just like it, sitting at a dining-room table that was three times as expensive as both chairs combined, protected by a lace tablecloth that was probably as proportionately expensive.

If Nova had been here, he'd have a different kind of headache. But she hadn't been here since the day of the attack.

Among Mal's instructions from Director Killiany was that the fact of Nova's telepathy was classified and only employees of the Ghost Program and members of the Terra family were to know of it. That meant that—unlike his interviews with the other Old Families—Mal could be direct with Clara.

"Ms. Terra, did you know that your sister was a telepath?"

"A telepath?" Clara looked up from behind her handkerchief. "That's ridiculous. Nova was no such thing."

And how nice of you to talk of your sister in the past tense. "I'm afraid she *is* a telepath, ma'am. There's no doubt of that." In truth, there was still some doubt, as the evidence was fairly circumstantial, but he saw no reason to share that with the sister.

"It's nonsense. If Nova was a telepath, I'd have known."

That, it seemed, was all there was to it. But Mal pressed on. "Ma'am, right now, Nova's a danger to everyone around her—but mostly to herself. I have to ask—have you seen her since the attack on your family?" He knew the answer was no, but he was curious as to what her reaction would be.

As she set the handkerchief down on the lace tablecloth, Mal saw a look of determination that might have been more fierce on the visage of someone who was better at it. "Agent Kelerchian, I agreed to speak to you because I received word from the Council itself that I was to cooperate with you in any way. But I will not see my sister spoken of in this way! Especially after the horrible tragedy that has befallen—"

"Yes, yes, the terrible tragedy that's left you and your darling fiancé in charge of the entire Terra fortune."

"What are you implying?"

Malcolm Kelerchian rarely smiled. He'd tried it a few times, and found that it never conveyed any sense of jocularity. So he saved it for occasions when he wanted to put the person with him completely ill at ease. "I'm not implying anything that isn't blindingly obvious to anyone paying attention. A bunch of rebels broke into the Terra Skyscraper—"

"Led by my mother's jig." Clara looked away and made a *tch* noise. "I *told* her not to trust that man. . . ."

Sure that Clara had never said any such thing to her mother, Mal ignored the interruption and proceeded. "—and killed the three people who stood between you and control of the Terra family, all at a time when you weren't home, because you were busy with your fiancé—who stands to inherit control of the entire Kusinis family fortune and businesses. That looks suspicious to people, given the likely prospect of your two families merging completely, instead of partially the way it would've been a week ago. Now *most* people wouldn't question a scion of the Old Families. But, as my presence in your apartment amply demonstrates, I'm not most people. I've got the Council's ear—" An exaggeration, but again, Clara didn't need to know that. "—and if I tell them that you're suspicious, they'll be all over you—and your fiancé. One way to keep me from telling them that is to *answer my damn questions.*"

Clara's lips set into a small line under her unnatural nose. "Very well. Ask."

In fact, Mal had already done so, but in the interests of moving things forward, he asked again: "Have you seen your sister Nova since your parents and brother were killed?"

"No." Clara let out a breath, and she seemed to deflate. "I can't imagine why she didn't come straight *to* me."

Mal drummed his fingers on the table. "Ma'am, it's my belief that Nova didn't know she was a telepath until she walked onto the roof of your family's skyscraper and saw Edward Peters kill the rest of the family—right before she killed him and his cohorts. A lot of telepaths' abilities don't get activated until they experience some kind of traumatic event."

Clara nodded. "This certainly qualifies."

"Exactly. I doubt very much that she was thinking straight, which is probably why she didn't come to you. Now I've gotta ask—is there anywhere she used to go, some kind of secret favorite place she didn't tell anybody about?"

"I'm afraid if she did, she kept it a secret from me. I must admit, Agent Kelerchian, we weren't as . . . intimate as sisters should be. She was much closer to her brother."

Yeah, but I can't really question him. Somehow, Mal managed not to say the words out loud. He reached into the inner pocket of his duster and pulled out a card. On it was encoded his personal comm code; placing that in a fone would transmit the user to his headset instantly. Normally, he simply gave out the cards in his outer pockets, which went to his mail cache, but on this case, he wanted instant gratification— even if it meant talking to this woman again. "If you think of anything else, or if you hear from Nova, or if there's anything you come across or remember that might help me find Nova—*please* call me immediately."

"Of course." Clara took the card and said the words in that noncommittal voice that drove Mal crazy.

Getting up from the chair, Mal pumped two doses

of the analgesic into his bloodstream to stave off the headache.

Wherever Nova Terra was, Mal was more and more convinced that it *wasn't* among the Old Families. Facial ID scanners had long since been set up at Giddings and all the other ground ports, as well as every train station in Tarsonis. They'd gotten three hits of women who looked similar enough to Nova, but weren't her—they were neither the right age nor telepathic. One had threatened legal action against the government, to which Mal wished her the best of luck and agreed to appear as a witness on her behalf, an offer she declined frostily.

If Nova went off-planet, she did it before the cordon fell—unlikely, as it was imposed within two hours of her disappearance from the puddle-jumper at Giddings. More likely, she was still on Tarsonis. But she wasn't among any of her peers.

So if I'm a telepath who was just confronted with the death of my entire family and hit with abilities I haven't the first clue how to control, where would I go?

The best answer Mal could come up with was: *As far away from my life as possible.*

Which meant Mal was going to have to check the Gutter.

CHAPTER 8

FIVE PEOPLE ARMED WITH GUNS ESCORTED Nova from the tiny apartment that Markus Ralian owned. She had awakened there after she blew up Billy's gun. Her first hope—that she was dead—was soon dashed, and she struck outward, wrecking all the furniture in the room before falling unconscious again.

When she woke back up, the room was empty.

She noticed that, when nobody was in the room, she had an easier time screening out everyone's thoughts. They were still there, but it was like the background noise of a crowd in a filled stadium, just a wall of mental noise.

But if someone came through the door, she couldn't hold the dam up. First it was Markus with his murdering father and angry mother and ex-prostitute sister and hatred for his boss and so much else, and that led to her hearing the thoughts of the couple in the next apartment who argued all the time but loved each other anyhow, the bruiser in the next room who secretly loved dancing but couldn't tell anyone for fear of ruining his reputation, the woman down the hall who kept trying to fix her holo because she couldn't afford to buy a new one or pay someone to repair it, the family across the way who were eating the last of their leftovers and didn't know if any of them would find work and thus be able to afford to buy food tomorrow, and *everything else. . . .*

Then Markus left, and she was able to silence the voices.

For a time.

It got worse when the bodyguard came in, but she was able to scare Tyrus Fallit enough that he left. Same for when Markus came back in.

Now, though, she was overwhelmed again, mostly with the four who escorted her, plus Markus.

This is a fine-(Damn, I hope Markus don't tell) lookin' curve. Gotta (nobody that my gun ain't loaded) get me some of her (I'm hungry.) when Fagin's all ('cause that'll get me in some serious crap) through with her. (with Fagin.) I can't believe we made it (Maybe I'll watch that holo tonight) through the (with Mom like I) night. Couldn't (promised her last week.) get a flickin' bit of sleep (Hope I can score me some hab after this, gotta) 'cause of that curve. She'd better be worth (get some hab or I'm just gonna) whatever Fagin wants (I'm hungry.) with her, or I'm gonna put the bullet (flickin' explode right here in the street, 'cause) in her brain my own self. (I gotta get me some!)

Nova closed her (*Need some hab!*) eyes and forced

herself to focus, (*A* nice *curve.*) to not think about (*I'm hungry.*) the thoughts (*Hope Mom remembers.*) that were pounding into (*Almost there.*) her mind.

The next thing she knew, the thoughts had gone away—no, not entirely. Just four of the five did. Markus was still there—and a new one.

She opened her eyes and looked up to see Markus and another man. He was shorter than Markus, but he seemed taller, somehow. Nova suspected that he'd always seem to be the tallest person in the room. He had a need to be in charge of everything he surveyed. He was a little taller than Nova herself was, with dark skin, a shaved head, and a full beard.

Even if she hadn't been able to see into his mind, she'd have recognized him from Markus's thoughts. "Your name is Jules," she said.

He laughed. "Not bad. Ain't too many people that know that name. But I'm called—"

"Fagin." She knew that already. She knew everything. "You named yourself after a character in an old novel called *Oliver Twist*—a novel you hated when you read it, but you liked the character of Fagin, and you hate the fact that your name is Julius Antoine Dale."

Markus looked over at Fagin—at Jules—in surprise at that. He hadn't known Fagin's whole name until now.

Now Fagin was angry. "Markus was right, okay? You are a teep. Which means I got only one question for you, curve."

"I just want to die."

This prompted a wide grin. "That may still be possible. But first, I gotta see if you're of use, you scan me?"

"Use people is all you do," Nova said quietly.

"That's right." The grin widened. "Now why don't we start with your name? I'm guessing it's something fancy—maybe with some money behind it—since your clothes are a lot nicer than most of what you see down here."

She saw where this was going before Fagin started talking. Tears streamed down her cheeks as she remembered her parents being killed. "You won't get any ransom. My family's all dead."

Suddenly, she remembered that Clara was probably still alive. She had forgotten all about her older sister. But still, she couldn't, she *daren't* let this monster know that. He had to believe that the entire Terra family was dead.

Luckily, that would be an easy fiction to maintain.

"So you *are* rich. Good, good. There's got to be *somebody*—"

"There's *nobody*!" she shouted. "They're all *dead*! I killed all of them!" Nova wasn't sure why she said that, but it had an immediate effect on Fagin. Running with what she saw in his head, she continued: "Why do you think I came down here? I killed my entire family, and I don't want the TPF to find me. So I came to the Gutter—cops don't come down here, from what I've heard." In fact, she'd heard no such thing—mainly because she hadn't cared enough to inquire—but she saw clearly in both Markus's and

Fagin's minds that the police left them alone as long as they didn't interfere in the world outside the Gutter.

Fagin rubbed his bearded chin. "So what you're saying is—you can kill with your brain, okay?"

"That's right. I can. But I won't do it for you."

"Oh, I think you will. Because if you don't—"

"You'll shoot me?" Nova said, though she saw that that wasn't what he was thinking. He was thinking that she would starve, which was a ridiculous notion.

"No, shooting'll be a mercy. You want to die, you said—I heard you say it. But that's not the worst thing that can happen to a rich little curve like you. No, the worst thing is to *suffer*. I'll bet you've never *sufferered*, have you, little curve?" He pulled out his pistol—a P220, apparently, the best handgun that money could buy—and pointed it right at her head. "Now I want you to leave here, little curve, and I'm gonna make sure that *nobody* helps you, okay? You won't get no food, you won't get no place to live, you won't get no drugs, you won't get *nothin'*, you scan me?"

Markus, Nova knew, was surprised at this turn of events—he thought that what Jules was doing was cruel and unnecessary. But he also knew better than to argue with him.

"Get *out*, curve! Out!"

Nova couldn't believe what she was hearing. A minute ago, he was convinced that she'd be the best weapon he'd ever had. Now, he wanted nothing to do with her. He was convinced that the only way she'd work for him was if she was on her own for a while—then she would come to him begging him to take her in, in much the same way his literary namesake took in Oliver Twist in the old Charles Dickens novel.

Right there, Nova swore to prove him wrong.

"All right, I'll leave. But first, let me tell you something, Julius Antoine Dale. You're never going to get your mother to love you. None of the twelve people you keep locked up in the back rooms even like you—they're just scared of you. Everyone thinks you look like an idiot with the shaved head, since that look went out of style ten years ago. And one of your most trusted lieutenants is going to kill you."

She made that last one up—well, not entirely. The image of killing Fagin was very clear in Markus's head.

Then she turned around and walked out.

As she moved past the four guards (*I'm hungry. What, she's leavin'? Gotta get my hab! Hope Mom's okay.*) and the other people in this large apartment—which was called a "square," she realized, because most of the low-income housing that the Confederacy built down here consisted of square-shaped apartments—she heard one final thought from Fagin. It wasn't anger at what she'd revealed to him because, she now understood, they were all things he already knew, and they didn't scare him, not even the fact that he'd die at the hands of a trusted lieutenant. Perhaps it was because that was how he rose to power, so he expected the same to be visited on him.

In any case, he had only one thought in mind:

She'll be back. And then she'll be mine.

Nova swore she would die before she let that happen.

Mal arrived at the Southwestern District Headquarters of the Tarsonis Police Force, knowing that he would be violating his director's orders when he entered.

He had already requested all the records from all the TPFHQs in the Gutter, and they'd told him nothing useful—as expected. That's because very little went on in the Southwestern and Southern Districts that made it into the records.

If he was going to find out what was really happening in the Gutter, he was going to have to talk to people.

Or, specifically, talk to a person.

He entered the main reception area. The walls were several unfortunate shades of green. The district HQs were first constructed shortly after humans settled on Tarsonis—the ruling class felt that keeping law and order was critical—and they were constructed from bits of the colony ships. Over the years, most of the HQs were replaced with more modern structures that reflected the growing prosperity of humans on Tarsonis.

But in the Gutter? Nobody bothered. Besides, the metal they built the HQ out of was designed to withstand the rigors of space, which meant it could stand up to whatever the Gutter could throw at it.

Not that the Gutter threw much. The cops down here were bought and paid for by the various criminal elements, after all. If nothing else, the salary for graft was a lot better than the one they got from the Council.

As if to prove that point, Mal saw that the sergeant in charge of the surveillance cameras was watching UNN on a screen on his desk. The other screens were showing empty alleys and streets; three weren't working. Mal assumed that someone paid good money to keep those three cameras down.

Still, just for the hell of it, he asked, "What happened to Cameras 4, 5, and 9?"

"Busted," the sergeant said without looking up from the UNN reporter. It was Mara Greskin, which Mal only knew because she'd interviewed him once or twice, and then asked him out to dinner. He'd said yes, which was a mistake, as the dinner was a disaster, like every date and attempt at a relationship Mal had ever made.

"I need to see Officer Fonseca."

Jerking his thumb behind him, and still not looking up from Greskin's story, the sergeant said, "Desk duty."

"Figures. Who'd he crack off this time?"

The sergeant shrugged. "I stopped keepin' track."

Yeah, that sounds like Larry. "Which desk is his?"

"The one up against the wall."

Anywhere else, Mal might have thought it odd that the sergeant never bothered to request Mal's credentials, or at least look up to see who it was. But this was the Gutter.

Mal walked past the sergeant through a long, dark hallway. He saw light fixtures, but they weren't working. He wondered how long they had been out, and if anyone even bothered to report their failure.

The hallway emptied out into a large room full of desks, all but one of which were empty. That figured. Most of the shift probably were out on patrol, were doing favors for whoever had paid for them, or had called in sick because they had better things to do today. In mid-shift, very few cops would be in HQ for any reason.

Unless, of course, they were on desk duty.

Officer Larry Fonseca was older than Mal, but beyond that Mal had no idea what his age was. He was white-haired and wrinkled, but that was the case when Mal first joined the TPF twenty years earlier. He was always just *old*, though it was possible he'd added a jowl or two, his white hair had gotten a bit thinner, and his belly had gotten a bit thicker.

"How you doin', Larry?"

Larry looked up from staring at the same UNN report the sergeant had been watching. His blue eyes were virtually hidden by folds of aged flesh, hovering over his bulbous nose.

"I'm doing for crap, Mal, whaddaya expect? What in the name of the sun in the sky is that you're wearing?"

Sitting down in the guest chair next to Larry's desk,

which creaked with his weight, Mal said, "Been transferred over to the confeds. Ghost Program."

"What'd they do a stupid thing like *that* for?"

"As soon as I know the answer to that one, old friend, I'll let you know."

Larry chuckled. "Yeah, that figures. So if you're a fancy-ass confed now, the hell you need to talk to *me* for?"

"I need to know what kinds of assaults have been happening down here the last four days or so."

Looking at Mal's earpiece, Larry said, "C'mon, you can get all that—"

Waving a hand in front of his face, Mal said, "I don't mean the records, I mean what's actually *happening* down there." He took a breath, then proceeded to violate several confederal laws. "What I'm looking for is a teep/teek. Got a Psi Index through the roof, and I'm pretty sure she's loose down here."

"Don't you got special fancy-ass confed equipment to help you find that stuff?"

Mal shrugged. "Yeah, sure, I can pick up her psionic wavelength pattern. Only one problem—I don't know what it is."

"Whaddaya mean you don't know what it is?"

Sighing at the digression, Mal leaned forward and said, "If you're looking for some mug's DNA, you can scan for it—and then you comp it to the database, right?"

Larry nodded. Then his eyes widened a bit, and he

nodded again. "Oh, I get it. You don't got nothin' to compare it to."

"Right. She's a renegade, never got into the program. I mean, I can do scans looking for a heavy wave pattern—and we have been, and I might find her that way, but I'm not about to count on that."

Again, Larry nodded. "Yeah, I can understand that. S'like a needle in a haystack."

"What's so hard about finding a needle in a haystack? Just run a magnet over the haystack, the needle'll pop right out."

As always when Mal pointed that out to someone, Larry got a confused look on his jowly face; then it brightened, as if he'd just received enlightenment. "Hey, yeah, that would work. Okay, so whaddaya need?"

"Anybody who's been attacked but left no marks. Or a DB that's bleeding out the eyes. Or just people being assaulted by a little girl who you wouldn't normally *expect* to get assaulted by a little girl."

"Yeah, okay. Gimme a day."

Mal smiled. He knew he could count on Larry. "So who'd you crack off this time?"

Shrugging, Larry said, "The captain. He wanted me playin' bodyguard for a turk shipment from the Heights. I told him to go flick himself, so he put me on a desk."

"You know, Larry, you could just take the money and be done with it."

Larry shook his head, then folded his arms over his chest. "Nope. Can't do it. Took an oath."

Shaking his head, Mal got up. "You're nuts, you know that?"

"Whatever." He went back to watching UNN.

For his own insane reasons, Larry Fonseca kept to his oath to keep the peace and uphold the law. He was also as good a cop as they came, so he always knew what was going on on his patrol and was always willing to cooperate with a fellow officer—even one who'd been transferred to the confeds—which made him a more useful resource than anyone else in the Gutter. The other cops here were all beholden to other masters, and wouldn't cooperate with Mal for anything short of cash that he wasn't authorized to provide officially and couldn't afford to provide personally.

In the meantime, Mal would wander around the Gutter for a while. Maybe he'd get lucky and get a headache. . . .

CHAPTER 9

NOVA HAD THOUGHT THAT STARVING TO DEATH
would be easier than this.

After leaving Fagin's place, she just walked until
she found an alley like the one Billy and Freddie
found her in. This one didn't have an AAI; but then,
it didn't have much of anything beyond a large trash
bin. Nova had been disgusted to see that they still
had trash bins down here—back home, the trash
was incinerated regularly right on the premises.
Apparently, down here in the Gutter it was collected
and then sent somewhere else to be incinerated,
which struck Nova as a colossal waste of time. Why
not just do it there?

She found a trash bin to lie behind, and fell asleep,
hoping never to wake up.

The problem was, she did wake up. And when she
did, she was very hungry.

Ignoring it proved impossible. Her stomach rum-
bled as loudly as the thoughts of the people around

her—which she was getting better at tuning out, even as she got worse at ignoring her hunger.

She tried to think of other things, but it just sent her back to food—or to things she didn't *want* to think about. Thinking about home made her think of the banquets Mommy used to put together. Thinking about her family made her think of how they died. Thinking about Morgan made her ill.

After two days, she got a distraction: a very small, very filthy tabby cat with half its left ear missing, who enjoyed foraging in the trash bin. The background noise of human thoughts around her had dimmed a bit, but when the cat came up to her, she found herself almost embraced by the cat's own rather straightforward thoughts. *Food? Not food. Find food. Sleep.* It never got more complicated than that. However, the cat decided that, even though she wasn't food, Nova was a decent enough sort for her to curl up next to when they both went to sleep.

By the fourth day of her Fagin-imposed exile, she had decided to name the cat Pip, after the kitten she'd had for about two weeks when she was a girl. Unfortunately, while Pip—who was a Siamese—got along fine with Nova, she constantly hissed at everyone else in the house, from the hired help to Zeb, and Mommy and Daddy both agreed that she had to go. Pip wound up with the family of the one servant the cat could stand—Rebeka, Nova's hairdresser. Nova visited her as often as decorum permitted a member of the Old Families to visit the home of a servant.

Whlie Pip wandered off occasionally, she always came back to Nova, unlike her namesake. At one point, she even offered a mouse that she had caught her very own self. *Food for big hairless cat* was her thought upon dropping the mouse in front of Nova. "Big hairless cat," Nova had soon realized, was how Pip thought of her. The idea of a creature other than a cat never entered her worldview.

She was very displeased when Nova refused to eat the mouse, and Pip disappeared for the better part of a day. Nova had wondered if she'd ever come back, and found that she was pleased when she did, almost twenty hours later. When Pip was around, it was easier to keep the other thoughts silent. Pip wasn't quite the dead zone that the AAI was, but that was better in a way. Getting used to the cat's thoughts provided good practice for human thoughts—at least that was her theory.

A small voice in her head said, *What difference does it make? You want to die anyway, right?* She ignored it.

On the fifth night, she awoke with a start, having dreamed of a very large steak with a three-color salad covered in the cook's mouthwatering mustard vinaigrette, all of it washed down with framberry juice.

She couldn't take it anymore. She had to eat *something*.

Getting to her feet, she looked down at her clothes. Her blouse, which was once white, now was streaked with gray and black and other colors she wasn't sure she wanted to identify. Her white denim pants had even more colors on them. Somewhere along the line, she'd misplaced her shoes; her white socks were riddled with holes, and her feet were killing her. Her hair felt like strands of wheat attached to her head, and her teeth ached. It had been days since her last shower or dental, and she probably looked terrible.

But it didn't matter because she had to eat something or she'd die.

You said you wanted *to die,* the small voice reminded her once again, but now it was drowned out by the much bigger voice that was reminding her of the steak dinner she'd just dreamed about.

Forcing her feet to move for the first time in several days, she inched out of the alley—

Why do I gotta (All these bills,) go to school? Ain't (I don't know how the flick I'm gonna) none of that (pay them all.) gonna do me (Now listen to this song, this song is) crap lotta good in (utter garbage, you won't believe) the real world. (how bad this song is, really.)

—and instantly regretted it. The thoughts beat into her head. She tried to force them out.

After a few moments, she was able to tamp them down to a dull roar. It was easier this time.

Pip sauntered up alongside her. *Big hairless cat go away?*

Crouching to give Pip a scritch on the neck, which she liked a great deal—her thoughts when Nova stopped were always *Why stop itch-go-away?*—she said, "I'll be back soon. I have to find some big hairless cat food."

With that, she stood back up and set out, determined to walk the streets of the Gutter until she
found *something* to eat.

Aside from hoverbikes, vehicles didn't generally
come down this way, except for the buses on the main
thoroughfares. Most of the streets of the Gutter were
walkways, with the neighborhoods divided by those
main thoroughfares.

When she turned the corner out of the alleyway
onto Decker Way, she saw a few stores, and several
AAIs imploring her to purchase a particular product.
She easily ignored the latter, paying closer attention
to the former—but none of them sold food.

And how are you going to buy the food once you find it?
she asked herself. *You don't have any money.*

Nova decided to worry about that when she found
a place. She started walking down Decker.

After passing a pharmacy, a pawnshop, and a bar—
which she considered, until the minds of the people
inside told her that they didn't have food, only alcohol, which was the worst thing she could have right
now—she finally went by a small place with a sign
that said MILTON BODEGA. The place was notable for two
reasons: It was the first source of food she'd found
since leaving her alley, and it didn't have an AAI outside its door hawking its wares.

She knew that the second word had its origins on
Old Earth and referred to what they called a neighborhood store. The first word derived from the owner
of this bodega, a couple by the name of Gray and

Alanna Milton. They'd bought the store five years ago from the previous owner with money they'd saved up working at the hoverbike plant owned by Nova's own father, the same one that was attacked by rebels the night of her fifteenth birthday. A tear streaked down Nova's cheek at the memory, which she wiped away with her filth-encrusted sleeve.

Neither of the Miltons were in the store at the moment, as they were asleep in a tiny apartment one floor above the bodega so they could run the overnight shift, since they didn't trust their hired help to mind the place during that time of night when the bad elements came in. They'd been robbed several times, all when the hired help ran overnight, so they decided to just take care of it themselves.

Nova also learned that the Miltons didn't have an AAI because they thought it was an extravagance. They were known in the neighborhood; the AAI wouldn't bring in enough new business, Gray said, to justify the expense. Their customers knew them, and word of mouth did the trick a lot more than one of those stupid machines.

Since it was still early evening, they had the hired help in the store: a boy named Benjy, who was Alanna's nephew, which was the only reason why he had the job. Benjy wasn't very bright, and was being lured by the easy money of the drug trade, and so Alanna convinced Gray to let him have the job to at least give him a chance.

Nova stopped. She realized that the only way she

was going to get food was to steal it. Which meant
that she'd commit a crime on Benjy's watch, which
meant that Benjy would fail in what he was supposed
to do—keep the bodega safe—which would get him
fired and back out on the streets and probably, before
too long, working for Fagin. She wouldn't wish that
on anyone.

So she moved on. She wouldn't do that to Alanna
and Gray, or to Benjy. They all deserved better.

Eventually, she reached the main thoroughfare,
which was called Colman Avenue. The side she was
on was called Pyke Lane, after one of the walkways
parallel to Decker; on the other side was the neighborhood called O'Callaghan, so named for the thoroughfare that divided it from Kitsios. Buses went
zooming by on Colman at high speeds. After a few
minutes of that, she realized that she was supposed
to go to one of the footbridges that went over
Colman.

Rather than do that—she didn't want to venture
too far from her trash bin, which had become rather
like home, mostly thanks to Pip's presence—she
turned up the walkway that was adjacent to Colman
and went up to the next street.

Fittingly, the next big street was Pyke Lane, and
Nova turned down it, hoping to find some food. The
steak dinner never strayed far from her thoughts.

An AAI implored her to get a new fone, with the
first day free; it stood outside a fone shop. Another
stood outside a jewelry store saying that these were

the best prices in all of Pyke Lane, a guarantee supported by a money-back promise.

The one that caught her attention stood outside a news vendor, providing the current feed from UNN, which was a male reporter with black hair and a Vandyke beard. Since the AAI didn't have thoughts, Nova had no idea who it was. *"Today, in a UNN exclusive, this reporter has learned that Sons of Korhal leader Arcturus Mengsk signed a treaty two weeks ago with the evil reptilian alien Protoss. This reporter has exclusive information that Mengsk has promised the entirety of the Confederacy of Man to the Protoss in exchange for letting him rule Antiga Prime as Monarch-for-Life. Mengsk and his forces took Antiga Prime three days ago, in part using mind-control drugs to suborn General Edmund Duke and his forces to his treacherous cause. UNN urges everyone to enlist now in the Confederate Army to help fight the combined menace of the terrorists of the Sons of Korhal and the foul aliens who stand against everything humanity stands for."*

Nova shook her head. She didn't know what scared her more, that UNN was saying this or that people around her were believing it. She knew from Daddy that the Protoss weren't reptilian, and they hadn't made contact with any humans—certainly not two weeks ago.

Half a dozen people were either in the news vendor or just outside it, and they were all watching the AAI.

That Mengsk (What crap. There's no) is such a panbrain. Where does (such thing as) he get off (I'm so scared.) getting into bed with (aliens, everyone knows) aliens? (that, I can't believe) I should sign (I'm so scared.) up right now, (they run this stuff on) and kick those aliens' asses! (UNN. It's just) Somebody should do something (embarrassing, that's what it is.) about all these aliens. (I'm so scared.) Where the hell is the (I hope Mengsk takes all the planets!) Council, anyhow?

The AAI then shifted to another image, that of a different reporter.

"For the first time since the murder of several members of the Terra family in the tragedy at their skyscraper, the lone survivor of the family, Clara Terra, has spoken."

Nova felt her stomach tie up in knots.

"Several attacks on members of the Old Families have been carried out in the past few days, but none so specatacular as the kamikaze raid on the Terra Skyscraper, where the evil terrorists—possibly affiliated with Arcturus Mengsk and his Sons of Korhal—took their own lives in order to wipe out virtually the entire Terra line, plus several hundred civilians in the surrounding area."

"That isn't true," Nova muttered. Edward and his cronies worked for someone named Cliff Nadaner, not Mengsk, and they weren't kamikaze at all—Nova knew from her history classes that that word applied to suicide bombadiers in one of Old Earth's wars. She forgot who employed them—the Germans, maybe? It was so hard to keep track of Old Earth's wars. . . .

In any case, that didn't apply to Edward and his people. And it was Nova who killed everyone else, not Nadaner's rebels.

"Today, Clara Terra gave a press conference, where she had this to say."

The AAI shifted to an image of Nova's sister. She was dressed in mourning black, which was appropriate. Under different circumstances, Nova would be doing the same for the six days following the death of her family. *Then again,* she thought wryly, *with all the dirt on my outfit, I'm most of the way there. . . .*

Clara spoke hesitantly. Nova's older sister had never liked public speaking—even though she was probably speaking in a studio where the only other people were technical personnel, and possibly her fiancé. The AAI wasn't sophisticated enough to show Clara's surroundings, but Nova expected that Milo would be standing behind her as a show of support. Clara didn't really care about Milo very much, except as a means to more money, but Milo was devoted to Clara. Nova had always thought it rather sad, really.

"I—I want to thank everyone who has consoled me in this—this terrible *moment of grief for me."*

"Moment?" Nova found herself uttering the stunned word aloud. Next to her, a woman, whose name, she now knew, was Donna, shushed her. Nova knew immediately that Donna eagerly followed the gossip regarding the Old Families—she apparently believed that Nova herself was having an affair with one of the Duke boys, whom she had never actually met—and would be mortified if she knew that she had just shushed one of the people whose life, and the lies told about it, she had obsessively followed.

"The death of my parents, their mistress and jig, and my two siblings—"

Until this moment, hunger had been the all-encompassing emotion smothering Nova's entire being. Now, though, it was replaced with outrage. *"Two* siblings!"

"—in this cowardly and—and brutal terrorist attack has been devastating. You can rest assured that my darling fiancé Milo and I intend to go ahead with our wedding, which we are dedicating to the fond memory of our departed family—my beloved mother and father, their jig and mistress, my dear brother Zebediah, and my darling sister November, all of whom were killed by those cowardly slikes. After the wedding, the combined forces of the Kusinis and Terra families will show those nasty terrorists and those icky aliens just what we can do!"

The AAI returned to the reporter. *"Ms. Terra went on to say that the investigation into her family's death has been closed, and she intends to hold a funeral ceremony for all six of her deceased family the day after tomorrow. Donations should go to Constantino Terra's favorite charity, which was—"*

"No! That's a *lie!*" Nova lashed out with everything she had, and the AAI exploded in a fiery conflagration of sparks and twisted metal.

Oh no. (We're gonna die.) She's some kind of (We're gonna die.*) freak! What is she? How'd (We're gonna die!) that happen? She's looks (We're gonna* die!*) really cracked off. I hope she (Oh, flick,* we're gonna *die!!!!) doesn't hurt us.*

Nova started (*We're gonna die.*) backing away from all the (*What did she do?*) horrible thoughts (*How'd that happen?*) directed at her.

The news vendor herself, Martina Dharma, came running out of her store, wielding a P180, which she pointed right at Nova, even though it wasn't loaded. Martina couldn't afford the bullets, but she kept the weapon itself to scare people. As far as Nova was concerned, she needn't have bothered, not only because Nova *knew* the gun wasn't loaded, but because she was plenty scared already.

She hadn't meant to destroy the AAI.

What she wanted to destroy was her sister.

How dare *she? Clara knows I'm not dead.* If nothing else, Nova knew she left bodies behind—she knew, because she stepped over them when she ran away. Nova's body wasn't one of those left, so Clara should have known that Nova was still alive.

"Hey! Blondie!" It was the empty-gun-wielding Martina. "Get your ass away from my place 'fore I fill you up with enough metal to open a shop, all righty?" (*Please don't hurt me, don't bust up my place anymore, I can barely afford the insurance and I don't know how the hell I'm gonna convince UNN to replace it without charging me. And please don't make me fire this empty gun. . . .*)

Nova turned and ran away as fast as her legs could go.

That wasn't especially fast, as it happened—days of lying next to a trash bin had left her legs rather rubbery when called upon to do anything more complicated than walk—but nobody gave chase. She could feel that much; everyone was too scared to get near her.

By the time she reached the intersection with Gladstone Way, she stopped and leaned against the side of a novelty store. She was horribly out of breath, and her hunger was now of epic proportions.

Across from the novelty store was another bodega. This one didn't have an AAI out front, either, but unlike the Miltons' place, Nova knew that it was because the owner didn't care if people got food from there or not. The back room was used for card games, ranging from poker to haunan, and the place was also a popular meeting/dropoff spot for Markus Ralian's people.

Nova decided she'd have no problem stealing food from this place.

Still out of breath, she went into the bodega. The owner was behind the counter, watching the same UNN reporter who had been talking about Clara, only on a flatscreen. He was now talking about the new security measures at Osborne because of the increased terrorist attacks and the alien threat.

"The rebels have proven with their suicide run on the Terra Skyscraper that they're not above killing themselves to achieve their evil goals."

Snarling with disgust, Nova lashed out at the flatscreen, which sparked and exploded in a very satisfying manner. So did the credit reader on the counter, which she hadn't intended to destroy.

"What the flick—" The owner shielded his eyes from the sparking, then looked at Nova. "Who the flick're you?"

"I need *food*." To her own ears, Nova's voice sounded desperate, which hadn't been her intent— she wanted to sound tough, although she had no experience in doing so.

It seemed to work, though. "Damn, curve, when's the last time you ate?"

"Shut up! I want food, *now*, or I'll blow up something else! You scannin' me?" She added this last because she remembered Fagin and his people using the phrase, or something like it; she hoped that it would help her blend in.

The owner—whose name was Terence, and who was older than Nova's grandfather had been when he died—laughed. "Curve, you got a lotta jones comin' in here and threatenin' me, but I gotta tell you that if you don't get your pretty little ass outta my place, you ain't *never* gonna get your pretty little ass outta my place, you *scan* me?"

Nova knew that Terence didn't take her seriously as a threat, mainly because he thought that the blowing up of the flatscreen and reader was due to their being of inferior manufacture. She was also really angry at herself for getting the phrase "you scan me" wrong.

Closing her eyes, she focused on where she knew Terence was standing, thanks to being able to feel his thoughts, and then scrunched her face in concentration as she tried to lift him.

She almost collapsed from the effort, but she got him up in the air—

—for about a second. Then he fell to the floor.

Pain sliced into Nova's head behind her right eye. She'd never tried anything that focused before, and it hurt like hell.

And it had mostly served only to crack Terence off. "You flickin' *curve*!" he cried as he clambered to his feet. He pulled a T10 out from under the counter. It was his prize weapon, one he'd been issued by the Confederate Army when he served in it sixty years ago. It didn't work very well, and it took Nova only half a second to jam the firing mechanism—after reading how to do it in Terence's mind.

Terence found that out when he tried to fire and the clip opened up unexpectedly and cut into the area between his thumb and forefinger. "Ooowwww!" He dropped the gun and shook his hand back and forth.

"I can keep this up all day, Terence," she said. "And not only that, I can tell Markus Ralian that you let a fifteen-year-old girl—*yes*, I'm only fifteen—make you look like an idiot. The only way to stop me is to *give me some flicking food*!"

Nova had never cursed in her life before. Somehow, though, it felt like the right thing to say just at the moment.

Cradling his injured hand in the other arm, Terence said, "Who the flick *are* you?" He shook his head. "Flick it, don't matter. Take whatever the flick you want, just get the flick *out* of my place when you're done. I don't ever want to see you in here again."

"Fine."

All of Terence's food was prepackaged: sandwiches, most of which looked like they had been on the shelf long past their date of expiration, so she skipped them; fruit and vegetables, most of which had gone bad, so she avoided them as well; mealbars, most of which were still good, so she took the three that were framberry-flavored; an assortment of drinks including, bless him, framberry juice, of which Nova took four bottles. Realizing she couldn't carry all that, she turned to Terence. "A bag?"

Terence, who was applying a salve to his hand, couldn't believe she was asking. "*Take* a flickin' bag."

She decided to try something. Closing her eyes again, she focused on the bags, which were on a rack next to the now-useless cardreader. She tried to bring them over to her.

The experiment was only a partial success—she actually grabbed the *entire* rack of bags, and she got them only halfway to her before they fell all over the floor.

Sheepishly, she bent over to pick one up. Terence was just shaking his head and wondering when the crazy curve was gonna get the flick *out* of his place.

Dropping the mealbars and the bottles of juice into the bag, she then took all ten bags of jerky that Terence had on the shelf—that never went bad, and the protein would be good for her—and a bag of camthar cookies, which she hadn't had since she was a kid.

About to leave, she had a thought, and grabbed Terence's entire supply of canned cat food: fifteen cans, ranging in flavor from salmon to tuna to eilik-fish. This would be better for Pip than the scraps she retrieved from the trash bin or the occasional alley mouse.

"You *done* yet?" Terernce asked angrily. At least, his tone was angry. In truth, he was scared to death.

Nova decided to keep him scared. She knocked over the entire fruit rack, sending the bruised and green fruit—which, like all his food, he only kept out for show, anyhow—tumbling to the floor.

She smiled at him. "*Now* I'm done." Then she turned on her heel and walked out, leaving Terence to curse her name, her parents, her ancestors, and who-ever she might have been related to back on Old Earth, while cleaning up the mess she made. He was also thinking about how he was going to pay for a new flatscreen and cardreader. . . .

Malcolm Kelerchian had to wait two hours to see Director Killiany. He would have just stormed into her office, but the door was coded only to open when it scanned the retinal patterns of either Killiany or her assistant, or when the latter touched a control on her desk. Said control was attuned to her DNA, so if any-one else touched it, the door wouldn't open.

Mal had spent the two hours he sat in the waiting

room trying desperately to ignore the holofeed from UNN and figuring out ways to subdue and/or kill the assistant and use her finger—preferably after it was violently and painfully removed from the rest of her hand—to touch the control.

Finally, the assistant—whose name Mal didn't really care about—said, "The director will see you now."

Rising from the uncomfortable couch, Mal gave her the most insincere smile he could muster—which was quite insincere indeed—and said, "Thank you *so* much."

She gave him an equally insincere smile back, though hers was due to training in always providing a smile no matter what, as opposed to the contempt that motivated Mal. "You're very welcome, Agent Kelerchian."

At her touch of the control, the door to Killiany's office slid open.

Ilsa Killiany fooled a lot of people. Short, skinny, weighing less than Mal's leather duster, with short brown hair, a hook nose, and a pair of spectacles that were wholly unnecessary in the age of Retinor, she gave the initial impression of being harmless.

That lasted right up until she opened her mouth. Her tongue was so barbed it had brought thirty-year veterans of the Confederate Army to their knees, and she didn't brook fools for more than about six and a half seconds.

Mal didn't consider himself to be any kind of fool, so he figured he was good for half a minute.

Killiany's desk was immaculate, which was one of several reasons why Mal had always assumed her to be more than a little insane. The only thing that broke the monotony of the shiny wood surface of the desk was her computer terminal and a holoprojection of UNN, which was currently paused, leaving the reporter—not Mara Greskin, so Mal didn't care which one it was—standing in mid-grin with her eyes closed. It looked both revolting and amusing at the same time.

Without preamble, he said upon entering her office, "Why the hell is Clara Terra going around declaring her sister to be dead?"

Killiany glared at him from over her spectacles. "I'm fine, Kelerchian, how are you?"

Mal took a seat in Killiany's guest chair. Her chair was made of very rare, very expensive leather. The guest chairs were rickety wood that felt like they'd collapse under you at any minute and, Mal knew, would do the watusi on his spine if he sat in it for more than ten minutes. Luckily for him, Killiany rarely let people stay in the office that long.

"Why is Clara Terra telling everyone who watches UNN that Nova Terra is dead when I'm picking up every rock in the Gutter trying to *find* Nova Terra?"

"And how *is* that going, exactly?" she asked in a sweet voice that lowered the temperature in the room by ten degrees.

"Lousy." Mal had never been one for equivocating. "All the Terra vehicles are accounted for, down to the hoverbikes, so she didn't take one of those. Her ID is on file at every train station, bus depot, and ship port in town, and she hasn't tripped a one yet. Plus—"

"She's a teep—*and* a teek. She can—"

Holding up a hand, Mal said, "She's an *untrained* teep/teek. If we were talking an actual Ghost, then yeah, she could fool people and scanners into thinking she was someone else, but as far as I can tell, *she* didn't even know she was a teep, and she definitely didn't have any training worth a damn—and before you ask, *yeah*, I talked to all the people here. Nobody did anything for the Terras on the side, and nobody *outside* here'd give her the right kinda training."

Killiany smirked. "Good work."

That brought Mal up short. Ilsa Killiany wasn't one for giving compliments. "Uh, thanks. Anyhow—she's probably still in Tarsonis, which means she's either uptown or downtown, and she ain't uptown."

"So you think she's in the Gutter?"

Mal nodded.

"You get files from the districts?"

Sighing, Mal said, "Nobody reports this kind of—"

"That isn't what I asked, Agent Kelerchian." The temperature went down another five degrees.

"Yeah, I got the files. Nothing. I also asked a cop I know in the Southwestern to look for signs of a teep working the area." *Five, four three . . .* "He hasn't heard anything yet, but I'm holding out—" *Two, one . . .*

Killiany leaned forward in her chair, setting her hands palms-down on the surface of the desk. "What the *hell* are you doing talking to a *grunt* about a *classified*—"

And zero. "Ma'am, do you want me to find Nova Terra?"

Tightly, Killiany said, "That is your assignment."

"Then let me find her. I can't work the Gutter blind, and without a psionic wave to compare hers to, our scans are just spittin' in the wind. I need someone who's got his ear on the street, and that isn't anyone in this department, it's someone who works the Gutter every day. Fonseca's a good cop, and he—"

"Oh, Fonseca?" Killiany leaned back. "Why didn't you say it was him? Never mind."

Mal felt like he missed a step. "You know Larry?"

"We've targeted him for recruitment plenty of times. For as long as we've been targeting you, actually," she added with another smirk. "Difference is, with you, we had a convenient crapstorm to use as incentive."

With an effort, Mal bit his tongue. "Incentive" wouldn't have been his first choice in words.

Killiany continued: "But Fonseca's got nothing we can hold on him. His jacket's clean."

Of course it is. He's in the doghouse all the time, but it's never anything that they can have paperwork on, since it's all connected to graft. Everyone knows about it, but with no record of it . . . "So it's okay that I went to him?"

"No. It would've been okay if you cleared it with me first." She leaned forward again. "Understand something, Kelerchian—you work for me. I know you don't want to be here, but it's way past time you got comfortable with several facts." The director started enumerating on the fingers of her right hand. "Fact: You're making more money and have considerably better benefits as a Wrangler than you ever did as a cop. Fact: If I hadn't pulled your ass out of the Detective Squad, your head would be on a pike outside the Tygore Estate, and you know it. Fact: As long as you are a Wrangler, you are answerable to me, and you do *not* break the mission specs without clearing it with me first, and the only way I'm going to clear it is if you provide full disclosure." Closing her hand into a fist, she added, "I'm not an idiot, Kelerchian. I know you have skills and your own methods. But this is a serious business here. We're training people who are the last line of defense for the Confederacy against scumwads like Mengsk and whatever these aliens are that have been showing up. We've lost two planets at least, and the only way we're gonna survive is with soldiers like the Ghosts. That makes our work *extremely* important, and I won't have you making it more difficult with your bull. Am I clear, Agent Kelerchian?"

Mal had spent Killiany's diatribe picking at a splinter on the arm of his chair. He'd stopped paying attention somewhere around the phrase "full disclosure," but he knew it was impolitic—if not suicidal—to tell the director that. "Plasteel clear, ma'am. Now would the director be so kind as to answer my damn question?"

The sweet smile came back, which was never a good sign. "What question would that be?"

"Why is Clara Terra going around saying her sister's dead when I'm trying to *find* her sister? My cooperation with the TPF, as limited as it is beyond Officer Fonseca, will be crippled if the TPF thinks the target is—"

"Agent Kelerchian, what happens if you find that Nova Terra is dead in some alley in the Gutter?"

"I'll—"

Killiany went on as if he hadn't spoken. "What'll happen is that the Terra family—or, I guess now the Kusinis-Terra family—will cover it up, pay off whoever needs to be paid off, and make like she died in the skyscraper with everyone else. Now, what happens if you find that Nova Terra is alive?"

"If that—"

"What'll happen *then* is that she'll be taken into the Ghost Program and trained. From that moment forward, November Annabella Terra will be, for all intents and purposes, dead, and she will be replaced with Agent X41822N."

Mal was more than a little disturbed by the fact that Nova had already been given a designation, since she hadn't actually been recruited into the program yet.

"So, Agent Kelerchian, what possible use is there in having Clara go on UNN and talk of her sister as if she were alive when the only possible outcome of your mission will be Nova's being dead, whether literally or not?"

Suddenly, Mal saw it. "You told her to go on UNN and make that speech."

"No, the Council did—but yeah, it was my idea. Set the record straight that Nova's no longer alive."

"What if she turns up alive somewhere else?"

Killiany frowned. "What do you mean? You said she hasn't left Tarsonis."

"I said she *probably* hasn't left Tarsonis. True, she hasn't tripped an ID scan yet. But no dragnet's a hundred percent foolproof. Yeah, she's just a fifteen-year-old kid with no training, but she's still a teep/teek, and who the hell knows how well she can use it? Sure, we *think* nobody trained her on the side, but how do we know that some renegade we don't know about hasn't been giving her pointers in the servants' quarters or something? Plus, she had a lot of hush money to throw around if she wanted to do something secret, and you know as well as I do that the Old Families can keep secrets better than anyone."

"What's your point, Agent Kelerchian?" Killiany asked in a tone that brought the room's temperature closer to absolute zero.

"My point is, she could be halfway to Tyrador by now and we may not know it. My point is, she could be any one of a thousand places where we won't find her. My point is, if we *don't* find her, and then she turns up alive somewhere, it'll be bad."

Shrugging, Killiany said, "It might be bad for the Terra family, but that's their problem, not mine. If she turns up alive somewhere, we take her for the program. Period."

Ilsa Killiany was completely certain in her words. *If the neat desk weren't enough, this proves it—she's crazy, just like every zealot.* In her case, she was a zealot for the Ghost Program. To Mal it was a job, and one he didn't even want; but for Director Killiany, running the Ghost Program was what she was born to do.

Or at least she believed it was, which was the same thing.

"Is there anything else?" she asked in a tone that made it clear that the answer to that question had best be in the negative.

"No." Mal got up from the uncomfortable chair and stretched his back, cracking a vertebrae or two. "I'll keep you posted."

"See that you do." Killiany touched a control on her desk, and the holograph started up.

"The Warp Drive gave a stellar performance at the Waits Amphitheatre last night, playing to a full house—"

Mal shook his head as the door shut behind him, cutting off the entertainment reporter. *Wouldn't have thought Killiany was a classical music aficionado. . . .*

TEN

FAGIN SAT AT HIS DESK, GRINNING FROM EAR
to ear.

It had cost him a year's supply of hab to three cops
in the Southwestern District for him to get access to
the traffic sensors, but it was worth it. The sensors
were used by the cops to monitor vehicular traffic. On
those rare occasions when they used them, it was
mainly to extort fines out of kids on hoverbikes or to
nail the bus drivers who were so drunk or stoned that
they couldn't drive straight—which was about half of
them. Usually that was only every three months or so,
when the Council did an audit and made noises about
efficiency, at which time the TPF levied some fines
and arrested some drivers; then, after the fuss died
down, business went on as usual.

By tapping into those sensors, Fagin was able to
survey his empire.

Today, what he wanted to survey was the little
blond curve that Markus brought him.

Oh, she'll be mine, that's for damn *sure. She just gotta learn a little.*

He'd programmed his sensor feed to alert him whenever it picked Blondie up. *Never did get her name.*

"F-F-Fagin?" the sleepy voice of Number Nine came from the futon behind him.

"Go to sleep, darl. Daddy's busy, okay?"

"Mmmph."

The alarm—a small beeping noise—went off right after he had finished a marathon session with Number Nine. It had been a long two days—Tenilee had been having some difficulty in her first few days on the job running O'Callaghan. It turned out that Manfred's betrayal ran much deeper than one street skimmer, and it had taken a great deal of work on the parts of both Fagin and Tenilee—who was eager to please and desperate not to meet the same fate as her predecessor—to straighten it all out. Several demotions, corpses, and broken limbs later, O'Callaghan had more or less settled down, though now Tenilee was getting complaints from the customers, and she was concerned that people were going to start going across Spring Street to Kitsios for their stuff.

As a result of all this, he'd had a stressful few days, and he found himself relieving much of it with Number Nine, who wasn't the best-looking person in his harem of twelve, but who had the most stamina.

Then, to his glee, the sensors finally found Blondie.

She was first picked up stumbling down Decker, a glazed look in her eyes. Fagin recognized the look instantly, of course: hunger. *I warned you that you wouldn't be able to stand it for much longer.*

Then she stopped outside the Milton Bodega before moving on. Now Fagin was confused. *Why didn't she go in?*

While she wandered, Fagin opened a desk drawer and took out his fone. He called Sergeant Morwood.

"Morwood."

"Fagin. My order come in?"

"You panbrain, I told you not to call me when I'm—"

"Did my order come in, Sergeant?"

"I'm still working on it. I'm hoping to have something for you tomorrow."

"I'd better. I'd hate for your wife's hab supply to suddenly disappear, okay?"

Fagin could hear Morwood gulp over the fone. "Look, it's not *easy* getting stuff from that department. You sure I can't get you something easier—a nuclear warhead, maybe?"

"Sure, I'll take the warhead—so I can shove it up your ass when you don't get me what I asked for, you scan me?"

Blondie had made it to Colman now. She turned and walked up toward Pyke.

Morwood was whimpering. "Fine, fine. *I'll* call *you* tomorrow. Now I've really got to go."

"I'd better hear from you." Not that Fagin had any doubts. Although he always complained and insisted he couldn't do what Fagin asked, Morwood always came through in the end. His wife was as bad off as any habhead in the Gutter; it was a need that could not be fulfilled on the salary of a supply sergeant in the Confederate Army. However, as a supply sergeant, he was in a position to get things Fagin needed, so he kept Diane Morwood in hab and her husband supplied Fagin with the occasional government toy.

Fagin disconnected with Morwood as Blondie went onto Pyke, stopping at a news vendor and joining the crowd watching the AAI that provided a UNN feed. All Fagin could see was the reporter—the sensor picked up only visual images, not sound, so Fagin couldn't hear anything. Not that he cared all that much—

—at least until the AAI changed into a teary-eyed woman who said a few things that had a profound effect on Blondie.

A second later, whatever doubts Fagin had about whether or not Blondie was a teek were dispelled by the AAI's exploding right after she screamed at it.

Frowning, Fagin reverse-cued the feed to a few minutes before, then focused in on the AAI.

The image it was projecting was a woman who was older than Blondie, dressed in the black of mourning. She was definitely related to Blondie—too young to be her mother, unless she had a *damn* good surgeon, so probably a sister.

And seeing her made Blondie go all panbrain. *So maybe your family isn't all dead after all.*

Fagin called up the UNN menu to see if he could figure out which story Blondie was watching.

Scrolling through a bunch of thumbs, he finally found one that showed the same face. The thumb had a caption that read: CLARA TERRA GIVES FIRST APPEARANCE AFTER FAMILY MASSACRE.

Crap.

Fagin played the story. When it was done, he was torn between breaking into a dance and shooting himself in the head.

On the one hand, Blondie—or, rather, Nova—did have family who could pay a ransom. In fact, they could pay a king's ransom out of pocket change, because she was from the Terra family, one of the Old Families.

The problem was—well, she was from one of the Old Families. They didn't pay ransoms. If you were stupid enough to kidnap one of theirs, they wielded their tremendous influence to crush you like a colony of cockroaches.

Fagin knew his limits. He was able to keep the cops off his ass down here because the cops didn't have a better offer, and because he kept off the sensors of anybody important. But he was just a little chip in the machine, and the nanosecond he came to the attention of someone on the Council or one of the Old Families, his entire life was gonna be as nuked as Korhal.

Besides, based on the story he just watched, Clara Terra thought her sister was dead. He couldn't be sure without an audio feed from the traffic sensors, but it was probably right around when she talked about her sister as a corpse that Nova decided to go all teek on the AAI and blow it to crap.

Speaking of which, Fagin started up the sensor feed again, which showed the woman who ran the news vendor running out with a gun. Fagin wasn't sure why a woman with a gun would scare Nova— certainly Fagin shoving one in her face hadn't had any kind of impact on her a few days ago—but now she ran away.

Eventually she wound up in Terence's place. *Stupid curve*, Fagin thought with a smile. *She's about to find out just how far my arm reaches.*

That smile fell in short order, however, when Terence allowed her to take food. To be fair, it wasn't until after Nova blew up his flatscreen and his cardreader, and after she picked him up and dropped his fat ass on the floor, and after she jammed up his T10.

Fagin grabbed his fone and called Markus.

Geena answered. "Chaneed, Fagin?"

"Where's your brother?"

"Goin' over the count."

Frowning, Fagin checked the time on his monitor, and saw that it was the time the day's cash came in. *Time flies when you're having fun.* "Tell him to cut Terence's percentage by ten."

"What'd he do?"

"It's what he didn't do, okay? Just make it true, you scan me?"

"Sure." Geena sounded like she didn't understand, not that Fagin gave a crap if she understood or not.

I told Markus to tell all *the stores to keep her from getting anything.* True, Nova made it hard on Terence, but Fagin didn't care. You start not following through, you may as well give the empire to someone who'll run it right, 'cause people stop listening when you don't follow through. Fagin learned *that* one early on when Grin started doing things like cutting only ten percent when he said he'd cut twenty, or breaking someone's arm when he said he'd kill them. In this business, that was a weakness, and weaknesses got you killed. That was why Fagin didn't have any.

He followed Nova carrying her new bounty back down to Decker. He lost her somewhere after Barre's Pharmacy. *She's probably been holed up in one of the alleys.*

Grabbing the fone, this time he called the Pitcher.

"Chaneed?"

"Got a target for you," Fagin said.

"Brutal. When and where?"

Pip was aloof when Nova first returned to the alley, but when she realized that the big hairless cat had provided some new food, she became very friendly, rubbing up against Nova's leg and purring. *Good food from big hairless cat. Happy.*

Nova set out a can of tuna for Pip, which the tabby commenced to consuming at a great rate. Then she sat down behind the trash bin and stared into the bag, realizing that she had no idea what to eat first. After not having eaten for days, she found herself with an embarrassment of riches.

Finally, she settled on the mealbar, figuring it was framberry-flavored and also would provide the most nutritional value.

Cautiously, she unwrapped it and took the first bite.

Seconds later, she ate the second one, having eaten the first down in three bites.

Once the dam broke, she found she couldn't stop. Before long, all the mealbars were consumed, and her stomach ached from being forced to digest after being inactive for so long. Her mouth dried up, and she grabbed one of the bottles of juice.

Leaning back against the wall, she drank half the framberry juice bottle in one gulp, and wondered how long she'd be able to keep this up. This food would last her a few days—maybe less if she kept going through it like this—and then she'd have to steal some more.

What does it matter, since you want to die anyway? the stupid little voice pointed out, but she had gotten as good at tuning out the little voice as she had the thoughts of those around her—at least those not in the immediate vicinity. More and more she was thinking that dying wasn't such a good idea.

But living didn't hold great appeal either. She had no idea what she was going to do.

Her old life was gone. Mommy and Daddy and Eleftheria and Edward and Zeb were all dead. Clara had callously written her off also. And how could she go back anyhow? If she did, she'd be imprisoned for the murder of all those people. There was no way she could get away with mass murder, there just *wasn't*.

So where does that leave me? Spending my days sitting in an alley with a moody tabby cat eating food I've stolen from crooks?

That didn't sound like much of a life.

But I don't want to die, either. She finally was able to admit that to herself. As terrible as life had become, the idea of not being alive was one that scared her more than anything—even more than the memory of what she had done at the skyscraper.

Edward dying with hatred in his mind, Gustavo dying looking forward to being with his family, Rebeka dying wondering why men were holding guns to her head, Marco dying wishing he'd told Doris that he loved her, Doris dying wondering why Marco never spoke to her, Walter dying thinking about how much fun it was to watch Gustavo kill the Terra family, Yvonne dying thinking that she hadn't finished cleaning the study yet and Ms. Terra would just kill her if she didn't do it, Derek dying thinking that—

"No!" she cried, forcing the memories out of her head, and also startling Pip, who jumped away from her can of tuna. *What's happening? Will big hairless cat hurt me?*

Once Pip realized that no harm would come to her, she went back to eating.

Nova pressed her fists against her eyes, tears squeezing out between the lids. Every time she'd thought she'd finally started having a handle on things, something would come up to make her realize that she had a long way to go.

It suddenly occurred to her what she needed: training. After all, when Clara, at age seventeen, decided she wanted to take her natural talent for the piano and hone it, Mommy hired the virtuoso Dee Palmer to train her. She later decided not to bother pursuing it, which Nova knew was because Palmer refused to respond to her outlandish attempts to flirt with him, but that didn't change the fact that when you wanted to learn how to do something, you found an expert.

Are there any experts on what's happened to me?

Nova thought about it a moment, and realized there *had* to be. She couldn't possibly be the only person who could do the things with her mind that she could do.

Which raised the question of where she would *find* someone to train her.

Not here. The Gutter was, she realized, the worst place to find such training. But sadly, she had nowhere else to go. And even this place was inhospitable to her—she could tell from the thoughts of Markus and the thugs he had guarding her that Jules Dale was the most powerful person in the Gutter. Without his patronage, she had no chance here; even with it, there were no guarantees.

But what else could she do?

With these thoughts swirling around in her head, she lay down in the little cubbyhole behind the trash bin that had become her bedroom of late. It was nice and warm—it was next to a cooling unit that kept the building that used the trash bin cool, so it pumped out warm air. The condensation from that unit had also provided her with water, albeit warm and icky water, her desperate sips of which often prompted the little voice to ask her why she was drinking this wretched stuff if she wanted to die.

She slept comfortably—well, as comfortably as possible in an alley behind a trash bin—and for the first time since her family died, she had no dreams.

Kill kill, maim maim, I love to take little girls and rip their tiny throats out, yes I do.

Instantly awake, Nova shot upward, hitting her head on the top of the cubbyhole. The intensity of the thoughts she suddenly heard was overwhelming.

She climbed out to see Pip hissing at the mouth of the alley. Glancing at her watch, she saw that she had slept for fourteen hours, which was the longest she'd been able to stay asleep in the alley. *Food is obviously good for my ability to relax*, she thought wryly.

Rubbing the top of her head where she'd hit it, she looked over to see what the cat was hissing at.

Can't wait to bite off her ear, yes, that'll be fun, ripping the ear right *off with my teeth, oh yes.*

It was a large man with piercings all through both ears, both lips, both nostrils, and both eyebrows. His heavily muscled arms were covered with holographic tattoos that showed a variety of acts of violence being perpetrated by large people upon small people.

Nova couldn't tell what his name was, because he himself no longer remembered it. He was referred to as the Pitcher because he once drank an entire pitcher of grain alcohol with no obvious ill effect—probably because he was already so fogged as to be clinically insane.

The little girl he wanted to kill right now was Nova herself.

He started moving down the alley toward her, with only her violent, brutal death in his thoughts. . . .

The little girl was right there in the alley, ripe for the taking, just like the bald man said she would be.

He loved it when the bald man gave him things to do. It provided him with a purpose that a bland and meaningless life had left him with no possibility of gaining on his own.

Or maybe it was the booze talking. It was hard to be sure.

He touched his arm, and that pumped the hab into his system. It had no effect. It hadn't had any effect the last six hundred and forty-nine times he'd tried it. That was what he hated about life in general, was that he got used to everything. But he was an optimist at heart—or maybe he was a pessimist at heart, he could never keep those two straight—and so he kept trying the hab in the hopes that *this* time it might get him high.

But it didn't. It never did anymore, and he wondered why he bothered taking it six hundred and fifty times when he knew, just *knew*, that it wasn't going to ever work ever again and there was just no *point*, dammit!

He forgot where he was.

He touched another part of his arm, and that sent the turk through his system. Turk made him more aware of his surroundings, which was good, because he couldn't possibly be *less* aware of his surroundings than he was right now and he didn't know where he was and wow the colors in this alley were so vivid it's a good thing he noticed that now because he didn't notice it before and the stonework was especially pretty except for the parts where it was cracked and ugly and filthy and dirty and covered in the fecal matter from assorted birds and rats and cats and dogs and whatever other animals came through here like that cat over there next to the blond girl who—

Sometimes turk made him *too* aware of his surroundings. But he remembered now. The blond girl. The bald man wanted him to kill the blond girl. The bald man promised a brand-new drug that was fresh off the market—hadn't hit the street yet, hadn't even been made illegal yet, it was so new—and the bald man promised that, once he killed the girl, he would get as much of it as he wanted for free, just like always.

The bald man was the only person who was ever nice to him. He liked the bald man.

He hated everyone else.

Except for Grandma, of course. She was always

nice to him to. In retrospect, killing her probably wasn't the smartest thing he ever did.

Thinking about Grandma made him sad, so he touched his arm again, this time giving him a combination of crab and snoke, which let him forget. As soon as he did that, he realized it was a bad idea, because then he'd forget—

Something.

He was supposed to do something.

It was something very important, too.

Incredibly important.

Yes.

He had to do it.

He had to do it right now.

What was it?

It probably involved violence.

That was pretty typical.

He was good at violence.

He wasn't good at anything else.

Especially remembering.

Whatever it was.

He was supposed.

To remember.

A cat meowed. *Brutal—now I remember.* He touched his arm again, this time to clear all the drugs out with caffeine. That had the added advantage of getting him all excited about whatever he was supposed to do—which he now remembered was to kill the blond girl who was standing next to the cat who just meowed.

He touched his arm again—what he needed was bog.

Bog wasn't anything that was on the market anymore. You couldn't even find it on Tarsonis, so he had been thrilled beyond all possible imagining when the bald man found it for him. It was a limited supply, so he was sure only to take it when he was about to kill someone.

And he was about to kill the blond girl.

The bald man had told him what her name was, but he forgot it. He couldn't even remember his own name. He knew he was called the Pitcher because of that time he drank the pitcher of grain alcohol. He killed the girl who called him that, but her nickname stuck, mainly because he couldn't remember what his own name was. Grandma knew it, but he killed her, so she couldn't say.

Of course, when the bog took effect, it didn't matter. Then the only thing he remembered was how much he loved little blond girls—especially when he ripped out their throats.

And her ear. She had a good ear. He'd enjoy biting that off. Maybe chewing on it.

"Get away from me."

He blinked. It took him a moment to realize that the blond girl had spoken. *How can she do that without a throat?*

Then he remembered—he hadn't actually ripped it out yet, he'd only thought about it. That was careless.

He started advancing on the blond girl.

"Don't come any closer—I'm warning you, Pitcher, if you come into this alley you'll—you'll regret it."

How'd she know my name? He decided to ask her. "How'd you know my name?"

"I know everything, Pitcher. I know how Fagin—"

That was the bald man's name. *Why can't I ever remember that?*

"—gives you free drugs so you'll do his bidding. I know how you killed your grandmother. I know that you want to rip my throat out and then bite off my ear."

He must have been talking out loud before. Except he didn't remember doing that.

"And I know that if you try to hurt me, I'll hurt you instead."

That was the funniest thing he'd heard all day. In fact, it was the funniest thing he'd ever heard. So he started laughing.

"*Bwah*-hah-hah-hah-hah-hah-hah-hah-hah-hah-hah-hah-hah-hah-hah-hah!"

His stomach almost exploded, he was laughing so hard. He couldn't believe that this little girl thought *she* could hurt *him*.

"Yes, I *can* hurt you."

Finally, he spoke. "Know't I did t'last girl?"

"You mean the one in the Firefly Club? The one who asked you where you got the ugly tattoo?"

Okay, now this was starting to really fog with his brain. There was no way—*no way*—that this little blond girl knew about what happened at the Firefly Club with that dark-haired girl. "You were there?"

"No. I've never been to the Firefly Club."

The blond girl's words were coming really fast out of her mouth now, and she was breathing heavy, like she was on something, and she was starting to cry. He was impressed—they usually didn't start crying until he got closer to them than he was right now.

She continued: "But I know that you put your hand over her face and kept it there until she stopped breathing. What kind of monster *are* you?"

He knew the answer to that one. "I'm th'one 'at's gonna kill you, curve."

"You're never killing anyone ever again, Pitcher. You hear me? *Never*."

He decided that this girl was even more fogged than he was—and he didn't think *anyone* was more fogged than *he* was—and the only thing to do was to start ripping her throat out.

Touching his arm to pump some more hab into him even though he knew it was pointless, he advanced on her.

He decided he was going to rip her arms off first. He wasn't sure where that thought came from, but as soon as it arrived, he knew it was very much the right thing to do. She'd stand there, staring at the stumps that her shoulders would be and then—yes!—then he'd beat her to death with her own arms. *Brutal—that'll be fantastic!*

For effect—and because it was easier for him to

walk that way ever since the accident—he stomped his feet on the pavement as he moved closer, hoping to scare the crap out of the little girl so she'd be sweating by the time he actually ripped her throat out.

No! Ripped her arms off. That was *much* better. . . .

He picked one leg—he was pretty sure it was his left one—up to stomp down.

Then he stopped.

He wasn't sure why; he just couldn't move. For some reason, he couldn't put his leg back down. Or blink. Or move his arms. Or *anything*.

His head started to hurt.

No, it was on *fire*. Like someone drove a hot metal spike right through his skull.

This was worse than the time he ran his head through a brick wall just to see if it would work, worse than the time he lit his hair on fire to see how long it would burn, worse even than the time he took raw turk for the first and last time.

"AaaaaaaaaaaaaaaaaaaaaaaaAAAAAAAAAAAAAA AAAAAHHHHHHHHHHHHHHHHHHHHHHHHHHHHH-HHHHHHHHHH*HHHHHHHHHHHHHHHHHHHHHHH-HHHHHHHHHHHHHH*!!!!!!!!!"

It had been easier than she thought it would be.

And that scared Nova more than anything else in the world could have.

Pip walked over to the Pitcher's body and sniffed it curiously. *Big hairless cat fell down.*

When she'd lashed out at Edward and everyone

else at the Terra Skyscraper, Nova did so without thought or focus, just throwing all her rage, all her grief, all her sadness, and all her anger out in one shot.

It was enough to kill three hundred and seven people at once.

This time, she'd focused very specifically on one mind instead of over three hundred, and smashed it to pieces.

It only took a few seconds. And then the Pitcher was dead. He screamed and then fell forward, his ugly, multiply pierced face smashing into the pavement with a bloody splat. Blood trickled out his ears.

Reaching out with her mind—she couldn't bear the thought of touching him—she managed to roll him over.

Blood was coming out his nose and eyes and mouth as well. Some of that was probably from the impact of his face hitting the ground, but she knew from home that when she killed someone this way, they bled out of every orifice in the head.

Nova collapsed to her knees, sobs now racking her body. *I shouldn't have left the alley. I should've stayed here and died.* Today she'd seen so much, from her sister declaring her dead to the miserable lives of the people around her to the casual vileness of Terence to the insane bruality of the Pitcher.

She didn't know how much more she could take.

Pip wandered up to her. *Big hairless cat hurt?*

Sniffing, Nova tried to wipe her eyes with her shirt-sleeve, then realized it was so dirty as to not be of much use. She used the back of her hands instead, though they were hardly cleaner.

"Mrow?"

"I'm sorry, Pip, I just—" She looked over at the corpse of the Pitcher. "I don't know what to do."

Fagin said that he was going to leave her alone, make her survive on her own until she came back to him, begging for forgiveness and a chance to work for him the way seemingly everyone in the Gutter did.

He'd lied to her. Instead of keeping his word, he sent a monster to kill her.

What was more, the Pitcher probably wouldn't be the last one he'd send. He had hundreds of hired thugs who did his bidding. She'd met some of them, from Markus and his dirty secrets on down to Tyrus and his dead sister.

Nova had just learned how easy it was to kill someone. Particularly someone as disgusting as the Pitcher. He, at least, had his insanity to blame for a lot of what was wrong with him—that and a frightening ability to metabolize drugs and alcohol.

But Fagin was considerably more disgusting, and didn't have the mitigating factor of being crazy.

Standing up, Nova made a decision.

"Mrow?"

"I'm going back to Fagin, Pip, just like he said I would. But I'm not gonna beg him for anything. I'm going to kill him."

CHAPTER 11

WHEN TWO HOURS PASSED, AND THE PITCHER never came out of the alley, Fagin assumed that the plan didn't work.

This really cracked him off. The Pitcher was both his most valuable enforcer and his most useful test bed for new drugs that came on the market. His metabolism was such that his response to a drug was about ten percent of how normal people would react. Back in the old days, Fagin had a source for some great designer drugs on Korhal IV. Sometimes, though, the stuff was too intense—you didn't want drugs that killed on the first shot, because then you don't get repeat business. So he'd use the Pitcher—if it made him sick, it'd kill anyone else, and so he knew which ones to put on the market.

(The day the confederals nuked Korhal IV was a bad day for Fagin. When Arcturus Mengsk started up the Sons of Korhal, Fagin had sent a rather generous contribution to Mengsk to further his cause, just because he was cracked off about the attack. . . .)

Three hours after the Pitcher went into the alley, Nova came out. The expression on her face was much different from the one a day earlier. Where yesterday she looked starved and desperate, today she looked angry and determined.

Between that expression and the fact that she survived an encounter with the Pitcher—something no one had managed in *years*—Fagin knew he was about to have bigger problems.

Someone knocked at the door. "Fagin, you got a package."

A protest that he'd left instructions not to be bothered died on his lips—the only exception to those instructions was if a package arrived. "Bring it," he said as he touched the control that would lower the force field and open the door.

Jo-Jo came in holding a shipping box with the holographic label MEDICAL SUPPLIES, and a return address from the Confederate Army Supply Depot in Grange Village.

Fagin grinned. *Morwood came through.*

After Jo-Jo put the package down on Fagin's bed, he left. Fagin grabbed the mailscan out of his desk drawer and ran it over the package; the mailscan's display showed him an alphanumeric code, which he then entered into the keypad on the package. With a pneumatic hiss, it opened, revealing a mass of

Pakstuf surrounding the item he had ordered from Morwood.

While reading over Morwood's note, he grabbed his fone and called Markus.

"Chaneed, Fagin?"

"I need you to grab every habhead who's short and needs a fix, and every little kid you can scrounge up, okay? I'm talkin' pre-acnoid here—and nobody hooked, I don't want no yous." He thought about who was on his list—the one of people who were a filament away from having their heads blown off by Fagin's P220. "And get Poppo, Jonesy, Two-Bit, and Mags down here, too, and tell them to bring *all* their guns. Get 'em all here in half an hour."

"What do we need little kids for?" Markus asked.

Fagin frowned. Markus wasn't usually one for asking stupid questions—or any other questions, it came down to it. "The hell do *you* care? Get it done, you scan me?"

"Yeah, okay." Markus didn't sound happy, though.

What the flick is wrong with him? Fagin shook his head. *Worry about it later—it'll keep until this business is taken care of.* Right now he had a crisis, but he'd also been given the perfect weapon to fight it.

After reading Morwood's note, he clipped his new toy onto his right wrist and stuck the head unit into his ear. Then he checked the traffic sensors. Nova was walking right toward here. At the rate she was going, it'd be an hour of walking before she arrived.

Grabbing his fone again, he called Wolfgang. Whenever there was a body needed taking care of before the TPF stumbled across it, Wolfgang was the one to call. Most crimes, the TPF would look the other way, but when bodies got knocked, they had to pay at least *some* attention. So he had Wolfgang and Wolfgang's girls remove the evidence.

After giving Wolfgang his orders—and making sure he brought *all* his girls, as the Pitcher had considerable mass—Fagin then called Jo-Jo in, and took him into the back room, where his harem had their pallets. All twelve of them were lounging about, some reading, some nibbling from a bowl of fruit, the rest sleeping. He woke them all up and had Jo-Jo take them to the other place. Most of them agreed right away but, typically, Number Three asked, "What's going on?"

"Ain't gonna be safe here." Fagin turned to Jo-Jo. "Anything happens to any of them, it happens to you times ten, okay?"

Nodding quickly, Jo-Jo said, "I scan, boss, no worries."

By the time Jo-Jo cleared all twelve of them from the room—some of them were a bit languorous in their movements, not enjoying being put out—Grotto came in.

"Poppo and Two-Bit're at the door, Fagin—they look kinda scared."

Fagin grinned. His complaints notwithstanding, Markus, as usual, did exactly what he was told. It was less than half an hour, and Poppo and Two-Bit were already here.

Five minutes later, Jonesy came in, quickly followed by Mags. Jonesy was the only one of the four of them who came with just one gun. Shrugging, he held up his Z50, which fired .70-caliber bullets. "I don't never need nothin' but Karla," Jonesy said with a smile.

His predilection for naming his weapons was one of several reasons why Jonesy was on Fagin's list.

The others had all packed at least four guns each. Two-Bit went overboard and brought ten. "I can't never figure out which one I wanna use, so I like to keep my options open, y'know?"

Fagin had 'em sit in the outer room. Ten minutes later, Markus showed up with Geena, Tyrus, and a bunch of kids—all pre-acnoid, which was exactly what Fagin wanted.

"Bring the kids into the back. Have Ty keep an eye on 'em."

Markus shot him a look. "What?"

Holding up a hand—this was a question Fagin could understand—he said, "It's clear back there. The kids're what you call a last line of defense."

Looking cracked off at something, Markus told Geena and Tyrus to bring them into the back room. "Geena, you take care of 'em—they need anything, send Ty up front."

Fagin looked at the other four recent arrivals. "There's a girl comin' here lookin' to do me harm. Your job is to stop her doin' me harm, okay? I don't care what you gotta do, but don't let her back into my room, you scan me?"

Three of them brightened. Bodyguarding duty was usually a choice assignment, especially since most folks knew better than to flick with Fagin. Either they'd find out pretty soon that this wasn't such a soft deal, or they'd surprise Fagin by actually stopping a teep/teek, in which case, they'd have earned their way off the list.

Poppo didn't brighten, though; he was the only one of them who was on the clever side of dim. "You need four of us to stop one girl?"

Hefting Karla, Jonesy said, "He won't, don't worry."

Sounding like he was getting his hopes up, Two-Bit asked, "Can we do anything to her 'fore we kill her?"

Mags snorted. "Only way you're gonna get some snap is if you kill her *first*."

"Yeah, well, your sister tells a different story."

"Stud, you couldn't keep *up* with my sister."

While the banter went on for several more seconds, Markus walked up to Fagin and talked to him in a low voice, his back to the other people in the room. "Are we talkin' about *that* girl?"

Fagin nodded. "Her name's Nova. I sent the Pitcher to take her out."

Markus blinked. "What happened to lettin' her starve on her own? You said—"

"Her name's Nova *Terra*."

Now Markus's eyes went wide. "Crap."

"Yeah, crap. Once I found that out, I figured best be sure. But she took the Pitcher out. So that means we gotta get creative."

"That why you wanted these four panbrains?"

Again, Fagin nodded. "See how she does there, then spring the trap."

Unsurprisingly, Markus looked confused. But this time, he didn't question. He knew what Nova was, after all. "What about the habheads? I got Preach, Seer, and Diva roundin' 'em up."

"She's a teep. Figure brains like theirs oughta be pretty distractin' to read while these four panbrains're shootin' at her, okay?"

Markus nodded. "Yeah, makes sense." He looked at the item from Morwood. "What's the new toy?"

Grinning, Fagin said, "Insurance."

"Look, it was terrorists, okay? You gummint types're supposed to stop 'em Nephews o' Korhal, or whatever they are, right?"

Martina Dharma was starting to seriously irritate Mal Kelerchian, which was frustrating, as she was the first real lead he'd gotten in a week.

Larry hadn't heard anything that sounded like Nova might have been responsible. A few reports of people being beat up by girls, but Larry knew who the girls were, so they couldn't have been Nova.

Then, finally, a news vendor reported that terrorists blew up her AAI. Problem was, no scorch marks on it. When Larry heard about it, he figured that might mean teek, so he called Mal.

The first thing Mal did was head to Dharma's place. It was a pretty standard vendor's: She sold chips with

the various magazines on them, plus subscriptions for
UNN feeds, all in a tiny space that barely had room for
the candy and drink machines. The charred remains
of her AAI were now piled behind the small counter.
Dharma—a short, shabbily dressed middle-aged woman
with fake red hair who had attempted to use cut-rate
surgery to remove her wrinkles, and got what she
paid for—had pointed to those remains when Mal
arrived, then stood angrily back there while Mal tried
to question her.

As soon as Mal arrived, his head started pounding.
It wasn't as bad as the Terra Skyscraper—he needed
only one dose of analgesic—but it was still pretty
intense. Nova, or another really powerful teep—and
that concept didn't even bear thinking about—had
been here recently.

But the Dharma woman was fixated on terrorists.

"Ma'am, can you just please give me a description
of who—"

"I don't know who! I toldja, it was them terrorists!
They're everywhere—saw on UNN that they took out
some of the Terra folks. If you can't protect *them*, how
the hell you gonna protect me?"

Mal tried not to grit his teeth and was only partially
successful. "Ma'am, I think you have me confused
with someone else. My job isn't to protect you, my job
is to find someone. She's a girl, fifteen years old, long
blond hair, green eyes, and—"

"I see lotsa people every day." Dharma folded her
arms defiantly. "Look, you're with the gummint, you

said? Well, I been tryin' to get the confeds to take my claim, 'cause my insurance contract says that acts of terrorism are covered, and it had to be them terrorists that did it."

Deciding to play along for the moment, Mal asked, "What makes you so sure it's terrorists, ma'am?"

Dharma swallowed, and her arms fell to her sides. "Well, stands to reason, don't it? I mean, they was talkin' about them Terra folks when it 'xploded. Betcha it was the same folks what killed the Terras, showin' that they'll stop the freedom of the press." She started gesturing, warming to her rationalization. "And—and what better way to do that than to take down the very *symbol* of freedom of the press? Right?"

Slowly, Mal started clapping his hands. He also sub-vocalized instructions to his computer. When he was done with that, he said, "Brava, ma'am. That was a fine performance. Only one problem—I happen to know for a fact that it *wasn't* terrorists who did this." He stopped clapping and leaned onto the counter. "Now ma'am, there's one of two ways we can do this. The first way is that you tell me what happened with the blond-haired, green-eyed, fifteen-year-old girl who came through here and blew up your AAI. The second way is that I report you to your insurance company as someone who's trying to defraud them. Take your pick."

Dharma swallowed again, more audibly this time. "Defraud?"

"That's right." He then conveyed the result of his

computer request. "The penalty for such a crime is a fine of whatever amount deemed appropriate by the judge, with the option of up to six months in jail."

In a very small voice, Dharma said, "Jail?"

"Oh, and no insurance company will give you a policy after that—which means you'll probably have to close the store."

Now her eyes went wide; that thought seemed to distress her even more than the jail time. "Close the store! I can't do that! S'my livelihood! 'Sides, Frobeet'd kill me."

Mal neither knew nor cared who Frobeet was. "So how're we gonna do this, ma'am?"

Dharma's mouth twisted around once or twice. "Yeah, okay, there was a girl like that. She started muttering and then screaming when they had the Terra survivor on, and then I pulled my gun."

Raising an eyebrow, Mal asked, "Gun?"

Reaching down under the counter, Dharma pulled out a P180 that had seen better decades. The stock was cracked, and the thing hadn't been polished or cleaned in months. Mal figured if she tried to fire it, it'd blow up in her face, even if she wasn't pointing it at a teek.

"I know whatcher thinkin'." Dharma no doubt read the expression on Mal's face, which annoyed him, as he didn't like his feelings to show that obviously—but then, the gun was in *really* rotten condition. "But I ain't got no bullets for it. Don't want to be shootin' nobody—just, y'know, threatenin' them."

Mal didn't see how anybody could possibly feel threatened by that weapon, but said nothing about it, instead returning to the topic of Nova. "What happened after you pulled the gun?"

Shrugging, Dharma said, "She ran off."

"Which way?"

Another shrug. "I dunno, down the street. You're not gonna report me, are you?"

"I've recorded this entire conversation, ma'am. As to what I do with that recording—we'll just have to see."

With that, he turned around, ignoring the squeaking noises that Martina Dharma was now making.

Nova probably saw Clara declaring her dead and went crazy. So where'd she go from here?

According to the report Dharma had filed with the insurance company—which Mal had read over before talking to her—the AAI exploded yesterday at 18.55, which was confirmed by UNN's Remote Feed Department. Mal therefore instructed his computer to provide him with all the traffic sensor feeds on Pyke Lane from 18.50 to 20.00 the previous night.

It would take a few minutes for the computer to request the files, verify his authorization, go into the files, extract the specific feeds required, and transmit to him, so he decided to question the receptionist at the surgeon who operated out of a storefront two doors down from Dharma's place. The person working there at the moment wasn't there the previous night, but his badge gave him access to the person's contact information, and Mal made a note to call him.

When he walked out, the computer spoke into his ear that the feeds he requested were no longer available.

"What?"

The computer repeated the information, but Mal interrupted and subvocalized a command for him to be put through to the Southwestern District's Traffic Control Center.

A bored voice said, *"Southwest Traffic, Sergeant Volmer."*

"Sergeant, my name is Agent Malcolm Kelerchian of the Wrangler Squad."

A pause, then Volmer spoke with more attention, having verified the source of the call. *"Yes, Agent Kelerchian, what can I do for—"*

"I just requested the traffic feeds for Pyke Lane yesterday at—"

"Uh, I can stop you right there, Agent Kelerchian—we've already wiped those feeds."

Mal couldn't believe what he was hearing. "Say that again, Sergeant—slowly."

"Uh, that's standard procedure, sir. At the end of each shift, we go over the feeds, and if we don't find any violations, we wipe 'em. There weren't any violations on Pyke last night, so—"

"Sergeant Volmer, if I look up the regulations governing evidence, I can guarantee you that I'm not gonna find a damn thing about how it's 'standard procedure' to—"

Volmer laughed nervously. *"Agent Kelerchian, that wasn't evidence."*

"And how do you know this? Did you verify that no crimes were committed? Did you run facial scans of every person on those feeds to see if they matched any known fugitives?"

"Uh, sir, we're traffic control—that ain't our job. The only evidence we care about on Pyke Lane relates to hover-bike violations and people bringing illegal vehicles onto the street. Otherwise, we can't spare the storage."

That, Mal knew was crap. "Sergeant, you can't tell me that you don't have enough storage—"

"Sir," and now Volmer sounded like he was trotting out a very old argument that he was tired of making, *"we've only got fifty kilomemes."*

"Fifty?" Mal was stunned. That was a quarter of what the Northern District—the precinct that also housed the Detective Squad—had, and they didn't *need* more than a quarter of it.

"Yes, Agent Kelerchian, only fifty. We've been requesting additional memory for the last three years, but the budget committee keeps telling us it's an 'extravagance.' The courts down here are backed up to three years ago, 'cause everybody contests their citations 'cause they know it'll take years to settle it. We have to keep those feeds around indefinitely, and it adds up, to the point where we can't keep files we don't need. There's a lot of traffic violations down here. I'm sorry you can't look at those feeds, sir, truly I am." To Mal's surprise, coming from a

Southwest cop and all, Volmer sounded sincere in that apology. The sergeant continued: *"But those feeds are gone."*

Mal let out a very long breath. "All right, Sergeant, thanks for your help." Then he hesitated before ending the call. After a hasty subvocalization to his computer, he said, "How sorry *are* you?"

Now Volmer sounded confused. *"Sir?"*

"You said you were truly sorry, and I'm asking you to put your money where your foot is. You sorry enough to do me a favor?"

"I, uh—I guess that would depend on the favor, sir."

"I just sent you a photo of a girl I'm trying to find. She's to be considered armed and dangerous. She's the one I know was walking down Pyke Lane last night, and who I was hoping to get a track on. Can your people check for her facial profile on your traffic feeds when you go through them?"

The sergeant hesitated. *"I can't promise anything, sir, but we will keep an eye out."*

Mal nodded. It was better than a poke in the eye with a sharp stick. That was about *all* it was better than, but he'd take it. "Thank you, Sergeant."

"You're welcome, Agent Kelerchian. And good luck."

Yeah, I think I'm gonna need it. Mal sighed and put a call through to the surgeon's receptionist.

Nova's stomach was killing her.

She should have realized that this was going to happen. After not eating for several days, she had stuffed herself worse than she did on her birthday.

Maybe I should just go back to the alley and to Pip.

No. Fagin had sent the Pitcher, he'd send someone else. Maybe several someone elses. She didn't want anyone else to die because of her.

Except for Jules "Fagin" Dale. She intended to do everything she could to make sure he suffered before she destroyed his mind.

But only him. She'd already heard the dying thoughts of three hundred and eight people, and she only wanted to bring it up to three hundred and nine.

She managed to keep the thoughts of the people around her out, though the effort to do so was giving her a headache to match her stomachache. The important thing was to focus.

By the time she got to the very building that Fagin Dale had kicked her out of days ago, she started to feel woozy. The thoughts she was hearing didn't make any sense at all. It was disjointed and full of weird stuff and colors *oh wow the colors are just so amazing and you can't believe that there are rats crawling all over the place and crawling right up my butt which looks so incredibly fat in this outfit what the flick was I thinking when I bought this outfit I hate this outfit it's the worst outfit ever I hate you and everything you stand for you panbrained slike and I'm gonna just run around in little circles that get smaller and smaller every time until I disappear into a singularity of nothingness and then everyone'll be sorry they ever made fun of me just because I only have one nostril I mean really is that fair at all to be doing that sort of thing to a* child *a* child *a* child *I never wanted and don't—*

"No!" Nova had stumbled to the street, clutching her now-pounding head.

Two people were standing around her. Nova clung to their thoughts as if they were a lifeline. The woman was named Dorian and was a housecleaner for folks in the middle-class neighborhood of Sookdar's Point— people who had enough money to not have to live in the Gutter, but not enough to be able to afford automated housecleaning—and had just come from her favorite client, the Frieds, who always left out cookies for her when she came to clean. The man was named Max, and he was a counter clerk at a laundry facility who hated his boss and had come up with seventeen different ways to kill him, none of which he would ever enact in real life, but the thoughts of which allowed him to get through the day.

"You okay?" Dorian asked.

"Yes, I'm fine," Nova lied. "I'm sorry, I just tripped."

As soon as Nova got to her feet, Max, satisfied that all was well, went on his way, the beginnings of the eighteenth way to kill his boss formulating in his head.

Dorian, though, lingered. "You sure?"

Putting on the same smile she used on Andrea Tygore when the old woman was being particularly patronizing, Nova said, "Yes, thank you, ma'am."

"Such a polite girl." Dorian was genuinely surprised and pleased to see a teenager with manners, especially considering that her own three boys and one girl never used the word "please" in their lives. "Your momma is raisin' you right," she added with regret that she hadn't been able to do the same for her own kids.

Nova tried not to think about the fact that her own mommy was dead, instead reveling in the domestic simplicity of Dorian's mind. She used it to steel herself against the insanity that was waiting for her at Dale's place.

After excusing herself from Dorian and thanking her again for her help, she kept walking, her teeth gritted, sweat beading on her forehead, as she tried to hold back the onslaught of drug-induced thought patterns.

Why do people do this to themselves? she found herself wondering. *It makes your thoughts all crazy. Why would anybody do that?*

She clung to her outrage, adding it to her considerable anger at Jules for making her do what he'd made her do, as well as her fury at Cliff Nadaner, a man she'd never met, yet about whom she knew so much, the man who ordered her family killed.

That anger allowed her to shove the drugged thoughts to the side, even when she approached Fagin's building and saw them all gathered there around the big metal door that led to the lobby. Some were standing, some were sitting, some were lying down, but all of them were high on *something*—or several things.

Stepping around or over them, she approached the front door—

—and knew immediately that four people were standing on the other side, ready to shoot her.

Cursing herself for missing that, she lashed out with her mind, going for the guns. She didn't want to hurt anyone—except Fagin—but she wasn't going to let herself get hurt, either.

She knocked the gun out of the hands of the one named Richard Roman, but whom everyone called Poppo because of his habit of popping chewing gum when he was a kid. He hadn't actually chewed gum in ten years, but the nickname stuck.

The other three were still holding their guns, and laughing at Poppo for dropping his, despite the latter's protesting that he hadn't dropped it.

One of the people on the other side of that door was Hieronymous Jones—usually called Jonesy due to people having trouble pronouncing "Hieronymous"—and he knew *everything* about guns. Nova clearly read in his mind the best way to keep a Z50 like the one he was carrying—which he called Karla after the first girl he ever dated—from firing. All she had to do was keep the bullets from moving into the chamber properly.

After she did that, she read ways of jamming the others' guns as well. Some she couldn't jam—she didn't know where the trigger switch *was* on Poppo's P30, for example—but she did the best she could. It was almost like a game. . . .

She felt the thoughts of the habhead who walked

up to her while she stood outside Fagin's door before he spoke: "Hey, curve, wha's the feed?"

Nova turned to give him a funny look. Nobody'd said "What's the feed?" since Nova was a baby.

The habhead—his name was Joey—was thinking that he hadn't had any good snap in *years* and Nova'd be a fine way to break the streak.

Just by thinking about it, Nova knocked Joey down.

"What the flick jus' happen'? Coulda sworn I was standin' a second ago." Joey studied the ground intently, as if it would provide some kind of clue, his desire for Nova already fading into his hab-addled brain.

From next to him, one of the other habheads who was lying on the pavement said, " 'Ey, flickface, getcherown bed. I'm sleepin' 'ere." Her name was Sharie, and she had been born addicted to hab, since her mother got hooked on it when she was pregnant with her by an unknown father (well, Sharie knew the father, she just didn't know which of the dozens of possible sperm donors whom her mother entertained was the culprit, since the money for a simple DNA test instead went to feed mother and daughter's respective drug habits).

Not to be confused with Eamonn, who fought in the Confederate Marines until he was dishonorably discharged for being drunk on duty, then wound up in the Gutter, having graduated to snoke following his court-martial; or Harry, who'd worked for UNN but was discredited when he made up a source on a story that supposedly exposed corruption in the TPF (not that the story was false—Harry knew it was true—but he didn't have a documentable source, so they fired him), and he wound up hooked on turk; or Maria, who had been an actor who spent more time going to parties that producers went to partaking of the snoke than she did actually acting; or Donna, who used to be a nurse before the stress of the emergency room led to her taking a hit of crab here and there just to get through the day, a habit that got worse and worse until she wound up here; or Michael, who dreamed of opening up his very own martial arts school but meanwhile kept on the turk because it got him peppy, at least until the sensei tossed him out on his ass for being high in class; or Jorge or Kara or Debbie or Wendy or Kelly or Marianne or Jim or Todd or Leia or Steve or Thomas or Chris or Sarah or Liza or—

"*No!*"

Shoving her fists into her temples, Nova tried to block the thoughts from her head, crying in pain and anguish, desperately clawing for some calm from Dorian, but unable to find it amid the cacophony of thoughts that assaulted her now.

Dimly, she registered that she had blown the door off its hinges and also physically thrust away several of the possessors of the thoughts that she felt. Turbulence was added to the thoughts as they tried to figure out who and what knocked them aside.

Then she heard voices.

"Crap, you all okay?"

"The hell happened to the door?"

"Hey, that's a blond curve! Think 'at's her?"

"Flick, I ain't waitin', let's shoot her."

Nova's ears rang moments later when all four of their guns jammed, resulting in two of them literally blowing up in their users' hands.

The pain that Jonesy and Mick Stanislawski, who was called Two-Bit, felt as shrapnel from their ruined weapons shredded their hands and forearms allowed Nova to focus and get her bearings. She got to her feet and stared at Poppo and Elois Magwitch, whose guns had simply jammed and stopped working.

Mags was furious as he took out another weapon. "Knock this curve!"

"Flickin' yeah," Poppo said, doing likewise.

Nova jammed those weapons as well, tears streaming down her cheeks. "Please stop, I don't want to hurt you." Jonesy and Two-Bit were screaming with pain, their blood all over the floor of the lobby to Fagin's building.

"Feelin' ain't mutual, curve." Poppo removed another gun, but that jammed to.

"Flick this noise." Two-Bit lunged at Nova.

She pushed him back with her mind, sending him head over heels to the rear of the lobby.

"Stay down." She was practically pleading now. "If you don't get up, I won't hurt you."

Poppo, realizing that there was no way for him to win this, dropped his weapon and held up his arms.

"Yeah, okay. Crap, Fagin ain't payin' me 'nough for this."

Two-Bit wasn't as bright as Poppo, and couldn't see past the fact that a teenaged curve knocked him on his ass without even touching him. He got to his feet and charged again.

Nova knocked Poppo into him and they both fell to the floor.

His anger now palpable Two-Bit whipped out his P100 and placed the muzzle right in Poppo's ear. "You flickin' with me, stud? Huh?"

"I didn't do nothin', I swear, Two-Bit, that curve did it, I'm tellin' you, I—"

"Don't do it!" Nova cried, realizing that Two-Bit intended to pull the trigger.

She wasn't fast enough to stop it.

Poppo's brains, skull, and blood splattered on the wall behind where he and Two-Bit had both fallen. His last thoughts before Two-Bit killed him were confusion as to why Nova had done that to him after he surrendered.

"I said no killing!" Nova screamed, even though she had said no such thing. But she'd thought it, *felt* it, *knew* it, that the only person who was going to die today would be Julius Antoine Dale.

Now Two-Bit had made a liar of her.

"Flick you, curve," Two-Bit said as he whirled around and aimed his gun at her.

She destroyed his brain, the same way she destroyed the Pitcher's.

It was even easier this time.

Nova couldn't bring herself to look at the bodies. Instead, she looked at Jonesy and Mags, who were still writhing in agony on the floor.

Mags said quickly, "Do what you want, curve—I ain't gettin' on *your* bad side, no flickin' way."

Jonesy, though, was livid. "You flickin' panbrain, didn't you hear what Fagin said?" He tried to get to his feet, made difficult by a right hand that was so much shredded meat and bone.

"Fagin can kiss my entire ass," Mags said. "Little curve, you do what you want. I'm stayin' far from you."

However, Nova was looking at Jonesy. "Stay down, Jonesy, or what happened to Two-Bit and Poppo will happen to you."

At that, Jonesy stopped—not so much from the threat, but from this curve he'd never met knowing his, Poppo's, and Two-Bit's names. He let himself collapse back onto the floor.

Nova walked to the back of the lobby and blew the door that led to the hallway off its hinges, too.

The main room Fagin used—the one from which he'd kicked her out onto the street—was just down this hall. She felt the thoughts of several of Fagin's hangers-on, including Markus Ralian, as well as several little kids—but no Fagin.

This was wrong.

Nova wanted to end this. Fagin had to be here, he just *had* to. She knew from the last time she was here that Fagin very rarely left his headquarters, having no real reason to. He was secure there, could have anything he wanted delivered to him, and so never needed to leave.

So where is he?

Bad enough that Two-Bit and Poppo had to die. They were not going to die while Fagin got away. Nova had sworn it, and she would *not* go back on that, not *ever*.

When she got to the door, she blew it away, too. She was getting rather good at this.

"Hey, those doors are expensive, okay?"

Nova's stomachache intensified. It was Fagin. But where was he? She couldn't feel him. . . .

He was standing right there. She could *see* him, but that was the only way she knew he was there. She also saw Jo-Jo, Markus, and somebody named Guy, but all her eyes were doing was confirming what her mind had told her before she blew the door off. She also felt Geena Ralian, Tyrus Fallit, and two dozen children in the back room.

"How can you be here?" she asked in a voice she recognized as being somewhat ragged. Her stomach was pounding, she'd killed two people today, and now Fagin was—was *doing something* to her.

"I *live* here, curve, okay?" He grinned, showing teeth that had been filed down to points. Nova found it somewhat gross. "But you can't read me, can you?"

"No," Nova said in a small voice. "How'd you—"

"I have *got* to start giving Morwood's wife the *good*

stuff." Fagin laughed—actually, it was more of a cackle. "What I'm wearin', curve, is—"

"Something you stole from the confeds." Nova couldn't read Fagin's mind, but she could read Markus's.

"Yeah, well, you ain't the first teep/teek, okay? Them confeds got to protect themselves against the likes o' you, curve. And this is one of the things they use to do that. And that means you can't touch me."

"Not exactly." There was a chair on the other side of the room. Nova sent it flying toward Fagin, but he managed to duck it.

"Nice try, curve, but you're gonna run outta crap to throw soon. 'Sides, I got me a backup plan. Tyrus!"

"No!" Nova screamed as she realized what Tyrus was going to do. Just as with Two-Bit, it happened too fast for her to stop it, and by the time she realized that Tyrus was going to shoot his T20 at the head of one of the little kids, he had already done it.

Tyrus's T20 blew up a moment later, but too late to save poor Mandy, a little girl whose father was a TPF cop and a turk junkie, and whose mother was dead.

Fagin was blurry now, because of the tears welling up in her eyes, but she stared at him and cried, "Stop it!"

"No." Then he pressed a button on his wrist.

Pain! It was like a laser saw started drilling through Nova's head, slicing through her eyes and forehead, like it was trying to split her skull wide open. . . .

Then it stopped. Only then did Nova realize that she had fallen to her knees. Her body was racked with sobs she could no longer hold back.

"See, them confeds don't just like to protect themselves, okay? They also like to keep you teeps in line. That's where the second setting comes in." Fagin knelt down next to her. "You try anything else, I'll leave it on longer *and* I'll kill another kid. Don't matter to me none, okay? But I figure it matters to you. Spoiled little Old Family kid like you, seems to me you don't know crap about death—or at least you didn't, till they done went and killed your whole family."

Nova whimpered. "I don't want anyone else to die."

Fagin hit her with another sharp-toothed smile. "Don't work like that, Nova. See, you're in *my* world now. In *your* world, people didn't die. Or if they did, it was neat—tidy. We don't do tidy here in the Gutter. We do ugly, we do nasty, we do mean—like what I just told Tyrus to do, or like what I did to you, or like what you did to Two-Bit, or like what Two-Bit did to Poppo. Or like what the Pitcher would've done to you if you didn't kill him."

Only a small part of Nova's mind registered what Fagin was saying. The rest was focused on little Mandy, a girl who never hurt anyone, killed just so Dale could teach her a lesson.

"I wanna die," she muttered between sobs.

"Not an option, curve."

Pain! Jules turned the other setting on again, and this time it seemed to last hours, days, *years*, before he finally turned it off again.

"So here's the scan, Nova. It's simple. You work for

me. Like I told you last week, I can use you. You're
going to do everything I tell you to do. Because if you
don't, I will kill another child and I will do this—" He
touched his wrist again.

She had hoped the pain would be easier to take
with more exposure to it, but the third time hurt
worse than the first two times combined. Every cell in
her body felt like it was attached to an electrical cir-
cuit, her skin felt like it was on fire, and her muscles
were as weak as boiled noodles.

Why couldn't I just have died?

"—over and over again, you scan me?"

After Nova didn't say anything for a second, Fagin
touched his wrist again.

"Yes!" Nova screamed through the bone-jarring
agony. "*Yes*, I'll do it, *yes!*"

The pain stopped.

Nova collapsed.

"I'll do it," she muttered. "I'll work for you."

"That's my good little curve, Nova." Julius Antoine
"Fagin" Dale stood up. "We're gonna do some great
things together, okay? Great things."

PART THREE

The best lack all convictions, while the worst
Are full of passionate intensity.
—William Butler Yeats, "The Second Coming"

CHAPTER 12

KEHL HAD BEEN HOPING THE MONEY WOULD get transferred today.

She called up her account on the crap-ass house computer that came with the tiny square that she shared with three other women. It was hard to push the right keys, seeing as how her fingers were shaking so damn much, but she made it happen, and she got into her account records.

Her balance still read in negative numbers.

Why the flick haven't they made the flickin' deposit yet? Flickin' panbrains . . .

She reached into her pants pocket to grab her fone. Rather, she tried to reach there, but she missed. After concentrating as hard as she could, she made her hands stop shaking long enough to go into the small pocket.

But it wasn't there. *Crap, what the hell happened to my—*

Then she remembered—she sold the fone to Pix so she'd have something to buy hab with last week. *That was stupid. Might need the fone again. Like, y'know, now to call the bank and ask them what the flick's goin' on. Stupid junkie.*

Standing unsteadily on her feet, not bothering to shut down the computer even though it ate up power she couldn't afford to pay for, she shuffled into the kitchen. She didn't trust the world not to tip over to the side if she actually picked a foot up.

Pix was out in the kitchen drinking a mug of tea—at least Kehl figured it was tea, since that was all Pix ever drank—along with Mai, who was yelling. "How come there ain't no *damn* coffee? How'm I supposed to get up in the *damn* morning and face the *damn* day if I ain't got no *damn* coffee?"

Mai's voice was drowning out the UNN anchor talking about the alien invaders on the flatscreen above the stove. Kehl shook her head. She'd let her subscription to UNN lapse in part because of this kind of "news" reporting. *Aliens—really. Trying to fog us with that crap.*

Of course, she also used the money that would've paid for the UNN feed to her room to buy more hab. She figured the hallucinations she sometimes got when she was high made about as much sense as the average UNN "news" report.

"I don't know and I don't care," Pix was saying in response to Mai's ranting and raving. "I don't drink that crap. Talk to Cisseta, it's her turn to buy the groceries." Then Pix looked over at Kehl. "You gonna have your share o' last month's rent 'fore next month's rent's due, Kehl?"

"I should," Kehl said in a ragged whisper. *Stupid junkie. Get it together.* She cleared her throat. "I need to call the bank and check something."

Pix looked at her with disdain. "So what's stoppin' you?"

"You have my fone."

Snorting, Pix said, "*Had* your fone. Sold that piece o' crap to Ayrie for some turk. All he gave me was one shot for that crap fone you had."

"What about my *damn* coffee?" Mai asked.

"Will you shut *up* about your coffee?" Pix winced as she asked, waving her hands back and forth like Mai was just a fly in front of her face. "Go out and *buy* some."

Mai put her hands on her wide hips. "We supposed to have some *damn* coffee in the house. I shouldn't need to be buyin' no *damn* coffee."

"Didn't I just tell you to talk to Cisseta?"

Stomping toward the door, Mai said, "The *hell* I wanna talk to that curve for? She ain't gonna get me no *damn* coffee, 'cause she always forgets. She's a *damn* panbrain, that's what her problem is." With that, Mai left the kitchen through the front door— presumably, Kehl thought, to get some of her *damn* coffee.

Kehl stood in the kitchen for several seconds. The UNN reporter was babbling about something else now. "*—six months after the death of most of the Terra family in a terrorist attack, the last survivor, Clara Terra, married Milo Kusinis in a beautiful ceremony held at*

Cortlandt Meadow in Ewen Park just outside Grange Village. Andrea Tygore was among the guests, making her first public appearance since her heart attack three months ago. The bride wore—"

Pix sipped her tea and then gave Kehl a look as if wondering why she still existed, much less was in the same room with her, still. "The hell *you* want?"

"I need to call—"

Rolling her eyes, Pix stood up and said, "Flick you, curve, you sold your flickin' fone, so don't come cryin' to me 'cause you didn't think nothin' through. I *told* you not to sell the fone, didn't I?"

In fact, Pix didn't, but Kehl didn't think it was such a good idea to tell her that right now.

Pix let out a real long breath, and then grabbed her fone off the kitchen table all theatrical-like, as if it was the biggest sacrifice any human being ever made to let Kehl use her flicking fone. "Yeah, okay, fine, you can use my fone—but you'd *better* just call the bank, you scan me? I find out you called anyone else, I'll tell Rowan who *really* took her brooch."

Kehl nodded nervously, sweat beading on her forehead. Rowan never even *liked* the brooch, so Kehl figured there wasn't any harm in stealing it—especially given how bad she needed the hab at the time. To this day, Kehl still didn't know how Pix found out.

Taking the fone, she sat down at the table. It'd take a while to navigate through all the menus before they'd let her talk to a person.

"—erate Army have been forced to abandon Antiga

Prime and regroup at Halcyon. Following the retreat, the
Sons of Korhal leader and current self-proclaimed ruler of
Antiga Prime, Arcturus Mengsk, sent out a message to all
Terran worlds."

Kehl muted the feed before it could switch to that
Mengsk guy. He scared Kehl, and she was scared
enough by real life without having to listen to
boogeymen on other planets.

She called the bank, first verifying that no credit
had been made to her account by Getreu in the last
three weeks. As she figured, the last credit from
Getreu was last month, and that was for the job she
did two months ago. But she knew she'd be paid late
for that one, and as a make-good, they said they'd pay
her this month right on time.

When she had finally gone through enough automated systems that she was permitted to talk to a person, she explained the problem. "Getreu said they'd
give me the money within three days of when I finished the job, and I finished it *four* days ago, and I still
don't have the money, you gotta help me."

"I'm sorry, ma'am," said the bored woman on the
other end, "but no credits from Getreu have been
made to your account. We can't make money appear
by magic, ma'am."

"Yeah, I *know* that, but you don't understand, I
gotta get my ha—"

She cut herself off. *Don't tell them you need a hab fix.*
Stupid junkie.

"Ma'am?"

"Uh, nothing."

"Ma'am, your best option is to call Getreu directly and find out from *them* what the delay is."

Kehl blinked. She hadn't even thought of that. It was always the bank's fault when money wasn't where it was supposed to be, but maybe it was just that Molina lied and they weren't going to pay as fast as they said they would. "Yeah, okay, I'll call Getreu."

She disconnected before the bored woman could say anything else, and called Molina's number.

Molina's voice said, "Hello."

"Look, Molina, the money did'n—"

"This is Louis Molina. I'm on vacation until the twentieth. Please leave a message and I'll get back to you on the twenty-first—or later."

A computerized voice then asked if she'd like to leave a message.

Kehl almost threw the fone across the room, but she managed to stop herself from doing it. Her body was shaking so badly, she almost did it anyhow. She *had* to have her hab fix! Molina probably never got around to putting the payment through before he went on vacation, and he wouldn't be back for another three days.

Three days!

Worse, now Pix was gonna be cracked at her because she called someone else besides the bank.

She dropped the fone on the kitchen table. Her intention had been to place it gently, but her arms were practically vibrating.

I gotta get me some hab. I don't get some hab, that's it for me.

But she had nothing left to sell. All her jewelry had long since been exchanged for money that paid for hab, as had every other useful possession. Every bit of income she scraped together went straight to one of Fagin's dealers for her hab fix.

The fone she'd sold to Pix was the last material possession of any value she'd had left.

It would be at least three days before Molina could straighten out her payment. By that time, she'd be dead, she just knew it, she'd be *dead* and then everything would be over.

She couldn't bear the thought.

There was only one thing to do. It was the one thing she'd sworn she wouldn't do. Kehl had always insisted on paying money up front for anything she bought. Never in her life had she taken loans or credit. Both her parents did that, mortgaging away their future to pay for their present—except that the future was when they really paid for it. They died in debt, miserable and starving.

Kehl wasn't gonna be like that. No way. She paid up front no matter what.

Except she didn't *have* any up-front. Not a flicking thing.

Fagin was always willing to extend junkies credit. Kehl had never taken him up on it.

Today, though, she had to. The alternative—well, there *wasn't* an alternative. She *had* to have her fix, and if that meant selling her soul to Fagin—well, it was the only thing she had left *to* sell.

Still afraid to pick her feet up, she shuffled out the door and headed down Juniper Way to talk to Francee.

Francee was a good person. Kehl had always liked her. Francee'd understand. She'd help.

First, though, she had to talk to Harold. You didn't talk to Francee unless you talked to Harold first. Kehl hated this part, because Harold *knew* he was the only way to get to Francee, so he held it over folks like his crap didn't smell.

This time of day—early in the morning—Harold was always in the Kenshi Kafé, a Japanese bistro that served really good tea that Kehl had never liked. Harold lived on the stuff, though—he was as bad with his tea as Mai was with her coffee—so he always spent his mornings here. Besides, he liked for people to be able to find him.

When Kehl finally shuffled over to the Kenshi, Harold was sitting at one of the outside tables by himself, talking on his fone, giving Kehl a pang of envy. *What were you thinking selling your fone, anyhow? How're you supposed to function without one? Stupid junkie.*

Even though damn little sunlight ever made it down here, Harold always wore huge mirrorshades that seemed to cover half his face. They were all the rage uptown about five years ago when solar flares meant people needed more protection for their eyes. Kehl remembered seeing a retrospective story about it on UNN before she let her subscription lapse. Most folks stopped wearing them, but Harold didn't. His sandy hair flopped over his forehead, resting on top of the glasses, and the bottoms of the glasses rested on his round cheeks.

He gestured for Kehl to sit in the chair opposite. The Kenshi had a dozen small, circular tables outside the café with four chairs at each—at least they were supposed to. Harold's only had two, and two other tables had five.

Trying desperately to keep her shaking from being visible, and only partly succeeding, Kehl sat down.

"Yeah, I know that. Yeah. Yeah. Look, Andres, I sympathize, really I do, but 'sorry' ain't gonna feed the Protoss, you scan me? Protoss—you know, the aliens that are kicking our asses out in space. Watch a damn UNN feed, willya, Andres? All right, look, if the shipment was damaged, the shipment was damaged, but getting that package to us is *your* problem, not mine. That means *you* gotta fix it. Whaddaya mean, when? I don't get that turk by tomorrow, it comes outta *your* ass, Andres. I told you, *you* gotta fix it. We don't make our count, I gotta tell Francee why, and I'm *gonna*. And then she's gotta tell Fagin why, and you know what *he's* gonna do? Damn right, he'll sic the Blonde on you. No, she's not a myth, you pan-brain, I met her. Fine, don't believe me, but I'm tellin' you, you crack Fagin off, and you get the Blonde fryin' you worse than any brain-pan the army's got, you scan me?"

Kehl had been hearing rumors about the Blonde for the last six months, but she didn't believe it any more than she believed that crap on UNN. Harold was obviously stupid if he thought that was real. The idea that Fagin had some kind of brain-fryer on the payroll was just as ridiculous as aliens.

"Look, Andres, you want proof? Don't get a new shipment tomorrow. Then you'll get the real story when Fagin hauls your ass up in front of him." With that, Harold disconnected, muttering, "Panbrained jackass." He then looked at Kehl. At least Kehl assumed he looked—it was hard to tell with the mirrorshades. "Chaneed, Kehl?"

"I ain't been paid yet and I *gotta* get some hab I need some credit from Fagin so I can get some." The words all came out in a rush, and Kehl wished she could have taken them back so she could say it slower. *Stupid junkie.*

Harold was rocking back and forth in his chair now, which was making Kehl nauseous. " 'Fraid that's gonna be a little bit of a problem, Kehl. See, Fagin ain't just givin' credit no more. He got kinda tired o' people taking credit and then dyin' on him—or just never payin' back 'cause they ain't got nothin'. So, since he's gotten the Blonde, he's got a new system in place."

Panic literally shook Kehl. This was terrible. How could Fagin do this to her now? She'd been good, she'd paid up front for *everything*, now he was gonna bring her to the Blonde.

No. Stop. The Blonde is just a myth. Harold's just fogging you. Stupid junkie.

"Damn, curve, you got it bad, don'tcha?"

Kehl gave up all pretense of hiding the shakes. Besides, if Harold saw how desperate she was . . .

And she was desperate. It was like her own brain was screaming at her: *WHERE'S MY HAB, DAMMIT?* If she didn't get some soon, she was half-convinced her entire body would just explode right there.

"Look, I'd like to help, I *really* would—"

Kehl didn't believe that for a second.

"—but rules is rules is rules is rules, and Fagin's been insisting that anybody wants credit, they gotta go through the Blonde."

He's just trying to scare me. Make me do something. "Harold, if I *had* the money, I'd—"

Shaking his head quickly, Harold said, "I told you, you gotta go to Fagin. Look, I gotta go over there anyhow, why don't you come with me?"

Kehl shook her head. "I told you, no money; I can't take no bus."

"I'll take you on my hoverbike."

At that, Kehl looked up sharply. Harold didn't let *anybody* ride on his bike.

"Look, Kehl," he said, "you been one of our best customers, and you always pay up front. That's good faith, and Francee an' me, we like that. If it was up to me, I'd give you credit right here and now, wouldn't even bother checkin' with Francee—that's how much we trust you."

Harold then leaned back in his chair and let out a really long breath that smelled like the tea he was drinking. "But it ain't up to me, and it ain't up to Francee, it's up to Fagin, and what he says he says, you scan me? Rules is rules is rules is rules, so we gotta get the okay from him—and from the Blonde."

Deciding enough was enough, Kehl said, "C'mon, Harold, there ain't no Blonde. Stop fogging me and—"

Slamming a hand down on the table so hard that Kehl almost jumped out of her skin, Harold yelled, "I'm *not* fogging you, you stupid curve! Now I'm tryin' to be *nice* here, but if you don't want it, then go die of withdrawal somewhere. See if I give a rat."

Realizing her only chance of getting hab was slipping through her fingers, she grabbed his wrist with her clammy hand and said, "No, no, it's okay, really, I'll go with, I just—" *Get ahold of yourself! Stupid junkie.* "I'm sorry, I just didn't believe—"

"Believe," Harold said emphatically. "I've met the Blonde. Not only that, I been on the receiving end. She's not only *real*, she's flickin' *scary*."

Kehl nodded. "O-o-okay. I'll go with." It wasn't like she had a *choice* or anything.

Harold picked up his fone. "I gotta make some calls. Meet me back here in a hour, all right?"

"An *hour*?" Kehl blurted out before she could stop herself. *Stupid junkie.*

"Yeah, an *hour*. I gotta make some calls first."

Quickly, she said, "Okay, fine," hoping that Harold wouldn't change his mind.

What the hell am I supposed to do for an hour? As she got up and shuffled down the street, she wondered if anybody was hanging out in VRcade. Sometimes she was able to score some free turk there—especially if Kenn was there, and especially if she was wearing a shirt that showed some cleavage. Wasn't the same as a hab fix, but it'd do.

She grabbed the neckline of her shirt and ripped about half a foot of material from it. *There, now I got some cleavage showing.* Satisfied that she would be able to trick Kenn out of some turk, she actually managed to pick her feet up to walk to the VRcade.

"Congratulations, Mal. It's now been six months."

Agent Malcolm Kelerchian had been dreading this meeting with Director Killiany for a week now. The only thing that had in any way ameliorated his dread was the hope, slim though it might have been, that he would actually *find* Nova during that week.

Which, of course, didn't happen. Hence his summons to the director's office.

"You look like absolute hell."

Mal found this hilarious, since Killiany wasn't exactly looking her best, either. Although he didn't know the specifics—mainly because he was too busy trying and failing to track Nova down to pay much attention to dispatches—he knew that the Ghost Program was heavily involved in the fight against the Zerg. The director had bags under her eyes, she'd let her close-cropped brown hair grow out to the point where it looked especially shaggy, and she no longer even bothered with the spectacles. It was as if she was too busy to look menacing.

Not that Mal was in any position to critique how someone looked. He had most, but not all, of a beard, and his own hair was uncombed and hadn't been cleaned in days. His eyes had bags of their own, and he was sure they were bloodshot as well. The latter condition was primarily due to his consumption of alcohol, which had increased exponentially over the last three months.

"Thank you, ma'am. Is that all you wanted to say to me?"

"Very funny." She shook her head. "What the hell are you *doing* down there, Kelerchian?"

"My job. Ma'am, I'm starting to seriously consider the possibility that Nova isn't in the Gutter—isn't even on Tarsonis."

Nodding, Killiany said, "We've been keeping an eye out on all the worlds we can. Sadly, that number's getting lower."

"Ma'am, I think—"

"I don't give a good goddamn what you 'think,' Kelerchian!"

Mal was taken aback. He'd never heard Director Killiany yell before. Speak softly and menacingly, yes. Snap, sure. Talk in a tight voice, once or twice. But yell? That didn't happen.

Things're worse than I thought.

The director continued. "Do you know how many PI8s we have in the program, Kelerchian?"

"Counting the guy in the basement? One."

"Actually, Agent X81505M died last week, so the answer is none." She stood up and started pacing behind her ultraclean desk—that, at least, hadn't changed. "Do you know how we're holding our own against the Zerg, Kelerchian? With Ghosts."

"With respect, ma'am, they don't seem to be doing that hot a job."

Tightly, she said, "I don't need you to tell me that, *believe* me." She peered at him in a way that would've carried more weight if she'd been wearing the spectacles. "We need more people in the program. We especially need *good* people. Right now, I've only got two people higher than a six."

"I understand, ma'am, but every lead has petered out. Nobody's seen her, there's no record of her on the traffic sensors, and no bodies've been found bleeding out the eyes."

"And nothing on the scans."

Mal nodded. "And nothing on the scans."

Still standing, Killiany leaned over to touch a control on her desk computer. She started reading off what she called up on the screen. "Six months ago—"

"Here it comes," Mal muttered.

"—you said you had a solid lead on Agent X41822N."

A complaint that she wasn't an agent yet died on Mal's lips: he saw no reason to put himself in worse trouble. Besides, Nova Terra had been declared dead. Her sister had even held an elaborate funeral for her and the rest of her family (nobody looked inside the coffin for Nova to see that it was empty, and Mal was sure the funeral staff were sufficiently compensated not to comment on how light the coffin was).

The director went on. "Had her sighted at a news vendor's where she blew up an AAI. What happened after that?"

"After that, I questioned all the neighboring shop-keepers and pedestrians, and nobody saw or heard anything, including the AAI exploding." Mal shifted in the uncomfortable chair. "Ma'am, this is the Gutter—the largest collection of blind, deaf, and mute people on Tarsonis. Unless she walks in front of a traf-fic sensor—which she hasn't done for six months—or drops a body—which, if she *has* done it, it's been off the grid—I'm not gonna find her without an army."

"Fine, you'll have an army."

Mal blinked. "I was speaking figuratively, ma'am."

"I wasn't." Killiany retrieved a fone from her pocket and pressed a single key on it. "Get me Ndoci."

Standing up, Mal said, "Ma'am, that's a little pre-mature." He'd heard about Major Ndoci, and the last thing he needed was having to ride herd on *that* psychopath.

Killiany said, "Good, thanks." After disconnecting, she fixed Mal with her nastiest glower. "Premature? You've had *six months*, Kelerchian. The TPF's been useless—"

"Officer Fonseca's been passing on all the useful intel he's gotten, and the traffic cops've been checking every day. I've also checked out all the usual places fifteen-year-olds wind up in the Gutter, but—"

"All of this has given you *nothing*. Dammit, Kelerchian, *we're losing the war out there*! Whoever isn't being mauled by the Zerg or disintegrated by the Protoss is being suborned by Mengsk. The Confederacy's falling apart at the seams, and the *only* way it's gonna stop is if we fight back with every weapon we've got. Agent X41822N is a weapon we *should* have, but we *don't* because *you* can't find her."

Killiany's intercom buzzed. *"Director, Major Ndoci is here to see you."*

Nodding, the director touched a control on her desk, and the door slid open.

Esmerelda Ndoci walked in. She was shorter than Mal was expecting, and less intimidating while wearing fatigues instead of the combat armor she was usually sporting in UNN reports about one of her victories in the field. Her dark hair was cut close to her scalp, her olive-skinned face drawn into a scowl that Mal knew had intimidated many a new recruit.

Ndoci was the CO of a ground unit officially known as the 22nd Confederate Marine Division, unofficially referred to as the Annihilators. They had the highest success rate of any division in the armed forces. In fact, Mal was rather surprised she wasn't off-planet blowing Zerg all to hell.

Her story was an odd one. She was an upper-middle-class girl, always good at sports, and considered a lock to become a pro soccer player, when she caught the eye of Gregory Duke, a scion of the Old Families.

Their marriage was an impressive affair, but Gregory died a year later, reportedly of a brain aneurysm. Scuttlebutt around the Detective Squad—which Mal had just joined at the time—was that she really killed him. After his death, she enlisted in the Marines, but she was made an officer. After all, she was still a member of the Duke family—though she had gone back to her maiden name after her husband's death, which was considered both scandalous and impractical, given how much trouble people had both spelling and pronouncing "Ndoci." (Rumor had it that new recruits to the Annihilators were forced to do sixty push-ups every time they mispronounced her last name.)

She quickly rose through the ranks, forging an impressive reputation—though Mal found it appalling, since carnage tended to follow in her wake—and eventually being promoted to major and taking over the 22nd.

Saluting, Ndoci said, "Major Ndoci reporting as ordered, ma'am."

Killiany returned the salute. "At ease, Major."

Ndoci shifted position slightly, but gave no indication that she was in any way at ease. In fact, to Mal's eye—long honed by his years in the TPF, not to mention his constant exposure over the last six months to the desperate residents of the Gutter—she looked ready to kill anything that moved the wrong way.

"This is Agent Malcolm Kelerchian, one of our Wranglers. You're assigned to him."

Giving Mal the same look one would give a diseased rat in one's dinner, Ndoci asked, "For how long?"

Turning the screen on her desk around so Mal and Ndoci could both see it, she said, "Until you find this girl." It was a picture of Nova Terra, a portrait provided by Clara Terra to UNN for the girl's obituary, taken only a few days before her fifteenth birthday.

"Ma'am, with all due respect, this is a waste of resources. We were rotated back here because of reports that the Sons of Korhal are mounting an offensive against Tarsonis."

At those words, Mal shot Ndoci a look. He hadn't heard anything about that. *Then again, I've been a little busy the last six months. . . .*

Ndoci was still ranting. "We need to be ready to—"

Killiany cut Ndoci off. "Major, I want you to keep three things in mind. The first is that this girl is a teep/teek, a PI8 or higher—something you should've known the minute you were summoned into this office and detached to a Wrangler—and is therefore a *lot* more dangerous than she looks."

"She'd have to be, ma'am," Ndoci muttered.

"My point is, she's a Class-A target."

That seemed to get Ndoci's attention. Class-A targets were to be apprehended totally unharmed, and if those tasked with the apprehension did the target even the tiniest harm, they were dishonorably discharged and jailed.

The director went on. "The second is that the Korhal attack on the planet will be made from space. The 22nd, the last I checked, was a ground unit. If Mengsk is able, by some miracle, to penetrate our defenses, then you'll be diverted to provide ground support, but unless and until that happens, I need you on this assignment." Putting her palms flat on her clean desk, Killiany leaned forward and said, "And the third thing is that if you talk back to me again, I'll bust you down to private and you'll be scrubbing waste extractors with your tongue on a freighter, do I make myself clear?"

Ndoci looked wholly unintimidated—which may have been a first for someone on the other end of one of Killiany's tongue-lashings—but she did stand at attention. "What's the mission profile, ma'am?"

"She's somewhere in the Gutter. You're to find her by whatever means are necessary."

At that, Ndoci smiled, which prompted Mal to frown. "My kind of mission, ma'am."

"That's what I thought, too."

"Ma'am," Mal started to say, "this is—"

Then he cut himself off. *What the hell am I objecting to?* He'd spent the last six months getting nowhere, as much because the residents of the Gutter had no interest in helping an agent of the government as anything. The cops down there were functionally useless, aside from Fonseca and the traffic cops, and they weren't nearly as helpful as Mal had thought they'd be at first.

Yeah, but the reason they're not helping is because the government hasn't done crap for them. Most of the people down there have gotten the short end of every stick the Confederacy's offered them. Hell, if Mengsk succeeds in taking Tarsonis, I bet it wouldn't make a damn bit of difference down there.

They don't deserve this psycho.

But Mal no more had a choice now than he did when he was turned from a detective into a Wrangler.

Mal was suddenly startled by the beeping of his earpiece, with his computer informing him that it was Officer Fonseca. "Excuse me, ma'am, I need to take this." Without waiting for Killiany to acknowledge this, he said, "Go ahead, Larry."

"I got somethin'—probably shoulda brought it to you sooner, but I figured it was crap like most—"

Mal didn't have the patience for this—not today. "Spit it out, Larry."

"Big talk on the street these days is someone workin' with Fagin—calls herself the Blonde. Some kinda enforcer."

"Fagin?" The name didn't ring any bells with Mal. "Who's that?"

"You don't know who Fagin is?" Larry sounded incredulous. *"He runs everything down here."*

Mal couldn't believe what he was hearing. "What do you mean?"

"He runs all the crap down here: the drugs, the protection rackets, the booze—it all flows through Fagin. I thought you knew that, Mal—how the flick could you not know that?"

"Larry, I never worked the Gutter, I don't know the players—that's what I came to *you* for."

"*Crap, I'm sorry, Mal, I just figured you knew all that already.*"

"Tell me about this blonde."

That got Killiany's attention. "What blonde?"

Mal waved her off as Larry replied. "*At first I figured it was the usual fogging you get—some stud's been killing all the habheads who don't pay their bills, some curve's been sleeping with Fagin for hab, the usual crap. My favorite was a guy called the Pitcher who worked as Fagin's personal enforcer. But they're all usually crap, and they're all gone in a few weeks. Hell, I haven't heard about that Pitcher guy in almost a year.*"

"But this blonde hasn't gone away?"

"*Nope. And the latest I heard was that she was a teep. I still think it's probably crap, but you may wanna check it out. But be careful—Fagin's nobody to flick around with.*"

Mal looked over at Major Esmerelda Ndoci. "I don't think that's gonna be a problem. Can I come talk to you in person?"

"*All right, but not in the usual spot. Fagin's got most of the Southwest firmly lodged up his ass, and I think they got the diner bugged.*"

"Come to my place. I'll reimburse the bus fare," he added before Fonseca could object to how much the fare to Mal's apartment in the Heights would be from the Southwestern.

"*Yeah, okay. I get off in two hours. I gotta get back, before*

*they notice I'm gone. Look, Mal, you'd better find this curve
already—I'm gettin' tired o' this spy crap. That's for you
confeds, not civil servants like myself."*

"Yeah, yeah." Mal disconnected, then turned to
Killiany. "I've got a lead. I need a couple of buscards
for fares to and from the Southwestern to my place to
give to Officer Fonseca."

"Sounded like you got everything we need," Ndoci
said tersely.

Shaking his head, Mal said, "Not yet. I've got a
name of someone who might be harboring her, but
nothing beyond that—and I need to get it all from
him, and not over an open line that the TPF can bug."
Before Killiany could point out that her department's
lines were secure, he said quickly, "They can listen to
what *he* says, even if they can't get what *I'm* saying.
The cops down there are corrupt, and from what
Larry told me, it's the main supplier of the graft
money that's got Nova."

Ndoci snorted. "Not for long he doesn't."

Mal glared at her for a moment, then turned to
Killiany. "I'll meet him in three hours, work out a
game plan, and report back."

"Fine." Killiany then turned to Ndoci. "Major,
you're on call until Agent Kelerchian reports in.
Dismissed."

Saluting, Ndoci turned and left Killiany's office.

As soon as the door shut behind her, Killiany said,
"This better be a good lead."

"Officer Fonseca hasn't let me down yet, ma'am."
Mal knew that was a lie. He couldn't believe Larry
had left out so important a piece of intel as this Fagin
character.

*And maybe I can come up with a game plan that won't
require Major Disaster to wipe out the entire Gutter.*

CHAPTER 13

MARKUS RALIAN WAS MORE AND MORE COMING around to the idea that he should've put a bullet in Nova's head as soon as she told him she knew what Dad did. Never told Fagin about her, just shot her and had Wolfgang and his girls take care of the body.

The last six months would've been much more pleasant if he had done that.

He was standing in Fagin's main room now. Also present were Jo-Jo and two of the dealers who worked for Markus in Pyke Lane, Jewel and Matt. As far as Markus knew, the pair had done nothing wrong—but that didn't matter much to Fagin these days.

"There's somethin' the Council does every once in a while, okay?" Fagin was saying. "Called a random audit. See, sometimes they just pick someone, anyone, and check 'em out. Make sure they've been payin' taxes, keeping their faces clean, not hidin' no bodies in the basement, that kinda thing, okay? Could be anybody. Every once in a while, they find somethin' they wasn't exactly lookin' for."

Fagin was pacing back and forth while he talked. Sweat beaded on his bald head—stubbled head, really, as Fagin had forgotten to take his follicle stunter again—and in his too-scraggly beard. His left hand kept going to his left ear, which was where he kept that weird gadget he got from his army contact.

As far as Markus was concerned, that gadget was as much part of the problem as Nova. Because that was what Fagin used to keep Nova in line, and he wore it *all the time*.

"Me, I like that idea, okay? I like it a lot. So you two are here not because I know you've done nothin' wrong. You're here so I can *prove* you've done nothin' wrong." He turned around. "Get out here!"

As bad as Fagin looked, Nova looked worse. When the curve first showed up on his doorstep six months ago, along with a seriously fogged-up Billy and Freddie, he thought she was pretty. A little young for Markus, but he could definitely see why Billy and Freddie had gone after her in the first place—good figure, nice features, lovely eyes, excellent hair.

That opinion no longer held. Her long blond hair only got washed periodically, and it had been a while, so it was hanging off her head like yellow strings. Her green eyes were bloodshot, her cheeks sallow, her lips cracked and chapped. She had lost so much weight that Markus suspected he could easily make out her rib cage if he saw her bare chest.

Certainly her wrists and hands—the only thing visible in the voluminous sweatshirt Fagin had given her to wear along with a pair of oversized denims—were thin and bony, to a degree that frightened Markus.

She walked slowly out of the side room from which Fagin had summoned her. "Please, Fagin, not today, I need—"

Fagin touched his arm.

"Eeeee-*yaaaaaaaaaaaaaaaagh*!"

Markus closed his eyes, unable to watch.

After a few seconds, Nova stopped screaming, but she was breathing heavily. Markus opened his eyes to see that Nova was looking at him, not with the defiance she'd occasionally show at first, but with a pathetic pleading expression.

Jerking a thumb at Jewel and Matt, he said, "Talk to me."

Nova stared at the two dealers blankly. "They're in love with each other."

Markus snorted. That wasn't exactly a secret.

"They like what they do. They think that UNN is telling the truth about the Sons of Korhal, but is lying about the aliens. They're scared that you're going to shoot them for no good reason, because they haven't done anything wrong. They were talking about whose place to sleep at tonight, hers or his."

Fagin held up a hand. "That's enough."

Then he pulled out his P220 and put three rounds into Jewel's chest.

"Nooooo!" Markus couldn't tell if that was Matt or Nova, then realized it was both of them.

Now aiming his gun at Matt, Fagin said, "Don't sleep with coworkers. Means you're spendin' all your time thinkin' 'bout flickin' and not enough time thinkin' 'bout workin', you scan me?"

Matt nodded quickly. "Yeah, sure, no problem, Fagin, no problem."

"Get your ass outta here."

"Sure, boss." Matt almost tripped over himself running out of the room.

"He's more scared now," Nova said, "and relieved that it was her and not him."

"Good."

Without another word, Fagin turned and went into the back room. Markus wondered which of the twelve would be unlucky enough to be on the receiving end tonight.

Jo-Jo and Nova were the only ones left besides Markus—and Jewel's bloody corpse. Markus looked down to see an expression of total shock on Jewel's round face.

She didn't deserve that.

To Jo-Jo, he said, "Dump the body."

Nodding, Jo-Jo said, "I'll call Wolfgang."

A thought suddenly fell into Markus's head, and before he could stop himself, he said, "No. Just dump it."

Jo-Jo blinked. "But—"

Now that his mind was on this track, Markus found

he couldn't stop it. "You hear Fagin tell you to call Wolfgang?"

"N-no." Jo-Jo seemed unsure.

"You really wanna take the chance on doin' somethin' he didn't say to do?" For emphasis, he looked down at Jewel's body.

Following his gaze, Jo-Jo let out a long breath. "Yeah, I scan. I'll dump her out in that alley."

Markus had no idea which alley "that alley" was, nor did he care. He just wanted Jewel's body gone from here. Her blood stained the floor as Jo-Jo hauled her out. *Hope he ain't attached to that shirt, 'cause it ain't gonna be fit to wear much longer.*

"You want the cops to find the body."

Looking over at Nova, Markus said, "What do you—?"

"You think that if the cops find Jewel's body and they pull out the bullets, they'll be able to match it against Fagin's P220 and they'll have to arrest him."

"That's crazy," Markus said, looking away from Nova, knowing that he was lying, because that was *exactly* what he was thinking. "First of all, the cops ain't got Fagin's gun. Second of all, no cop's gonna arrest him, even if they *find* her body."

Yeah, right. So why'd you tell Jo-Jo not to call Wolfgang? he asked himself.

It was Nova who answered, having heard the question as clearly as if he'd said it out loud. "Because you want him to get caught. You want him to go away. But this way isn't going to work, Markus. You have to do to him what your father did to your mother—your *real* mother."

"Shut *up!*" Markus pulled out his own P220.

"I know all about what happened, Markus." Nova's voice was a croaked whisper. "And I know how much you want Fagin gone."

Markus lowered the weapon. "Yeah, well, nothin' I can do."

"Yes there is."

He raised the gun again. "No, there *ain't!* He's the boss, you scan me, curve? And I ain't doin' *nothin'* to change that!"

"Then more people are going to die. The ones he doesn't shoot, he'll make me kill for him. I've already killed seventy-four people for him, Markus."

Eyes widening, gun dropping again, Markus whispered, "What?"

"Seventy-four. The first one was a cop who'd been skimming. His name was Lonnie Ursitti, he was assigned to the Southwestern District, and he was keeping five percent for himself for the last two years. The second one was—"

"Stop it." The last thing Markus needed right now was a list of all seventy-four.

But Nova was on a roll. "—a habhead named Ariana Manning who kept promising to pay off her debts, but never did it. Then there was Vic Cox, who said something Fagin didn't like when he was drunk and regretted it, but Fagin didn't care and told me to kill him. Then there was Dion—"

"Stop it!" Markus raised the gun again, and took the safety off. "I swear, if you don't shut up, I will shoot you in the face!" He didn't want to hear any more, especially after hearing about Vic. He had thought—

"No, Vic didn't die in a bus accident," Nova said. "That was what Wolfgang's girls set up so Fagin had something to tell Vic's daughter."

The entire time, Nova hadn't moved from where she had been standing when she told Fagin what Jewel and Matt were thinking. Her voice was a ragged whisper, and Markus had to wonder how long it had been since the last time she—

"He fed me this morning, and there's a water tap in the room. I just didn't feel like having anything."

Markus shook his head. "You ain't—"

"I know he won't let me starve myself. *I* won't let me starve to death. I tried that once."

Putting the safety back on and returning the P220 to his jacket pocket, Markus shook his head, thinking everybody would've been better off if she *had* starved to death—and he didn't care that she heard him think that.

"There's a way to stop all this, you know," Nova whispered.

"Yeah, I put a bullet in your skull." He let out a long breath. " 'Cept that'll just mean I get knocked, too."

The door slid open to reveal one of Fagin's kids— Markus couldn't remember which one. He supposed Nova knew, but he didn't feel like asking.

"It's Orvy," she whispered.

Six months, and that *still* creeped the crap out of him. "Chaneed, Orvy?"

"Harold's here. He's got some junkie curve with 'im. Says he got an appointment."

Markus put his head in his hands and started rubbing his forehead. Harold wouldn't have come all the way from Kitsios if he didn't have an appointment. Hell, you practically needed laser surgery to get Harold's ass out of that chair he liked so much at that café with the stupid name.

"Yeah, okay, let him in."

Orvy nodded, and then Harold came in, with the saddest-looking curve Markus had ever seen. She was skinny as hell, with stringy brown hair, sunken eyes, and clothes that hadn't been washed since before Korhal was nuked. Markus suddenly felt the need to breathe through his mouth.

"The hell she doin' here, stud?"

"She wants credit," Harold said with a shrug. Even though they were inside, he was still wearing those shades—which you'd *also* have to laser-cut off his damn face. "I hadda come here to talk about the party tomorrow night, so I figured I'd bring her along, since she's gotta go to the Blonde."

"Fine, I'll—"

"Get out."

That was Nova. "Shut up," Markus said, "you'll just—"

"Get out *now*!" Nova got to her feet, her green eyes

fixed on the junkie. "If you stay, I'll have to tell him what I see in your mind, Kehl, and he'll know that you'll *never* pay him back because you'll just buy more hab with whatever money you get and you only need the credit because you sold everything you have and a few things you didn't have but took money for anyhow and you won't ever pay and he'll kill you right now and he'll make me do it and why are you standing there, *get out*! *Get out! GET OUT!*"

The junkie turned around and ran out faster than Markus had ever seen anybody move.

"What the flick is this crap, Markus?" Harold asked. "This is—"

"You leave, too." Now Nova looked at Harold. "Trust me."

Harold stared at her through his shades. "I got an appointment."

"Fagin's busy. If you interrupt him now, he'll shoot you—or he'll make me kill you. I don't want you to be number seventy-five."

"Sevent—" Harold turned his gaze on Markus. "What the flick is she talkin' 'bout, Markus? This is—"

Guiding Harold toward the door, Markus said, "Just listen to her, Harold. You know how he's been."

"Don't be touchin'!" Then Harold seemed to deflate. "Yeah, okay, fine. I'll be gone. But we *got* to talk about the party. I can't be—"

"Wait outside till Jo-Jo gets back. He'll set you up."

Harold looked over at Nova. Then he shook his head. "Yeah, okay, fine. Damn."

He walked slowly out.

Markus looked at her. "You're panbrained, you know that, right?"

"You have to kill Fagin, Markus. It's the only way you'll live. Because otherwise, he's gonna make me scan you and I'll have to tell him." Tears welled up in her green eyes. "I'll *have* to tell him, because I can't do anything else, he makes my brain *hurt*!"

Unable to stand hearing her anymore, Markus got out of the room almost as fast as that junkie had. *What'd she say her name was? Kehl? Flick it, I'm goin' home.*

He barreled past Fagin's assorted kids and went outside, only to find the junkie seated on the front step.

"Harold just walked out," she said. "Got on his hoverbike without me. Left me here. Guess I should just sit here until I die."

Markus was seriously considering joining her. Instead he said, "Get up."

Kehl stared up at him with her bloodshot eyes. Her pupils were dilating. If she didn't get a hab fix soon, she was gonna deet out right there on Fagin's step. That was no good.

"I said get up, curve! Come with me, I'll take care of you."

Not saying anything, Kehl got unsteadily to her feet and grabbed Markus's left arm like it was a lifeline.

Crap, it is a lifeline for her. Crap.

He led her to his hoverbike, guided her into the sidecar.

As he drove back to Pyke Lane, he wondered what he was going to do with this habhead.

It beat thinking about what Nova said to him.

CHAPTER 14

"WOULD YOU MIND TELLING ME WHY THE *flick* you never mentioned this Fagin guy?"

Larry Fonseca stood in the doorway of Mal Kelerchian's apartment, greeted not by a hello, nor by a query as to his health, but with this question. Under other circumstances, Mal would have apologized for the rudeness, but just at the moment, he didn't give a good goddamn about politeness.

"I told you, Mal, I thought you knew—"

"Well, I didn't. Never heard of the panbrain before." He shook his head. "Come in. Don't mind the mess."

Mal stepped over the readers, music, and food containers that lined the floor. Larry did likewise. Mal threw some clothes onto the floor to clear a spot on the chair for Larry to sit, though he remained standing. If not for the mess, he would've paced.

"Dammit, Larry, who *is* this guy?"

"He's—he's Fagin."

"Please tell me that isn't his given name."

Larry shook his head. "Nah, he started callin' himself that after he took over from Grin."

Starting to feel lost, Mal asked, "Who the hell's Grin?"

Now Larry rolled his eyes, as if *Mal* was the idiot in this conversation. "I told you—he's the guy Fagin took over from."

"So besides having a Dickens fetish, who is this guy?"

"What's a Dickens?"

Waving his hand across his face, Mal said, "Never mind. Just answer—"

"I told you on the fone. Fagin runs all of it in the Gutter. Drugs, booze, sex—you name it, it goes through him. You got anything to drink?"

"No." Mal leaned against the wall, seeing no reason to let Larry have any of his precious Scotch supply. That was, at present, the only libation he had in the place, and he didn't have much of it left. "Go on."

Larry shrugged. "What more you want?"

"I wanna know who this guy is, I wanna know where he lives, I wanna know who his pets are, and I wanna know why the *flick* you didn't tell me about this guy sooner!" Without giving Larry a chance to respond, Mal swept his arm around the room. "*Look* at this place! I used to be a neat-freak. Everything in its place and put away and organized. Six months of wandering around the Gutter like an idiot, and I've turned this place into a biochemical experiment, and now you're tellin' me—"

Standing up, Larry pointed an accusatory finger at Mal. "I'm tellin' you somethin' *I thought you already knew*. Don't give me this crap about how this is *my* fault, Kelerchian. All you asked me to do was keep an ear out for blond teep/teeks hurtin' people. I brought you every tip I heard, just like you asked. You wanna be cracked at me, go right ahead, but this ain't *on* me, it's on *you* for not doin' your police work."

Mal recoiled as if he'd been slapped. "What're you—"

Larry shook his head. "Dammit, Mal, you used to be a good cop. A good cop *knows* his territory."

In a weak voice, and knowing it was foggy as the words came out of his mouth, Mal said, "I never worked the Gutter."

"Then you shoulda *learned*. Dammit, Mal, you used to be good police, and good police know how to work a neighborhood. Here's a clue: You *don't* do it by talkin' to people with a big sign on your flickin' forehead that says you're a confed."

"You're right." Mal put his head in his hands and started rubbing them up and down his face. "Dammit, Larry, you're right. I'm sorry, I shouldn't have blamed you." He started pacing, kicking food containers and readers aside. "It's this damn job, y'know? Got me chasing down teeps like I'm some kind of dog-catcher. Just bringin' 'em—" He stopped. The specifics of the Ghost Program were classified, not that Mal gave that much of a crap about that—still, telling Larry could get the officer in trouble, and Mal had done badly enough by him today. "Anyhow—now I *am* asking. Where can I find this Fagin guy?"

Larry unhesitatingly gave an address in the Duckworth section. "That's where he runs his whole operation. He owns the whole building, rents out some of the squares—but the ground floor's all his. Word is he keeps some boys and girls in the back room for his own use, if you know what I mean—and he's apparently got the Blonde back there."

"And you think the Blonde is my target?"

Shrugging, Larry said, "The hell should *I* know? But she fits the profile you gave me. You remember—the part you actually *asked* me for."

"All right, all right." Obviously Larry intended to get his entire pound of flesh out of Mal. "So he just operates out in the open?"

"Why the hell not? Nobody's gonna bust him. Most of the cops that work the Gutter are on his payroll—and that'll keep up, long as he pays 'em better'n the Council does. Especially now with the freeze."

Mal frowned. "What freeze?"

"You ain't hooked up to crap anymore, are you?" Larry gave Mal a disdainful look.

Tightly, Mal said, "I've been busy."

"They froze all our salaries. They even gave the bosses a pay cut—all to fund the alien war, they said." Larry shook his head. "Not that they give a crap about us down there anyhow. It just means studs like Fagin got it easier, 'cause the payoffs he gives keeps 'em happy."

Finally, Mal sat down, not even bothering to remove the laundry from the coffee table, just plunking down on it. It wasn't as if he cared how his bodysuit looked—that was why he wore the duster outdoors. "Now it all makes a sick sort of sense."

"What does?" Larry sounded genuinely confused.

"Why I couldn't get anywhere. It wasn't just that I'm a confed—that didn't help, but it wasn't just that. If Nova's with Fagin, and has been this whole time, nobody was gonna tell me. They like him down there—he provides all the good stuff that the Council and the Old Families won't give 'em."

Mal was startled by a staccato sound. He looked up to see Larry giving him slow, sardonic applause. "Congrats, Mal. Took you half a year, but you finally figured out the Gutter." He stopped clapping. "Know what else that means? You ain't gonna get no help from nobody down there. Including me—I can't be seen helpin' you out, or I lose what little cred I got."

For the first time, Mal was grateful for the director's saddling him with the psychopath. "That won't be a problem. I've already got an army."

Larry's eyes went wide. "What?"

"I said I got an army. When you called me earlier, I was in my boss's office, where she was giving me an entire Marine division to use whatever way I see fit to bring in my target." He smiled. "I'm gonna use them on this Fagin guy."

That just made Larry's eyes go even wider. "Are you outta your mind? Mal, that ain't gonna help."

Standing up, Mal said, "I'm not *trying* to 'help.' Dammit, Larry, if people wanted my 'help,' they shoulda told me where Nova was six months ago. But I've gotten fogged up to my ass. Well, I've had it. I've got the Annihilators, and I'll use 'em if I gotta to get the job done."

Larry put a hand on Mal's arm. "Look, Fagin's a slike, no question. Worst of the worst. But he keeps a lid on things—keeps the order that the Council won't let the cops keep. You knock him, and we got a war on our hands while everyone tries to take what was his."

"We already have a war on our hands," Mal said with a discontented sigh. "What's another one?"

"Yeah." Larry let out a low rumble. "Whatever. Look, you need anything else?"

Mal shook his head. "I'd say we're done, Officer Fonseca." He held out a hand.

Larry glanced at it for a second before accepting the handshake. "Glad to be of help, Agent Kelerchian."

After breaking the handshake, Larry headed toward the door, then stopped. "Hey, what about my bus fare?"

Chuckling, Mal walked over to the chair where he'd draped his duster. Reaching into the pocket, he pulled out an envelope that contained two buscards. "Here you go," he said as he handed them over.

"Thanks."

The officer turned and the door slid open.

"Larry?"

He stopped and turned back around. "Yeah?"

"I'll try to do it without bloodshed. But at this point, I can't promise anything. I don't bring this girl in, they'll level the Gutter to get at her. I know my boss—giving me the Marines was the first step to taking me off this." He shook his head. "As it is, I'll probably get chained to a desk for a year for screwing this one up."

"You could just quit."

"So could you."

Shrugging again, Larry said, "I took an oath."

"Yeah." Mal let out a long breath. "Me too."

Markus Ralian watched the girl from Kitsios take her hab. Kehl, that was her name. She was sitting on the sofa in his living room. A transformation came over her face, as her nervous expression became a beatific smile, her nervous twitching became a relaxed slump, and her muscles, which had been wound tighter than a spacesuit, loosened right up.

She looked over at Markus with bleary eyes. "Thaaaaaank you. I *really* needed that."

"Yeah." He sat down on the sofa next to her. "Was it true, what the Blonde said?"

"Whaaaaaa'd she say? Don't 'member."

"She said you sold everything you owned to get hab, and you don't got nothin' left—s'why you were goin' to him for credit."

"Yeaaaaaaaah, that sounds right. I don't got nothin'

left 'cept the clothes on my back." She looked heavily down at her clothes. "And they ain't much."

"Got *that* right." Markus got up, as much to get away from the stink of Kehl's unlaundered clothes as anything. "You realize that the Blonde would've told Fagin that, and he woulda killed you, right?"

Sounding unconcerned, Kehl said, "I dunno."

He moved over to stand in front of her. "He would've. Guaranteed. Hell, even if she didn't tell him, he probably woulda killed you." Walking off, he muttered, "S'all he does anymore. Ever since he put that damn thing in his head to control her . . ."

"So why don't he take it off?"

Before Markus could give that stupid question the answer it deserved, his fone beeped. He pulled it out of his pocket, and saw that it was Jo-Jo. *The hell he calling me for?*

"Chaneed, Jo-Jo?"

"Markus, you gotta help me. Fagin, he gone *crazy*. He come runnin' out the back room, yellin' and crap, an' he asked me where Harold was, that he was supposed to talk about the party. I told him Harold left 'cause you weren't around and didn't wanna be disturbed, an' he made me bring Harold back here, so I did, an' Harold said it was *my* fault that he left."

"You weren't even in the room." Markus wasn't surprised—Harold was always a backstabbing little panbrain.

"I *know* that. I *told* Fagin that, and then he just

went and shot up Harold, and then he told *me* to go to Kitsios to tell Francee."

"So?"

"So how the *hell*'m I supposed to tell Francee what happened?"

Markus was about to point out that it was a pretty straightforward exercise, when he remembered the history between Francee and Jo-Jo. "You still think she's cracked off about that?"

"Flick, *yeah*, she's still cracked off about that. I tell her that Harold's dead, I swear she'll knock me right there, stud!"

"Where you right now?"

Jo-Jo hesitated. "Outside your square, man."

Markus rolled his eyes and disconnected. He went to the front door to see Jo-Jo yelling into his fone. "Markus, you there? You—" He looked up. "Oh."

"I'll go with you." He turned around. "Geena!" Back to Jo-Jo. "Give me a second." Turning back around to see no sign of his sister, he yelled louder, "*Geena*!"

From the kitchen, the muffled voice of his sister cried back, "What?"

"I gotta go do somethin'. Keep an eye on the junkie in the living room."

"What?"

"I said—"

The kitchen door slid open to reveal a very cracked-off-looking Geena. "The hell's a junkie doin' in the living room?"

"Same thing all junkies do, Sis—gettin' high. Make sure she don't throw up or steal or nothin'. When she comes down, give her another batch and send her on her way." He hesitated. "She's on credit from Fagin."

Geena held up a hand. "Fine." She looked past her brother. "Chaneed, Jo-Jo?"

"Markus here, he helpin' me out with somethin'."

"Great." Geena fixed Markus with a look. "Don't forget to be back here by—"

"I *know* when I need to be back here! I know how to deal with things, so don't *you* start lecturin' me! I was doin' this when you were a junkie just like her!" He pointed to Kehl, who was intently studying the living room ceiling. "So don't go *tellin'* me what to do! I already *know*!"

Geena looked like he'd slapped her, but Markus frankly didn't give a crap. He was sick of all of this today, and he just wanted it all to end—Fagin, Nova, Jewel and Matt, Harold, Kehl, *everything*.

Without another word, he turned and stomped out of the square, not waiting to see if Jo-Jo was following him.

CHAPTER 15

"WELCOME TO TARSONIS AND YOU, THE SHOW *that gets behind the news to tell you what's really happening in the Confederacy. I'm your host, E.B. James. The latest reports coming out of Antiga Prime indicate that the alien Protoss have engaged the alien Zerg in ground combat, with Terrans, as ever, stuck in the middle. Here to discuss these latest developments with me are Edward Heddle, aide to Councillor Shannon, and Jennifer Schlesinger, who covered Antiga Prime for UNN before being forced to evacuate following the Sons of Korhal's takeover of that world."*

Fagin paced quickly in the back room. He'd grown weary of Number Six. He simply wouldn't do what Fagin said to do, which meant he had to go. Fagin decided he was better alone anyhow. But he still had a ton of nervous energy, so he put on UNN, hoping it would give him a distraction. Unfortunately, they were showing one of those stupid talk shows. Fagin hated those. They didn't talk about anything that mattered to Fagin—especially right now. For all Fagin knew—or cared—Antiga Prime didn't even exist. Hell, sometimes he wasn't entirely sure anything existed outside Tarsonis City.

But he left the holograph running in the middle of the room anyhow. He wasn't sure why.

"Ed, what's the Council's position on this latest revelation? They had previously announced that the Zerg were allied with the Sons of Korhal, yet the Zerg have been attacking the planet indiscriminately."

Heddle jumped up and down in his chair, a bundle of nervous energy—something Fagin could relate to. A pudgy, brown-haired man with a thin goatee, Heddle gestured wildly as he spoke. *"Obviously, the Korhallians have learned the lesson that should've been self-evident: Aliens aren't to be trusted. I mean, they're aliens! Sure, what they're doing to Antiga is inhuman, but let's face it—so are they."*

"This is assuming you buy all this," Schlesinger, a pretty woman with dark hair and thin-rimmed spectacles, said. *"Personally, I didn't see any evidence that the Zerg were allied with* anyone *on Antiga Prime. They're just a bunch of killing machines. Arcturus Megnsk is simply taking advantage of their attacks to further his own cause."*

Heddle smirked. *"And that's exactly the kind of treasonous actions that show Mengsk to be the reprobate we've always said he was."*

Fagin laughed. He'd never heard anybody use the word "reprobate" in real life before. "Now that's some funny crap, stud. Funny, funny stuff, ain't that right?"

Nobody answered. That confused him.

He turned around and looked at the bed. Number Six was right where Fagin had left him.

Except for the large bullet wound in his chest.

Funny, I don't remember *shooting him.* "Jo-Jo!"

"Mengsk may be a reprobate," Schlesinger was saying, *"but that doesn't make him wrong."*

"Are you out of what passes for your mind?" Heddle looked ready to jump out of his chair and attack Schlesinger, which Fagin was actually rooting for, as it would spice things up. *"Everything he does is wrong—he stands against everything we hold dear."*

Getting annoyed at the lack of response, Fagin yelled louder, "Jo-Jo! Where the flick *are* you?"

"What Mengsk stands against is the Council's inability to help its own people and to defend them against the alien attacks, and its actions on Korhal IV. So you're saying that the Council stands for murder?"

Heddle made a sound like a bursting pipe. *"That's a sensationalistic oversimplification—but then, I'd expect no less from a so-called journalist."*

Fagin was starting to get seriously cracked off. He walked over to the door, which slid open at his approach. "Jo-Jo, where the *flick* you at?"

One of his kids—he couldn't remember which one it was, but was pretty sure it was Sam—ran down the hall to him. "Jo-Jo ain't here, Fagin. You told him to go tell Francee about Harold."

"What the *flick* he do that for?"

The kid blinked. "Uh, like I said, Fagin, you told him to."

"Flick that, okay?" He took his P220 out of his jacket pocket and pointed it at the kid's nose. "You get his ass back here right *now*, okay? Or I will shoot you in the face, you scan me?"

Nervously, the kid said, "No problem, Fagin." She backed off slowly while taking her fone out of her pocket. She called a number, waited a second, then: "Hey, Jo-Jo, it's Dani."

Eyes widening, Fagin started muttering to himself. *Coulda* sworn *it was Sam.*

"Yeah," Dani was saying into the fone, "Fagin says to come back to the square. Yeah, I *know* that, but now he wants you back. Okay." She disconnected and looked up at Fagin. "He's comin' back."

"Good." Fagin then fired seven shots into Dani's chest. She fell to the floor, dead. "That's for pretending to be Sam."

He went back into the room, where Heddle was saying, *"Mengsk's actions are treasonous. In light of these alien attacks on our soil, we need to come together as confederates. Instead, he's weakening us by not throwing his support behind the rightful leaders of humanity."*

Fagin was really getting tired of the way everyone was acting. He didn't get it; it was like they all went crazy all at once. He never used to have to kill people before. Sure, having Nova around made part of the difference—thanks to her, he knew what people were *really* thinking.

Schlesinger laughed. *"Rightful? By what right, exactly? The Council doesn't work with any kind of mandate from the people. Like it or not, plenty of confederates like what Mengsk has to offer a helluva lot more than the Council's been able to manage. Mengsk has promised freedom and liberty—"*

Snorting, Heddle said, *"Like he'd be able to provide that."*

"Doesn't matter if he can, he's simply got to convince people that he'll do a better job than the Confederacy has. Right now, that's a pretty convincing argument, since all the Confederacy's provided people is poverty, death, destruction, and invasion."

That, Fagin realized, was the problem. People weren't able to keep their thoughts to themselves, and they hated that, so they got all crazy—so crazy that Fagin just had to kill them. Wasn't nothing to be done about it.

"If it weren't for the Confederacy," Heddle was saying, *"the human race would be dead now. When we crash-landed—"*

Fagin aimed his P220 at the holograph. He kept firing after it exploded into a fiery shower of sparks that made spots dance in front of his eyes. He stopped firing only when the weapon dry-clicked. *How'd I run out of ammo so fast?*

"Dani!" *No, that's right, I just killed Dani for pretending to be Sam. Stupid curve.* "Sam! Sam, get your ass in here, okay?"

A few seconds later, Sam came running in. "What happened to Dani?"

"Flick Dani, okay? Find the Blonde, get her in here."

"O-okay." Sam sounded nervous.

"What's wrong?"

"*Nothing!* Honest, Fagin, nothin's wrong, not a damn thing, really, don't worry."

"Good." As Sam turned around to go fetch Nova, Fagin called out, "And get me some more ammo!"

Dropping his P220 on the floor, Fagin started rubbing the bridge of his nose between his thumb and forefinger. The headaches had been getting worse lately. The 'jections he was taking weren't doing crap. *Time to find me a new pharmacist, this keeps up.*

When Nova came in, Fagin laughed. Most of her pretty was gone, which was how Fagin liked it. When it came to sex, he wanted pretty, but when it came to his kids, he just wanted them to do what they was told. As far as he was concerned, Nova—or, rather, the Blonde, since he liked the idea that her ID had been wiped away—was one of his kids, and she looked like hell. Bags under her green eyes, her skin all pale, her hair a mess. *Perfect.*

"It won't work, you know," she said without preamble.

"What won't work?"

"Any of this. Everything you've done since you forced me to become your teep has just made your position worse. And it's going to end badly for you."

"You don't know that."

"I know everything, Julius Dale."

He pulled out his P220. "Shut *up*! That ain't my name!"

She smiled. "Your gun's empty."

Oh crap. A shiver of fear ran through Fagin's body, as he thought that Morwood's device had stopped working and she could read his thoughts, and that meant he had no protection—

"Calm down," she said. "Sam said you needed ammo."

Fagin breathed a sigh of relief. Then he touched a control on the wrist of the device.

Nova was good enough to scream really really loudly and collapse to her knees. Fagin never got tired of seeing that.

Through clenched teeth, sweat beading on her brow, her face turning red, Nova said, "It's going to end soon."

He stopped the pain. "What makes you say that?"

After taking a moment to catch her breath, Nova stared up at him with tear-streaked green eyes. "I can't read your thoughts, but I can read everyone else's. Remember six months ago when we first met? I told you that one of your most trusted lieutenants is going to kill you. That's going to happen soon."

Barking a laugh, Fagin said, "Don't go foggin' me, curve. You're a teep. I been readin' up on you. You can read minds and stuff, but you can't see the future. Nobody can do that. Future's what we make it."

"I know that. And I know what future you've made for yourself."

Giving her a dismissive wave, Fagin said, "Get the hell outta here."

Nova slowly got to her feet and left without a word.

She's been useful, but damn, *she makes me crazy.*

Markus stared as his fone for a long time before he finally decided to connect to the person he wasn't supposed to call.

"Sergeant Morwood," said the voice on the other end.

"Morwood, this is Markus Ralian."

Sounding irritated, the sergeant said, "Look, I don't know who—"

"I work for Fagin."

A pause. "What the flick do you want?"

"Look, I need to know about a piece of equipment you supplied him about six months back. Specifically side effects if you keep it on too long."

"I really can't talk about this over the—" He sighed. "Look, as long as he doesn't wear it more than the recommended seven hours at a time, he'll be fine."

Markus hoped like hell he was hearing the sergeant wrong. "Seven *hours*?"

"Yeah. Why, how long does he keep the thing on?"

Biting his lip, Markus said, "Sergeant—he ain't taken the damn thing off since he opened your package."

"What?" Morwood muttered something Markus couldn't hear. "He hasn't taken it off at *all*?"

"Not that nobody's seen."

"Oh, no." Now Morwood sounded scared. "You

gotta get him to take it off. The warning on that thing—which I gave him, by the way, so don't go saying this is my fault—it says you shouldn't wear it for more than seven hours at a time. I don't know of anybody who's worn it more than twelve, and she suffered some memory loss. For six months . . ."

Suddenly, a lot was making sense to Markus. He'd had a feeling that thing he used to keep Nova in line was eating away at Fagin's brain something crazy, but he had no idea it was this bad.

Morwood started talking again. "Look, I'm amazed he isn't a vegetable by now. Seriously, I don't see him being able to stand upright for much longer. You gotta do something."

"What the hell am I supposed to do?" Markus asked defensively, mainly because he'd been asking himself the same question for months now.

"I don't know, but you'd better flicking well do *something*. Listen, you low-life panbrain, I've done good work for you people. This ain't my fault, and I ain't lettin' you cut Diane off to—"

Markus disconnected. He didn't care about Morwood's wife or the sergeant's deal with Fagin. Hell, it was looking pretty likely that Fagin wasn't going to remember who Morwood *was* for much longer.

If he hadn't forgotten already.

He had just returned from talking to Francee—alone, since Fagin had called Jo-Jo back for whatever reason—when Geena, aghast, said that Dani was dead. *How many did Nova say it was? Seventy-five now?*

He wasn't even sure anymore. And Dani had been dedicated to Fagin; no way she was disloyal, Fagin's usual excuse for a pointless death these days. Markus could barely reconcile the Fagin who'd made a long speech about killing not being a deterrent with the one he now worked for.

And then he found out that the hab supply was critically low. Nobody seemed to know when the next re-up was coming. In the years since Fagin took over from Grin—hell, in the years since Grin took over with Fagin as his right hand—the hab supply had *never* gotten this low.

Which was why he called Morwood. Because there were only two things that changed six months ago, and one of them was Morwood's little toy taking up permanent residence on Fagin's head.

Now that he'd gotten the truth, he knew what he had to do.

Walking out into the hallway toward the front door, he passed Geena, who was talking to that junkie Markus had rescued.

"Hey, Markus, Kehl here wants a job."

Markus frowned. "What?"

The girl looked up at him. She had gone through her hab high, and was relatively straight for the time being. "I wanna work for you. I need a job, and I—"

"Fine," Markus said quickly. "Don't we need a new barker for Greene?"

Geena looked at him funny. "I thought we got Andy for that."

"We did—and Billy, Freddie, Ryon, *and* Elizabeth all been complainin' about him nonstop. Let her take over."

Kehl ran up to him and embraced him fiercely in a bear hug. "*Thank* you, Markus. You're the *best*! *Thank* you!"

Pulling her out of the hug, Markus looked harshly down at her. "Listen to me—you do what the dealers tell you to do, you scan me? No matter what it is, you do it when they tell you to do it, and you do it right. Think you can program that?"

"Definitely," Kehl said with an enthusiastic nod.

"You do that, you'll be able to have all the hab you need, and maybe buy some of your crap back." *Assuming we ever get the damn re-up, anyhow . . .*

Nodding so emphatically that Markus thought her head would fall off, she said, "I won't let you down."

Markus said, "Good." Then he looked at Geena. "Set her up. I gotta go take care of something with Fagin."

That prompted a look of concern from his sister. "Be careful, Markus. Fagin, he's—" She hesitated.

"I know," Markus said quietly. "That's part of what I gotta take care of."

Nova lay curled up in a fetal position in the corner of one of Fagin's rooms. She wasn't sure which one, and didn't care all that much.

She didn't want to die, but she didn't want to live, either. In school, a lifetime ago, she learned about different myths from Old Earth, including several beliefs in an afterlife where bad people suffered for all eternity after they died. Tartarus, Hell, Sheol—whatever they called it, it was a place of endless pain.

Nova was in Tartarus now, she felt.

There were two things she'd learned over the past six months. One was the ability to screen out the white noise. If someone was in the room with her—and wasn't Fagin, with his flicking mental screen—it was impossible for her not to know what the person was thinking, but otherwise, she'd toned it down.

The other was a confirmation of a belief: that she was not alone.

She had managed to sneak some time on Fagin's computer when he was asleep here and there, and had done some research. There were lots of telepaths around, but only people with a Psi Index of eight or more also had her ability to move things with their mind, which was called telekinesis.

Nova had no idea what her PI was—she'd never been tested, which, in retrospect, was odd, since most kids, even scions of the Old Families, were tested at a young age. In practical terms that meant that while Fagin was protected against her doing anything to his mind, he wasn't protected from her doing anything to his body.

The problem was, she had to pick her moment. If she failed, he would cause her pain again. Every single time he used the device that way, it was worse. She feared that sometime soon, it would outright kill her.

But she would find that moment. That was why she repeated what she had told him.

The trusted lieutenant who was going to kill Fagin was Nova herself.

CHAPTER 16

THE FIRST THING THAT MAL KELERCHIAN noticed about the Annihilators is that not a single one of them had a neck.

The 22nd Confederate Marine Division numbered, ironically enough, twenty-two: Major Ndoci, a captain who served as her second-in-command, five sergeants, and a mixture of corporals and privates rounding out the remaining fifteen. The division was broken into five companies, each led by one of the sergeants. Formally given the prosaic designations of A, B, C, D, and E company, they had each taken on nicknames of their own. Mal hadn't learned them yet, and after meeting the 22nd—the smallest of whom was Mal's height and twice his weight in shoulders alone—he didn't want to know. *Probably named after rabid animals*, he thought with a shudder.

They were in a Confederate air base in Holyktown, standing outside a Valkyrie that would take them to the Gutter. The Valkyrie—which was used as both an air combat vehicle and a troop transport—sat thirty in the rear section, which was currently unoccupied. The various members of the Annihilators were milling about in groups of five or fewer, occasionally shooting disdainful looks at Mal. He overheard one private making a remark about the "confed asshead." Mal had to bite back a retort about how a Marine would know all about people with their heads in their asses, which he was mainly able to do out of an intense desire not to talk to any of them. The Marines were a tool to help him finally finish the damn mission, nothing more, nothing less.

Esmerelda Ndoci walked up to Mal. In Killiany's office, she was wearing fatigues, but now she, like the rest of her people, was in full combat armor, minus only the helmet. Mal knew that the helmets weren't usually affixed until it was absolutely necessary—to wit, just before insertion—in order to preserve the suit's power and air supplies.

"Director Killiany said we had a plan."

"*I* have a plan, yes. We've got a probable location on where the target is. This plan has two parts. The first part is where I go in and ask for her."

Ndoci actually laughed at that. "That's funny, Agent Kelerchian. Very funny. Now what's the *real* plan?"

Dead serious, Mal said, "That *is* the plan—or, rather, the first part."

"Dammit, Kelerchian, the director said we're supposed to be *part* of this." As Ndoci spoke, the holster embedded in the right thigh of her armor extended

sideways with a whir to provide the major with access
to her firearm—a P500, military issue, and which Mal
had thought hadn't been cleared for field use yet.

The action was meant to intimidate, but while Mal's
bodysuit wasn't as impressive-looking as the Marines'
combat armor, it had considerably more toys, including a force field that would protect him from anything
short of a nuke. It was the main reason why he could
walk around the Gutter with impunity for six months.
The major could shoot him until her fancy-shmancy
weapon ran dry and Mal wouldn't feel a thing.

"You *are* part of this," he explained only semi-
patiently. "Specifically, as far as the first part of the
plan goes, you're the threat. I'm gonna walk into the
house of this guy—who is, by the way, the major
crime lord in the Gutter, a position he couldn't have
gotten by being stupid—and explain to him that the
Marines are going to drop the entire Gutter on his
head if he doesn't hand the target over."

Mal wasn't sure why he was calling her "the target." He couldn't bring himself to go Killiany's route
and refer to her by her designation, but for some reason he refused to use her real name in front of the
Marines. *Like I'm betraying her somehow.* He shook his
head. *What a ridiculous notion.*

Ndoci's holster reembedded itself in the suit, putting the P500 out of immediate reach. "And when this
panbrain tells you to go flick yourself?"

At that, Mal smiled. "We go to the second part of
the plan."

"Which is?"

"You drop the Gutter on his head."

Rubbing her chin with a gloved hand, Ndoci asked, "Any reason why we can't do the second part first?"

Mal had expected this question, and had prepared an entire argument about how real people not involved in this might get hurt, but at the last minute he realized that it would be wasted on Ndoci. *She's a major; you're in charge. Act like it.* "Because I said so, Major. You have a problem with it, take it up with Director Killiany. I'm sure she'll be happy to replace you as CO of the 22nd."

That caused the major to roll her eyes. "Don't push me, Wrangler. You really think your little teep squad can do anything to *me*?"

"You really think Ilsa Killiany can't bend the universe to her will?"

Ndoci just stared at Mal for a second. Then she turned around. "Captain Spaulding!"

The captain, a young man with a large nose and a small mustache, snapped to attention. All the other Marines stopped talking.

"Yes, ma'am," Spaulding said.

"Let's get a move on, Captain."

Spaulding smiled. "Yes, ma'am. Ten-*hut*!"

All the Marines snapped to attention.

"Fall *in*!"

With the exception of the two in charge, each Marine entered the Valkyrie through the rear hatch in rank order: first the sergeants, then the corporals, then the privates.

Ndoci looked at Mal. "It's your mission, Agent Kelerchian."

"Then let's get to it, Major." Mal climbed into the Valkyrie and took a seat on one of the two benches, each of which sat fifteen, on either side of the rear compartment. Mal took the seat on the right side closest to the front, which required him to walk past twenty Marines who refused to make eye contact with him.

As Ndoci and Spaulding followed him in and took up the seats facing each other at the rear end of the Valkyrie close to the hatch, Mal subvocalized to tell his computer to patch him in to the pilot.

"Yes, sir," came the voice of the pilot, an older woman with the appropriate name of Fleet. She was up in the cockpit, along with the copilot and the Valkyrie's medic.

"Lieutenant Commander Fleet, this is Agent Kelerchian. We're ready to go at your discretion."

"Roger that, sir." At Fleet's command, the hatch closed. *"Prepare for takeoff."*

Spaulding then barked out, "Who's the best?"

As one, the twenty soldiers of the 22nd said, "The Annihilators, sir!"

"Who's the best?"

"The Annihilators, sir!"

"Who's the best?"

"The Annihilators, sir!"

"Who's not the best?"

"Everybody else, sir!"

"Let's do it."

"Yes, sir!"

With that, the Marines put on their helmets and started running their final systems and weapons check, as the Valkyrie took off with sufficient smoothness that Mal barely felt it—just a mild amount of pressure against his feet and rear end. He made a mental note to commend Fleet on her piloting skills when this was over.

Figuring it couldn't hurt, Mal told his computer to do a check on his bodysuit—particuarly the psi-screen, which he'd activate as soon as they arrived. In particular, he wanted to make sure the force field worked properly.

He had a bad feeling that bullets were going to fly before this day was over.

Markus almost gagged when he went to the back room. Dani's body was still lying there in the hallway. *Dammit, he couldn't even call Wolfgang?* Deciding it was best to call him, he pulled out his fone before he went into the back room and did so himself.

But Wolfgang didn't answer. That was weird—Wolfgang *always* answered his fone. Markus left a message, then went on back to see Fagin.

The man in question was pacing back and forth in his back room, occasionally kicking the charred remains of his holograph. To Markus, destroying that was one of the few things Fagin had done that made sense. UNN wasn't talking about nothing that wasn't the damn alien invasion—which Markus didn't even think was *real*—and he'd come pretty close to blowing up his own holo this morning.

Fagin was also muttering to himself. Markus couldn't make out what he was saying, and all things considered, he figured he was better off not knowing.

Finally, when he'd been standing in the doorway for half a minute without his boss's noticing, Markus said, "Fagin."

Whipping out his P220, Fagin stopped pacing and pointed the muzzle right at Markus's head. *"What?"*

Holding up his hands defensively, Markus said, "Take it easy, Fagin. Listen, I gotta talk to you." He decided to cover the business first, figuring it would be better to ease into the other thing. "We almost out of hab. When's the re-up coming from Halcyon?"

"Ain't no re-up comin'." Fagin lowered the gun and started pacing again. "Flickers on Halcyon cut us off last month. The Blonde read that one of their couriers was planning something, okay? I shot the guy as a *favor* to them, and what do they do? They cut us off. I'm *this damn close* to renting a shuttle and killing the whole flicking bunch."

Slowly, Markus said, "So, we find a new supply yet?"

That got Fagin to stop pacing again. "What?"

"A new supply."

"New supply of what? Stop sounding like a pan-brain, Markus, I ain't in the damn mood, okay?"

"We need a new supply of hab, Fagin, or—"

"We got Halcyon, we don't need nothin' else."

Damn, damn, damn, it's worse than I thought. "Fagin, listen to me—you gotta take that thing off your head. You *got* to!"

Fagin started laughing. "You *are* a panbrain! I take this off, the Blonde'll fry my brains like an egg. Nah, stud, I *got* to keep this on, or—"

"I talked to Morwood—you're only supposed to wear that thing for seven *hours* at a time, or it causes—"

The P220 came back out. "What the *flick* were you doin' talkin' to Morwood?"

"I wanted to ask him about the thing you wearin'. Fagin, *listen* to me, it's done something to your *head.* You been killin' people for *no reason.* The hab supply's gonna run out. Profits are down all over 'cause people are scared you gonna be shootin' 'em. Everybody's convinced you're gonna do something else all panbrained. I'm not even sure it's gonna work, but you *gotta* take the thing off!"

"I ain't takin' *nothin'* off, okay? And you ain't answered my flickin' question yet. What the *flick*—"

"Hey, Fagin!"

Moving the P220 over to the door, Fagin yelled, "*What?*"

Out of the corner of his eye—he refused to take his eyes completely off Fagin—Markus saw Jo-Jo standing there.

"There's some stud at the door with the gummint. Least, that's what he *said.*"

"No, that's what I *meant.*" Another figure came up

behind Jo-Jo, a tall man dressed in a leather duster over a pristine white thing that covered his entire body, and a holographic badge.

Whirling around, Jo-Jo said, "Crap, stud, I *told* you to wait—"

"You don't tell me a damn thing, kid. I'm a Wrangler—Agent Malcolm Kelerchian—and I'm here to remove Nova Terra from these premises."

"Flick you!" Fagin fired his P220 at the doorway, bullets hitting both Jo-Jo and the confed.

Jo-Jo fell as bullets ripped into his chest and arms and head.

The confed just stood there, bullets stopping right before they would have hit him, then falling to the floor.

As if Markus needed more proof, this indicated that Fagin was seriously fogged. The confeds had the best toys, everybody knew that—especially Fagin, whose mantra had always been never to get on the confeds' sensors.

Calmly, the agent said, "You finished?"

"Get the flick out of my square, you flickin' slike!"

Markus shivered as he saw the look in Fagin's eyes. *He's lost it. He's completely lost it.*

Fagin emptied the rest of his ammo into the confed's force field. The bullets collected at Kelerchian's feet.

After he'd dry-clicked a few times, Kelerchian asked, "*Now* you finished? Nova's been tagged for the Ghost Program. That means the government wants her, and that means you don't get to keep her. Don't try to deny that she's here—I've had a pounding headache since I walked in the door, so I *know* she's in the building. There are two ways this can go. The first is that you turn her over to me like I asked. The other is that I bring the Marines down on your head."

"What?" Fagin was just staring blankly at the confed.

"I got a division of Marines waiting to take this place down. Only thing holdin' 'em back is me. So—you gonna give me Nova Terra?"

"What do you want with me?"

Markus whirled around to see that Nova was standing in the door.

Kelerchian turned around. "Ms. Terra, I'm Agent Mal Kelerchian. I'm a Wrangler—my job is to find telepaths and bring them to the Ghost Program. I've been searching for you for six months." He turned to look at Fagin. "But you've been pretty hard to find."

To Markus's surprise, he started to reach into his jacket pocket for his own P220. *What the hell—?*

"She's mine," Fagin said. "She's mine, you flickin' confed slike, and you ain't takin' her from me, okay?"

Of its own accord, the P220 raised. Markus tried to stop it, but his arms were no longer under his own control.

"You have only two choices, Fagin," Kelerchian said with a hard stare at him. "You give us to her or we take her from your corpse."

"What is the Ghost Program?" Nova asked.

"Shut up, curve!" Fagin shouted, his eyes wild, his arms gesticulating crazily.

His thumb hitting the safety button, Markus started to pull the trigger.

He could have shouted out. He could've warned his target. But he realized that he was under Nova's control. *She never could do this before.*

Besides, he found he didn't want to stop her.

A snarl started to form on Fagin's lips. "Flick you!"

Then Fagin convulsed from the seven bullets that slammed into his back.

Nova stared down at Fagin's corpse. "Six months ago, I told him that one of his trusted lieutenants would kill him."

"Then you lied," Markus said, lowering his arms and grateful for having the ability to do so again. "Two of 'em did."

"I was just doing what you've wanted to do for months now, Markus," Nova said. "Every time we were in the same room together, I couldn't feel anything else, because your desire to kill him was so strong. But I knew you would never do it on your own."

The confed had just been standing there watching this. "I see you've been busy since you killed the people who killed your family."

Nova's eyes went wide. So did Markus's, both at what Kelerchian said and at Nova's surprise. Nova had never been surprised by anything anyone said— except for Fagin, of course.

Shaking his head, Markus thought, *Of course, he's a*

confed. He's got the same toys they all do. Probably wearin'
one of them things that made Fagin fogged.

"How did you know that?" Nova asked in a small
voice. "I saw my sister on UNN, she said—"

"She said what we told her to say." Agent Kelerchian's voice got surprisingly gentle as he went on.
"You've got nothing left, Nova. I can't believe that living here is something you want, given what you just
made this young man here do. And your family's all
gone. We're your best bet." He took a breath. "I'm
wearing a psi-screen. It's—"

"I know what it is," she said quickly. Pointing at
Fagin's corpse, she said, "He wore one."

Kelerchian looked in surprise at where she pointed.
"Where the hell'd *he* get one?"

"Fagin's contacts go all over Tarsonis, stud," Markus
said. "Or they did 'fore that thing made him fogged. He
got it from a guy in the army to keep Nova in line."

"He had people in the *army*?"

Markus nodded, amused at the agent's surprise.

"No wonder I couldn't find crap for six months."

"Problem was, he didn't never take it off."

Now Kelerchian's eyes widened. "*Never*? For six
months?"

"Nope."

"I was wondering how a panbrain like that could
be as powerful as he's supposed to be."

"He wasn't always that panbrained." Markus
looked down at the man who had once been such a
good boss. "He got greedy, I guess."

"They always do," Kelerchian said. Then he turned back to Nova. "Look, I'm gonna turn my psi-screen off. You can read me, learn everything there is to know about the Ghost Program. You'll see it's the best thing for you."

Unlike Fagin's screen, Kelerchian's didn't require him to touch anything. He just nodded, and Nova stared at him.

Then she straightened up. Whenever Nova stood these days, she was all slumped over, like she was trying to protect herself. But when she'd first showed up, Markus had noticed that her posture was damn near perfect. *With her background, that would figure*, he had thought at the time, but six months with Fagin had fogged that posture right up.

Until now. Tears welling in her green eyes, she smiled. Markus hadn't seen her smile since the last time she'd stood up straight.

"Is it true?" she whispered.

Kelerchian frowned. "What was that?"

"Is it *true*? At the end of the training program, you'll take my memories away? *Please* tell me."

"That's become SOP lately." Kelerchian looked concerned now. "Is that a probl—"

The confed's words were cut off by Nova's running up to him and wrapping her arms around his chest. "Thank you thank you thank you *thank* you, Agent Kelerchian, you don't know what this means, thank you *so* much!"

Awkwardly, the confed patted Nova on the back. "Uh,

that's fine, really. Didn't figure that to be the big recruiting incentive. Hell, usually that's the biggest drawback."

"Why the flick not?" Markus asked with a certain heat. "Ain't nothin' down here but crap flowin' down from on high. Only folks that get anythin' here get it for themselves, and most of 'em can't. S'why they all take hab and turk and the rest. They're tryin' to forget. Crap, if there was some way you could give me a brainpan, I'd take it in a flash, it means I can forget this life."

Nova pulled out of the hug; Markus figured the agent was relieved. After sniffling, she said, "Agent Kelerchian, I've killed three hundred and eighty-two people, and felt thirty-two more, including my *family*, die in my head. I can tell you *everything* about *every single one* of those people—*all* four hundred and fourteen of them—including what they were thinking at the moment they died." Her voice was getting louder with each sentence, but then it broke. "What makes you think I want to remember any of *that*?"

A shiver went down Markus's spine, and not just from Nova's words. He tried to imagine what might've been going through the mind of his mother—his *birth* mother, not the woman his father married later—when his father killed her. He wondered if his father's being able to know that would've changed what the man did.

Probably not. Crap, he probably would've enjoyed it more.

Kelerchian nodded. "Fair enough. I'll call—"

Nova suddenly slumped again. "Something's wrong." She put her hands to her head. "No!"

Then the world exploded around Markus.

CHAPTER 17

MAJOR ESMERELDA NDOCI HATED MAL Kelerchian from the moment she set eyes on him.

This had nothing to do with Kelerchian. Esmerelda hated *everyone* the moment she set eyes on them. It saved time.

She had read Kelerchian's file, and knew he was a former cop. Esmerelda hated cops. The bad ones were corrupt leeches who eroded the system of justice from within, and the good ones were arrogant asses who thought they were better than everyone else because of their stupid calling. They were also the most territorial slikes in the whole damn Confederacy.

Kelerchian was one of the good ones, which meant he treated Esmerelda and the Annihilators like something he'd accidentally stepped in. He wasn't going to use them as his Plan A.

Under the right circumstances, Esmerelda could admit that Kelerchian's plan was a good one—if one wanted to avoid bloodshed. But this was not a situation where bloodshed was to be avoided. If it were, Esmerelda would never have been summoned to Director Killiany's office in the first place.

Obviously Kelerchian was trying to cut the Annihilators out of his op, even though he'd been ordered to make them part of it.

That really cracked Esmerelda off.

As a general rule, Esmerelda tried to kill anyone who cracked her off. That option didn't always present itself, especially after she joined the Marines, as she was bound by her orders. In the old days, things were different. She was always grateful that nobody had ever traced any of the bodies back to her. Amusingly, the only death people actually suspected her of—her late, unlamented husband Gregory— was one she was not truly responsible for. Had the brain aneurysm not claimed him when it did, it was perfectly possible that she *would* have eventually engineered his demise, but his sudden death relieved her of that burden, and freed her to find a better channel for her aggression than either soccer or being a wife in an Old Family was ever likely to provide.

Right now, though, her orders bound her to be under Kelerchian's command. He was a Wrangler, so killing him would probably cause difficulties she couldn't work her way out of. The Council took the Ghost Program way too seriously for that to be as easily brushed under the rug as, say, Colonel Tabakin.

The comm unit in her helmet crackled. She was

still sitting in the Valkyrie's rear section, waiting for a signal from Kelerchian.

She'd given the Annihilators leave to remove their helmets. The Wildebeests—A Company—were continuing their perpetual poker game, with the biggest pile of chips remaining in their usual spot in front of Corporal Deaton, though Private Carver had just taken a big hand from Sergeant Vincent, to the sergeant's irritation. Carver would, Esmerelda suspected, be doing early-morning calisthenics for a week. The Bengals—B Company—were doing their usual arm-wrestling competition with D Company, better known as the Dragons. Reigning champion Private O'Neill was going one-on-one with the newest recruit, Corporal Mitchell, with neither of them gaining ground, though the betting had two-to-one odds on O'Neill. The Razorbacks—C Company—were silently cleaning their weapons for the nine thousandth time, as Sergeant Mack was a stickler for cleanliness. As for the Wolverines, most of E Company was hitting Corporal Flanigan with pop-quiz questions, as the corporal was studying for the sergeant's exam. The exception was Sergeant McGillion, who was chatting with Captain Spaulding about sports.

Activating her comm, Esmerelda said, "Ndoci, go." She noticed that Spaulding cut off his conversation with McGillion in the middle of one of the sergeant's tired rants about the Tarsonis Tigers' defensive line, so the comm was going into his headset as well.

"Major, this is General Ledbetter. Your orders have been changed, effective immediately. The Sons of Korhal have penetrated our orbital defenses, and we need you to defend the city."

That got Esmerelda's blood boiling. She never liked the Slikes of Korhal, as she preferred to call them, and the way they were using the deaths of good Confederate soldiers to further their treasonous agenda. "We're to return to base immediately, sir?"

"No." Ledbetter sounded pretty cracked off about that, which meant it wasn't his order, but that of someone over his head. Since the number of people over Ledbetter's head could be counted on the fingers of one hand, that was going some. *"However, you are to complete your current mission with dispatch, Major. Agent Kelerchian is no longer in charge of the op."*

Ndoci grinned. Spaulding never smiled, but he did give a satisfied nod.

"You're to retrieve Nova Terra by whatever means are necessary, and bring her back to Holyktown within thirty minutes."

Ilsa Killiany was one of the people you could count on that hand. They obviously wanted this Terra girl pretty bad, enough to temporarily hold back their best ground unit to defend an invasion at the heart of the Confederacy. Esmerelda could understand why—the Confederates were losing their two-front war against the Zerg and the Protoss, and the only reason they were keeping *any* ground was because of what the Ghosts were doing. But they were also dying—or, in the case of that treasonous slike Sarah Kerrigan, defecting—at a great rate, so new recruits were vital.

"Roger, sir. You'll have her. Ndoci out."

Spaulding immediately got to his feet. "Ten-*hut*!"

The poker game, pop quizzes, weapon cleaning, and arm-wrestling all ceased and the twenty Annihilators stood at attention.

"Boys and girls, we're going in in two. The bosses want the Terra girl back in Holyktown in half an hour—we're gonna do it in twenty. Suit up." Opening a line to the cockpit, she said, "Fleet, prepare for insertion. Head for the roof."

"Roger that."

Two minutes after she gave the order, they were all helmeted and standing at attention, ready to go in.

Spaulding yelled: "Who's the best?"

"The Annihilators, sir!"

"Who's the best?"

"The Annihilators, sir!"

"Who's not the best?"

"Everybody else, sir!"

"Let's do it. Plan Bravo."

"Yes, sir!"

Esmerelda and Spaulding had put together a series of plans for hard-target searches. Bravo was the one where a) the target was in a multistory building and b) collateral damage was very much not an issue.

Certainly nobody was going to give a damn if they trashed the Gutter. Hell, if they didn't have to retrieve the target alive, Esmerelda would've let the Annihilators stay at camp and nuked the whole Gutter from orbit, and made Tarsonis a better place.

Fleet put down on the roof of the building, and the back bulkhead of the Valkyrie opened into a ramp with a whir.

Esmerelda looked at her troops. "You all have the target's profile. I remind you that Nova Terra is a Class-A target. Anybody here gives her so much as a paper cut, they'll be in the stockade by nightfall. Am I clear?"

All the Annihilators said, "Yes, ma'am!"

"Anybody else you encounter is expendable. These people are Gutter trash—they contribute nothing of value to the Confederacy, except for a cheap labor force, and that's a resource that's infinitely replaceable."

Sergeant Mack raised a hand.

Esmerelda nodded. "Sergeant?"

"Ma'am, what about Agent Kelerchian?"

"What part of 'anybody else' wasn't clear, Sergeant?"

Nodding, Mack said, "Yes, ma'am. Question withdrawn, ma'am."

"Good. Wildebeests, go."

Sergeant Vincent led A Company down the ramp, their armored boots clanging on the metal of the ramp in perfect time. They would secure the roof and upper floors.

"Fleet, bring us to the middle floors."

"*Roger that.*"

Moments later, the rear of the Valkyrie was facing the side windows. "Bengals, go."

Sergeant Hammond didn't lead B Company down—Mitchell went first, firing on the windows with his wrist cannons, blowing them inward to clear the way. The rest of the Bengals followed, with Hammond taking up the rear.

Moments later, C Company did the same on the other side, Mack leading the way with his incredibly clean wrist cannon.

The Valkyrie—which was a stealth craft, and so would be unseen and unheard by those inside, though the breaking glass and armored troops were creating something of a ruckus—landed silently outside.

"Spaulding, you and the Dragons secure the perimeter, ten meters around the building. Anyone crosses it, shoot 'em."

"Yes, ma'am," Spaulding said.

"Fleet, get back on the roof, be ready to go at a moment."

"Roger that."

Spaulding took D Company out to secure the street. Esmerelda saw some people running away, others milling around, others staring blankly.

"Wolverines, with me."

"Yes, ma'am," said McGillion.

As Esmerelda led E Company toward the front door, she caught in her peripheral vision someone walking toward O'Neill. "Hey, what the flick you people—?"

O'Neill raised an arm.

The man held up his hands, but kept walking forward. "Hey, look, I don't want no trouble, just want to know what the flick—"

As soon as he got within ten meters of this Fagin person's building, O'Neill fired a dozen rounds from his wrist cannon into the intruder, who fell to the ground in a bloody heap.

People started running away after that. Esmerelda smiled. Although she had a thing for carnage, sometimes just one death did the trick properly. Luckily for her, the Marines had provided her with opportunities for both.

Unholstering her P500—which she'd used to kill quite a number of Zerg these past few weeks—Esmerelda shot a hole into the front door control, and then kicked the now-useless door in with her armored boot.

Four people in a small receiving area of some kind jumped up. Two were armed. The others were counting money. Esmerelda put a bullet in each of their heads. Actually, the power of the P500 was such that the shots destroyed their entire heads north of the jawline, with the exception of the third person she shot. He moved a bit, so the round took only about half his head off. One dead eye looked up at her as brains oozed out of the halved skull.

She looked around at the sound of gunfire. Apparently B and C Companies were getting resistance.

Then the ground shook and plaster started falling from the ceiling. Just the fact that it *was* plaster made Esmerelda realize that she had made a tactical error. *Dammit. Forgot these buildings were put together on the cheap. The structure can't handle—*

The rest of the thought was cut off by the ceiling collapsing on her head.

When he saw the ceiling collapse, the first thing Mal did was tell the computer to put his force field on full.

The second thing he did was dive for Nova to protect her. She was a Class-A target, after all.

Besides, leaving aside the consequences of letting a Class-A come to harm, it would just be embarrassing after six months of chasing to let her die now that he'd finally found her.

That Ndoci and her merry band of demolition experts surprised Nova with their attack was to be expected, since their helmets were equipped with the same psi-screens that Mal was using—and, for that matter, that the late Fagin had been using. However, it was also a surprise to Mal, by virtue of the fact that he didn't order it.

If I live through this, Major, I am definitely getting Killiany to crawl right up your ass. I don't care who you used to be married to, this is crap, and you're gonna pay for it.

Nova was already on the floor, having collapsed to her knees just before the ceiling buckled, so it was easy enough for Mal to blanket her with his body, using the force field to protect them.

"Creatures coming everywhere, can't stop them, everywhere you go, they consume it all . . ."

Mal's back started to hurt as much as his head was. The head was a lost cause—five doses of analgesic didn't even begin to slow it down while he was in the same room as Nova—but the back might be a problem. The force field could withstand most any force in theory, but it was as subject to gravity as anything else. It felt like the entire ten-story building was weighing down on Mal's back. The advantage armor had over a force field was that the former enhanced one's own strength, allowing one to, for example, get up from a prone position with a ton of plaster and wood and steel on one's back by simply pushing it off. Sadly, the force field did nothing to provide Mal with the ability to do that. Had he been standing, he might have been able to force his way through, but being stomach-down on all fours like this provided him with no leverage whatsoever.

". . . death and destruction, they're everywhere, swarming all over the place, oh no, Markus, he's dead, he died hating me and wishing I would die and wishing he could've killed his father . . ."

Mal remembered that Markus was the young man whom Nova had telekinetically manipulated into shooting Fagin. A pity Markus was dead, as he had seemed a more reasonable person to deal with, and might have been able to bring the stability to Fagin's organization that Larry Fonseca had been afraid to lose.

That, however, was the least of Mal's problems. Nova was becoming rapidly more incoherent, and now the computer was telling him that the force field was starting to show indications of failure, and recommended that it be shut off for maintenance.

That's not gonna happen.

Since his mouth was right next to her right ear, Mal said, "Nova, I need you to focus."

". . . dying everyone, all around me, nobody living, everybody falling apart . . ."

This time he shouted. "*Nova*! Listen to me!"

The sudden loudness got her to at least stop talking.

"You need to get us out of here." He thought as loud as he could, in the way that they'd trained him to do when dealing with teeps, *Nova, focus on me and on getting us out of this predicament.*

The computer warned him that force field collapse was imminent, and to shut it down to avoid irreparable damage to the suit.

Mal was a lot more concerned about irreparable damage to the suit's wearer. *Nova, listen to me, you have to get this debris off of us before—*

"I understand," she whispered. "Be quiet, please, I'm concentrating."

"Good."

Then the force field failed, and pain smashed into Mal's back and crushed his rib cage against his spine and something hit the back of his head so hard that his head swam and he couldn't feel his legs, and then he mercifully blacked out.

Malcolm Kelerchian's pain sliced through Nova's mind, and almost stopped her from lifting the debris of ten stories' worth of building off her. But then she moved past it and pushed with everything she had.

It didn't work.

So she pushed harder. She thought about Fagin and what he did to her, and Markus and how he always was nice to her and killed Fagin for her, and Pip and her worry about what happened to the poor cat that she was never allowed to return to find (though Nova had asked, *begged* Fagin to let her), and Clara and how much she hated her for lying on UNN, about Nova dying, and all four hundred and twenty-eight people whose deaths she felt, from her family and Gustavo McBain on down to Markus and thirteen others who had just been knocked by a group of Confederate Marines, and the Marines themselves and Nova's fury at them for almost getting her killed.

All of that helped her focus her energy on getting the debris off.

She stood up to find herself in a disaster area. Most of the building's superstructure jutted into the air like the bones on an animal carcass, the steel beams were charred and pitted in spots, and the plaster-and-wood meat for those bones was piled in jagged pieces all around her.

The minds of the Marines were not entirely clear—

they had psi-screens, but they weren't as good as the ones Agent Kelerchian or Fagin had, so Nova could hear bits and pieces. She did know that the leader of this group was Major Esmerelda Ndoci and that she hated Agent Kelerchian.

An armored form was stomping through the debris, moving awkwardly. "I found her!" the Marine said. After a second, Nova figured out that this was Corporal Flanigan; he was part of E Company, which was nicknamed the Wolverines after a wild animal from Old Earth, he was studying for his sergeant's exam, he was convinced he would fail it, he hated his younger brother because the corporal's childhood sweetheart married his brother instead, and he regularly had sexual fantasies involving Major Ndoci and chocolate sauce.

Two more armored figures approached a minute later. One was Sergeant McGillion, who always wanted to be a doctor, but washed out of medical school and joined the Marines to avoid the ridicule of his family. His psi-screen was better than Flanigan's, probably because of his superior rank, so while she knew all that, she didn't know McGillion's first name.

The other armored figure was Major Ndoci. The only thoughts of hers Nova could detect were relief that Nova seemed unharmed and glee that Agent Kelerchian was a bleeding mess sprawled across the only part of the floor that wasn't covered in debris.

"You're Major Ndoci," she said. For the first time in over six months, she managed to summon up the tattered remains of her highborn station, and tried to channel as much of Andrea Tygore into her voice as she could. "My name is Nova Terra. Agent Kelerchian just saved my life from your people destroying this building. I know from Agent Kelerchian's thoughts that violation of my person is a criminal offense, and also that, as at least a PI8, my reading of those thoughts will be considered in evidence at your court-martial. I also know that you can't do a thing to me, because if you don't bring me back intact, it'll be as good as violating the Class-A directive. I'm telling you this because if you make sure that Agent Kelerchian gets medical attention and if he survives and recovers, I won't provide that testimony."

Major Ndoci said nothing at first, and Nova couldn't read her thoughts through the screen. Finally, she spoke: "Not bad for a little girl. It's a deal."

"I stopped being a little girl when I became the slave of a crime lord down here. The only reason why I haven't torn the armor you're wearing apart is because I *want* to go into the Ghost Program. In fact, if you had just waited another five seconds, Agent Kelerchian would've told you that himself. That is something else I will withhold from the authorities, unless Agent Kelerchian dies."

"Fine. Fleet, get the Valkyrie down to my position, and have Scheeler standing by."

Lieutenant Commander Fleet was the pilot of the conveyance that had brought Agent Kelerchian and the Marines to the Gutter; Sergeant Scheeler was the conveyance's medic. Moments later, the air vehicle silently came down to hover about three meters above the debris line, expertly weaving between the beams of the superstructure. A ramp folded out of the back to hover one meter above the debris line. As soon as it finished unfolding, a woman in armor—Scheeler—came down. Her armor was similar to that of the Marines, except that it was all white, with the traditional red cross of the medical community on the shoulders.

While Scheeler put Agent Kelerchian on her stretcher, Nova turned to Major Ndoci. "Thank you."

"You're not welcome. If it was up to me—"

"If it was up to you, Major, you would just have nuked the Gutter from orbit, and you're right now thinking of ways to do it anyhow." Before the major could say what was on her mind in response to that, Nova said it for her: "And you hate telepaths."

"Get on the Valkyrie before I shoot you, and flick the consequences."

Nova came within a hairsbreadth of killing the major herself, but she had seen more than enough death, and she suspected she'd see more.

Because what made her collapse on the floor right before the Marines attacked wasn't the Marines.

It was the Zerg. They were on Tarsonis.

Nova had known of the Zerg only from the incomplete and misleading reports on UNN, but now that they'd arrived on her homeworld, she knew everything she needed to know about them.

Right now, humanity needed people like Major Ndoci—and, if it came to that, Nova herself—to kill the Zerg before they destroyed the entire human race.

CHAPTER 18

WHEN MAL WOKE UP, THE FACE OF A SURLY-looking nurse was gazing down on him.

"You're awake," the woman said in a dull mono-tone. "Doctor'll want to talk to you."

With that, the nurse walked off. Mal realized he felt funny, as if his body were trying to float up off the bed, which was about when he realized as well that he was lying on a bed—which only made sense, given that he was being looked down on by a nurse.

Then he remembered why he would be in a hospital.

What he didn't know was why this hospital was fly-ing through space. At least, that was his assumption, based on the slightly lighter gravity and the way the bed was vibrating ever-so-slightly. It wasn't something easy to notice, but Mal had always been prone to space-sickness, which was one of about a thousand reasons why he stuck with a job that kept him dirtside.

A man in a uniform Mal didn't recognize came into his view. He held a status board in one hand and a cup in the other. Tall, with sandy hair and blue eyes, the man looked like a recruitment poster model. "Good to see you're awake, Agent Kelerchian. I'm Commander Hunnicutt of the Dominion Navy Medical Corps. You're on the *Pasteur*."

That was an organization Mal didn't recognize, but he did know the ship—it was a hospital ship assigned to the Confederate Army. He tried to speak, but his throat was dry.

Hunnicutt handed him the cup. Weakly—his arms felt like they were made of rubber—Mal reached for it. The cup was cold to the touch.

"Ice chips," Hunnicutt said. "Should help lubricate you."

Mal nodded in response and started gulping down the ice chips. His teeth ached with the chill, but his throat felt better.

"I'm sure you have many questions."

"Yeah, I do." Mal didn't recognize his own voice, so scratchy was it. "What the flick is the Dominion Navy Medical Corps, and how'd you guys get the *Pasteur*?"

Hunnicutt smiled, showing perfect teeth. "I'm afraid there've been some changes over the weeks you've been unconscious. The Confederacy of Man is no more—it's been replaced by the Terran Dominion. Director Bick will fill you in on the rest when he arrives."

"Director Bick?"

"Your boss." Hunnicutt took a stylus and made some notes on the status board. "He's been alerted that you're finally conscious, so he's shuttling over from the *Scimitar*."

The *Scimitar* was another Confederate Army vessel. "What the hell're you—?"

Holding up a hand, Hunnicutt said, "I'm afraid I'm not authorized to answer anything nonmedical, Agent Kelerchian."

Mal sighed. "Fine, then, what's wrong with me?"

"Not much anymore. You should count your blessings, Agent Kelerchian. Your spine was fractured, and you had dozens of broken bones. If the Marines hadn't gotten you to the medical facility on Osborne when they did, you might've been paralyzed for life even if you survived. However, you'll be happy to know that I foresee a full recovery, with some spinal treatments, a few new bones, and a few months of physical therapy."

This, like everything that had come out of Hunnicutt's mouth, confused Mal, particularly the notion that he owed his life to Ndoci's goons. "Why was I brought to Osborne?"

"It was the only orbital facility that was still secure, and it was the flash point for the evacuation." Hunnicutt paused, seeming to weigh his words, then stopped. "I've said too much."

In fact, he hadn't said nearly enough as far as Mal was concerned, and Mal fully intended to get the truth out of him. "When'll we be returning to Tarsonis?"

Hunnicutt suddenly became intent on his status board. "Director Bick will be able to answer those questions."

Mal had conducted enough interrogations in his time to read the doctor's expression—going back to Tarsonis was not on the agenda. *Mengsk must've gotten through.*

The doctor whispered some instructions to the nurse, who had rematerialized without Mal's noticing—or caring that much—and then looked toward the bed. "I'll be back to check on you later."

"I'll be counting the nanoseconds."

Smiling insincerely, Hunnicutt said, "So nice to see you're regaining your sense of humor." Then he left, the nurse following behind.

Mal looked around. It was a pretty standard-looking hospital room—no windows, but that wasn't surprising if they were on a ship. Usually only generals—or admirals, he guessed—got the use of plasteel in their cabins, and maybe their offices. Otherwise, he was hooked up to a monitor the display of which was facing away from him—perish forbid he should actually know aspects of his own health before a doctor does.

He also had the room to himself. There were no other beds, and Kelerchian wondered what he had done to deserve the VIP treatment.

The vibration in the bed changed, and Mal got a little queasy. Then, after about a minute, the vibration went back to what it was. Mal figured that was this Director Bick person's shuttle docking.

I wonder what happened to Killiany. He suspected he wouldn't like the answer one bit.

A moment later, the door slid open to reveal a

bulky man in a suit. He had shaved his head, and the stubble on his head indicated that, if he hadn't, he'd be mostly bald anyhow. He had a round head balanced on a round body, and piercing blue eyes.

"Agent Kelerchian, good to see you up and about," he said in a scratchy voice. "My name is Kevin Bick. I run the Ghost Program."

"What happened to Director Killiany?"

"There've been a few changes since—"

"So Commander Hunnicutt said."

Bick turned to glare at the door. "He wasn't supposed to tell you anything."

"He didn't reveal the *nature* of those changes, just that there were some—which, frankly, I would've worked out on my own by his rank, his uniform, and the name of the service he's in."

"Fair point." He took a breath. "The Confederacy of Man is no more, Agent Kelerchian. Tarsonis fell to the Zerg—"

"To the *Zerg*?" That shocked Mal. He thought that it was Mengsk who was threatening the homeworld, not the aliens.

"Yes. With the Council destroyed, the human race has been united under a new leader, who will bring us to salvation from the alien hordes that are trying to destroy us."

Mal rolled his eyes. "Let me guess—King Arcturus I?"

"Emperor Mengsk is not someone to trifle with, Agent Kelerchian," Bick said frostily. "You'd do well to remember that. In any case, the emperor saw no reason to dissolve the Ghost Program, though it has moved its headquarters to the Ghost Academy on Ursa. That's where we're headed."

"Who's 'we' in this case?"

"We've picked up some refugees from a few worlds that have been overrun by the Zerg who've asked for Dominion help. We've also got some new Ghost recruits for the program."

"What about Nova?"

At that, Bick smiled. Mal hadn't thought it was possible for Bick to be any uglier, but the smile went and proved him wrong. "She's our star pupil. I've never seen anyone so determined to make it through this program."

"Director, I've been a Wrangler for over a year, and I have no recollection of you having anything to do with the Ghosts in any of that time, so I'm curious how many people you've seen in this program at all."

The smile fell. "Get some rest, Agent Kelerchian. You've got a long recovery ahead of you." He turned to leave.

"You haven't answered all my questions, Director."

Bick stopped and turned around. "What question haven't I answered, Agent Kelerchian?"

"What happened to Director Killiany?"

A pause. Then: "If the human race is to survive, Agent Kelerchian, it needs unity. Old rivalries must be set aside. People who can't do that—"

"Are expendable."

"We understand each other," Bick said with a nod. With that, he left.

So Killiany refused to play ball with the new emperor. Either Mengsk had her arrested, or she ate her gun. Figures.

He still had many questions, but he wasn't so sure he wanted the answers to them. If Tarsonis really had been overrun by the Zerg, right after Mengsk was rumored to be attacking Tarsonis's defenses, it meant that the Confederacy's seat of government was set up by the new monarch in order to facilitate his takeover.

Funny—he never once said he wanted power, merely wanted to stop the Confederacy's abuses. Probably refused the crown twice before accepting it, too. That lousy slike.

He wondered what happened to the Gutter. Whatever the evacuation plan was, he doubted anyone down there was part of it. Whoever the Annihilators left alive were probably killed by the Zerg. Fagin's people, Martina Dharma, Sergeant Volmer, Larry Fonseca . . . *Are any of them still alive? Probably not.*

Mal stared at the ceiling for a long time before the nurse came in and pressed a few buttons, and then Mal found himself involuntarily drifting off to sleep.

Weeks later, Mal found himself on Ursa, undergoing grueling physical therapy sessions in order to make his legs remember all the things they used to do naturally. Mal had never realized just how much *work* walking actually entailed.

When he wasn't in physical therapy sessions, he

floated around in a convalchair, which not only kept him off his weakened legs, but had nanoprobes that monitored and repaired and maintained his battered body parts.

He'd been thoroughly debriefed by Bick, who also filled him in on the specifics of what had gone on in the weeks he was unconscious. To Mal's regret, Major Ndoci and her Annihilators were still going strong, now part of the Dominion Marines, and boasting the best Zerg kill rate among all the Marine divisions.

Mal also checked up on Nova, though he never spoke to her. He would spend time in the observation rooms that were located above the training center, watching her learn various martial arts skills each morning, practicing her psionic skills in the afternoons, and working on weapons training in the evenings.

One day, while he was watching Nova and four other trainees running an obstacle course under the watchful eye of Sergeant Hartley, Mal was joined by an imposing figure with a thick mustache. Looking up at the man from his convalchair, Mal recognized the face instantly. "Mr. Mengsk. Or should that be 'Your Holiness' now?"

A smile peeked out from under the mustache. " 'Mr. Mengsk' will do for now, Agent Kelerchian, as long as it's the two of us in the room. In public, I prefer 'Mr. Emperor.' "

Mal nodded. "That's good—you don't insist on a title like 'Your Highness' that elevates you too high. 'Mister' is a common honorific, the same one used by democratic governments for their politicians. Keeps your man-of-the-people image intact, despite being an absolute monarch."

Mengsk chuckled. "I'm impressed, Agent Kelerchian. None of the Wranglers I've met—the ones who survived the Zerg attack on Tarsonis, anyhow—are especially intuitive. They simply use the tools at hand." Another chuckle. "Which raises the question of why it took you six months to find that young girl."

Turning away to watch the five trainees doing twenty push-ups on their fists, Mal shrugged as best he could in the convalchair. "Maybe I'm not as smart as you think I am."

"I suppose anything's possible."

"Anyhow, you know the answer to that. When authority doesn't help the people, the people don't help *them*. Nobody in the Gutter wanted to help me find a little girl, especially after she became the tool of someone the people in the Gutter liked and respected." Smiling wryly, he added, "You understand that—it's why people are calling you 'Mr. Emperor' now. The Council and the Old Families only cared about themselves and only did things for themselves, so when the Zerg and the Protoss showed up, the people in charge were completely unequipped to do anything for the people they were supposed to serve. They were so busy improving their own position, they forgot about what the position was. In the end, it killed both them *and* the people. Paving the way for you."

"A remarkably canny observation for someone who

was on a hunt or unconscious when most of this happened."

Mal snorted. "Been catching up on UNN a lot the past week or two. Nice of you to keep it intact."

"The people deserve to know the truth."

That prompted a bark of derisive laughter from Mal. "The next time UNN gets anywhere near the truth will also be the first time."

To Mal's surprise, Mengsk came back with a more genuine laugh of his own. "Perhaps."

"No 'perhaps' about it." He turned to watch the trainees. They had switched to a different type of push-up, with their fists together on the floor, their legs spread a bit wider, and pushing up and down so their chests landed on their wrists. "I see you kept the program intact."

"There were a few elements of the Confederacy that were worth keeping. The Ghost Program was one of them. I know firsthand how effective the Ghosts are."

"I'm sure you do. It's 'cause of you that trainees have their memories wiped when they graduate."

Putting his hand over his heart, Mengsk said, "I had nothing to do with Sarah Kerrigan's defection to my cause, Agent Kelerchian. She did that of her own free will. I merely took advantage of your own inability to hang on to her."

The trainees were now doing the push-ups on one fist, the left one. Their right hands were gripping their left wrists. All but one of the trainees were struggling mightily with this configuration, the exception being Nova.

No, that wasn't fair—she was struggling, but she

wasn't letting it stop her. The others were collapsing onto the floor, getting themselves yelled at by Hartley or simply unable to rise, which resulted in a similar outcome, but Nova refused to give in to her own body's frailty.

"Of course, not everything's the same," Mal said, as much to see how Mengsk reacted as anything. "New person in charge, for a start."

"I can assure you, Director Bick believes in the program as much as his predecessor."

More of the party line from the man who drew it. "No he doesn't. Believe me, I'm the first person to list Ilsa Killiany's faults, but she viewed her role as head of this program as a calling, because she believed in the Confederacy and wanted to protect it from those that would destroy it. That's probably why she didn't fit into your new world order. Bick, though, he only believes in whatever his superiors tell him. He couldn't care less about protecting the Terran Dominion, he just wants to keep you happy so he'll stay employed." Raising a hand to cut off Mengsk's likely rebuttal of this, Mal quickly added, "Hey, I'm not complaining. Bick's type is a lot easier to work for." Then he looked up at Mengsk. "Assuming I am working for him."

Smiling enigmatically, Mengsk said, "We'll see."

Then he left the observation room, leaving Mal alone to watch Nova train.

CHAPTER 19

THE PART OF THE GHOST ACADEMY THAT NOVA found herself looking forward to the most was the physical training in the morning.

Well, no, that wasn't entirely true. The part she *really* was looking forward to was the end of it, when she would be relieved of having to remember her past life.

But until that time, what she was anticipating most eagerly every day was the physical training.

The other stuff was certainly useful. The afternoon training in her psionic skills was something she wished someone in her family had the foresight to give her years ago. So much of her childhood made more sense now—especially why she always seemed to know how other people felt when nobody else did. She had gone through her youth thinking Zeb in particular to be horribly insensitive—which he was, at least by her standards, but she now knew it wasn't by choice. Mommy had always called her ability to see

the servants' points-of-view "empathic," but Nova
had always assumed her use of the word to be figura-
tive. Being taught by other telepaths and telekinetics
was very useful. The latter were more scarce, as one
needed a PI8 or higher to be telekinetic. Nova was not
a PI8. The Wrangler had simply guessed she was at
least that because of her telekinesis, just as she herself
had when she'd done her surreptitious research into
her abilities. In truth, she was a PI10, the highest in
the program. That made her afternoon studies all the
more important.

The evening work with weapons and target practice was all fine, though Nova was very bad at it. She
rarely hit the targets she was supposed to hit, and had
trouble holding the bulky hand weapons properly.
Sergeant Hartley yelled at her a lot. The other trainees
were terrified of Hartley, but after six months with an
ever-more-fogged Julius Antoine Dale, it was impossible for her to be at all intimidated by Hartley. Of
course, that just made him yell at her more and push
her harder, but that didn't bother her, either, since she
wanted to be pushed hard—especially during the
morning training.

It wasn't because she was especially good at it. In
fact, she was as bad at the martial arts as she was the
weapons work. Exercise had never been a concern
when she was a scion of the Old Families—they had
other people to do things for them, after all, so indo-
lence was very much the order of the day—and it was
even less of a concern in the Gutter, where she spent

most of her time curled up in a corner being afraid of
Fagin.

As a result, on her first day at the Academy, she
couldn't even do one push-up on her palms, much
less the twenty on her fists that Hartley demanded.
Hartley had explained that the push-ups were to build
upper-arm strength and to toughen the knuckles so
that, as he put it, "you only need to punch someone
the once."

When one of the trainees pointed out that Ghost
uniforms had gloves, so that the toughness of the
knuckles was irrelevant to their training, he was
forced to do an additional forty push-ups.

But Nova hated the fact that she couldn't do those
push-ups, and not because Hartley yelled at her or
because he prodded her to go beyond what she was
physically capable of doing as a malnourished fifteen-
and-a-half-year-old, but because she didn't want anything getting in her way.

For the first time in her life, Nova was able to
choose her own future. Malcolm Kelerchian had told
her of a way she could finally live with the telepathy
that had become her curse, could live a life that had
the positive aspects of the luxurious life she'd lived as
a daughter of the Terra family—such as regular meals
and access to the best technology the Confederacy (or,
rather, the Dominion) had to offer—without the
polite-society expectations that being a scion of the
Old Families entailed.

Besides, if she couldn't do the physical elements,

she couldn't graduate, and she couldn't be brain-panned.

So she pushed herself. When Hartley taught her a sequence of punch combinations that she needed to know, she did not rest until she got it right. When Hartley told her to do forty push-ups on one fist, she forced herself to do them, no matter how much her shoulders and biceps burned with fatigue and how much her muscles refused to cooperate.

Of course, she had to accomplish the other things, too, but she wasn't concerned about that. Time and practice would show her how to hone her telepathy and telekinesis—a process she'd already started in the Gutter, where she had taught herself, under awful conditions, how to manipulate Markus's arms so he'd shoot Fagin—as well as how to handle the weapons. Those were disciplines of the mind, at which Nova had always succeeded in the past.

No, it was her body she wanted more than anything else to be in proper shape for what she was to do.

Besides, she got to wear a psi-screen during the physical training.

She wore it during some of the weapons training, too. The first year, all trainees wore psi-screens when they were training in groups, to avoid distractions. Many of the weapons sessions were one-on-one, so she didn't wear it then, but the physical workouts were always in groups, so they were protected from each other's thoughts.

Her fellow trainees had complained about it, but she loved the peace and quiet it gave her.

After six months at the Academy, she was already farther along than the ones who'd been doing it for a year. She could do forty push-ups on one fist without being too out of breath, could fieldstrip a Torrent shotgun in under a minute, had scored above ten with the Lockdown gun (only the trainees in their final year ever scored as high as ten), was able to effectively screen out the thoughts of anybody in the room (the hardest trick for as powerful a telepath as her wasn't reading minds, but *not* reading them), and had a decimeter's precision with her telekinesis. Hartley had even let her start training on a Vulture, even though that wasn't supposed to come until the second year.

She knew what the other trainees thought of her. Every once in a while, at night in her bunk—trainees slept alone, as it was felt that roommates would be distractions—she would open up her mind and listen to everyone around her. *Teacher's pet, always (I bet she's sleeping with Hartley) sucking up to Hartley, that kinda (how else would she rate this treatment?) thing just makes me sick. (Nobody's really that good, she's just) I so want her, that (faking it with her teek powers, probably) supple body, especially now that (moving around the psi-screen some-how,) she's all toned, mmm, that's (probably working with that confed) nice. Maybe if I can get up the courage to talk to her, (who brought her in, the lousy slike.) something will happen.*

But it didn't matter. All this was a means to an end—specifically, the end of her memories. Because, while she had mastered the art of closing off her mind to the thoughts around her, the thoughts in her head wouldn't go away that easily.

. . . Mommy and Daddy and Zeb and Eleftheria dying at the hands of the rebel group . . .

. . . Edward, Adam, Tisch, McBain, Geoffrey, Paul, Walter, Derek, and all the other rebels she killed . . .

. . . Maia, Natale, Rebeka, Marco, Doris, Yvonne, and all the other servants she killed in her grief . . .

. . . Ursitti, Manning, Cox, Dion, and the other seventy people Fagin ordered her to kill . . .

. . . Jewel, Jo-Jo, and all the other people Fagin killed in front of her . . .

. . . Markus dying when the Marines destroyed Fagin's building . . .

She needed the voices to *stop*. Brain-panning was the only way it was going to happen, and the only way she'd get that brain-panning was to finish her training.

One morning, on her way to breakfast, she saw Agent Kelerchian.

Nova had heard that he had been in a conval-chair, but apparently he had moved onto the next stage of healing, as he was now walking with bracers on his thighs. It made his steps awkward, but she knew that they were an aid to making his legs work again.

"Agent Kelerchian. It's good to see you well." She

couldn't read his thoughts, as she had already turned on her psi-screen.

"Same here," the confed said with a nod. He joined her on the way to the mess hall. She was kind enough to slow down to keep pace with his slower gait. "I wanted to talk to you before I shipped out."

That surprised her, given that he hadn't made a full recovery. "You're leaving?"

"There's a report of a teep on the Sakrysta Mining Base—it's low-G, so my legs can handle it a little better." He chuckled. "And I have *got* to get out of here. I spent six months spinning my wheels looking for you, then another six months sitting in that damn chair. I need to get my ass back out in the field, and apparently His Holiness has decided that I'm still worthy of being a Wrangler."

"What would you have done if Emperor Mengsk had decided not to keep you?"

A clouded look came over Kelerchian's face, and Nova found herself switching off the psi-screen for a second.

I sure as hell (This coffee tastes like crap) hope they don't have waffles (Why won't she look at me?) again, I **(Mengsk wants me dead.)** *swear I will murder (One of these days, Hartley is just gonna have to die, I mean, die really.) somebody if I have (really slowly.) to eat another waffle.*

Kelerchian recovered and lied: "I'd just get a job as a cop somewhere. I was a good detective on Tarsonis, I can be one somewhere else."

Nova understood. This was a dangerous mission, one the emperor didn't expect Kelerchian to return from. If he did, by some miracle, then Mengsk might reconsider his decision.

I'm never going to see him again, she thought as she turned the psi-screen back on. He deserved his privacy, and he obviously wanted to keep up a brave face for her. But even if he survived this mission, when she was brain-panned after this was all over, she wouldn't remember him.

"Thank you for everything, Agent Kelerchian."

He smiled. "It's Mal."

She smiled back. "But you hate the name Malcolm."

That got a chuckle. "Hence my preference for Mal. In any case, I didn't really do anything for you."

"You saved me, Mal. I'll always be grateful to you for that." She hesitated. "Well, okay, I'll be grateful to you until my training's done."

"Fair enough." He held out a hand.

She grabbed the hand and pulled him into a hug. "*Thank* you, Mal. I mean it—you did save me."

"Glad I could do it for *somebody*."

Nova wondered what he meant by that. Then she remembered Tarsonis, and just nodded into his shoulder.

Suddenly she broke the hug and looked into his scared brown eyes. "You wanna join me for breakfast?"

He opened his mouth, closed it, then opened it again to say, "Yeah, okay, sure."

They went into the mess hall together.

It was the one and only time in all her two and a half years at the Academy that Nova was ever late for her morning session. Sergeant Hartley said, "Arrive late and you'll *be* late," one of his infamous aphorisms, before making her do fifty push-ups as punishment.

But it was worth it.

EPILOGUE

The darkness drops again. . . .
—William Butler Yeats, "The Second Coming"

The average Ghost Academy trainee graduated after four years. Attempts to accelerate the program had proven disastrous, as rushing training of this nature simply resulted in bad Ghosts, which did the Dominion no good.

However, the program was such that an above-average trainee could graduate sooner, maybe in as few as three years. (A below-average trainee simply was removed from the Academy permanently.)

In the entire history of the Academy, under two different human governments, only one trainee had made it out in as few as two and a half years: Nova Terra.

Not that she was out yet. As she stood in the jungles of Tyrador VIII trying to figure out the best way to kill Cliff Nadaner, she found herself wishing this was over, and that she was brain-panned already.

But first she had to kill Nadaner.

She had almost laughed in Emperor Mengsk's face

when he summoned her to his office. He had been wearing a psi-screen, of course—it wouldn't do for his thoughts to get out—and had said to her: "You've done quite well for yourself, Ms. Terra."

As if she hadn't already known that.

"One thing we've added to the Ghost Academy training since we took it over from the late, unlamented Confederacy is a graduation exercise. A field mission, as it were, that shows you're able to apply the classroom to the real world. This is especially an issue with you, who went through the program so fast."

Nova had said nothing. This was the emperor, after all, the one who wanted Mal dead, the one who'd stopped the Confederacy all by himself. If she was honest with herself, she knew he was also indirectly responsible for her family's death, since the Sons of Korhal had inspired a huge number of copycat rebel groups, including the one run by Cliff Nadaner.

So she had been rather surprised by Mengsk's next words.

"Your assignment is to kill Cliff Nadaner. We've tracked his location to Tyrador VIII. He's been agitating against the Terran Dominion, and it has to stop."

He had said more things, but Nova had barely paid any attention to them. Besides, she had known that everything he said would be in a file prepared for her perusal. *Nadaner. The man who ordered my family killed.*

Interestingly enough, Mengsk had not mentioned her family at all. She still wondered if he knew or not.

Not that she cared all that much. Whatever the reason, Nova had found it fitting that the last mission she'd undergo as herself, so to speak, was to kill the man who'd been responsible for destroying her life.

"Good luck, Ms. Terra."

"Thank you, sir," she said with all the politeness her tutors had taught her during her first fifteen years, skills that she was surprised hadn't atrophied in the three years since she'd used them last.

Then they brought her to Tyrador VIII.

Nadaner had started telling another story. It was an even bigger lie than the previous two.

Nova came to a decision.

The exact location of Nadaner and his people was a few meters below a metal hatch that was hidden by the overgrowth of the jungle, as well as the damping field that had led her here. Reaching out with her mind, she ripped out the overgrowth and tossed it aside. Then, using the techniques they'd taught her at the Academy, she looked for teek traps—defenses against telekinetic tampering, booby traps that would go off right in Nova's face if she wasn't careful.

After a moment, she realized she needn't have bothered. Nadaner hadn't anticipated a telekinetic. *More fool him.*

She ripped the hatch off its hinges and tossed it aside. It was heavy, so it took some effort, but she managed it.

Cocking her assault rifle—which she had brought as backup in case she encountered unexpected opposition or wild animals—she leapt down into the hatch, having telepathically determined that Nadaner and his people weren't right under it.

They were about ten meters to the right of the hatch, and they were very surprised to see a young blonde in a white-with-navy-blue-trim bodysuit, holding a very large gun, leap in through the hole where their hatch used to be.

Twelve people leapt to their feet, some less steadily than others. All of them had had something to drink—except for Cephme, who was allergic to alcohol—and many were very drunk.

A second later, they were all dead. Steve, who was looking forward to another opportunity to kill many people at once. Pratikh, who joined up because Arcturus Mengsk killed his cousin, and he wanted Mengsk dead in revenge. Cephme, who hated not being able to drink with the others. Yvenna, who loved hearing Nadaner's stories, even though she knew they were lies. Ray, who wanted to be back home on Halcyon with his girlfriend. Geraddo, who wished Nadaner had some *real* drinks tonight instead of his usual swill. Alexandra, who was starting to get hungry. Thom and Joan, who'd just gotten married. Joel, who'd just gotten divorced. Alessio and Peter-Michael, the twins who secretly hated each other, but never did anything apart. And David, who hated everybody and everything, and joined Nadaner's cause so he could have a focus for that rage.

She killed all of them in a second. The first time she

deliberately killed someone—the Pitcher—it had taken a supreme effort. Ursitti, the cop who'd been skimming, had been even more difficult. Now, though, killing thirteen people was easier than snapping fingers.

Nova hadn't wanted to kill anymore, but she knew there was no choice.

Besides, these slikes targeted my family.

The only one who hadn't risen was also the only one she didn't kill. This was Cliff Nadaner. A tall, broad-shouldered man with receding dark brown hair and a hook nose, Nadaner didn't look like all that much.

But she knew better. She felt his hatred for the governments of humanity, making no real distinction between the Confederacy and the Dominion. He was a self-proclaimed anarchist, though he didn't believe in the true chaos that was required for proper anarchy.

Most of all, though, she felt his fear. He looked around at the corpses suddenly at his feet, blood oozing out of every orifice in their heads, then looked frantically up at her.

"What are you?"

She smiled, and started walking slowly toward where he sat. "I'm what you made me, Cliff Nadaner. I'm the product of your psychosis. You hate the idea of anybody being more successful than you, so you take it out on them. Koji at the factory wins employee-of-the-month more than you, so you arranged for the accident that crippled him. But it didn't work, they just gave the award to Mika instead. So you joined the Marines. But you couldn't succeed there, either—passed over for promotion *six* times, then they drummed you out. With nowhere left to go, you formed your own little band of rebels—but never got Mengsk's press. There were the Sons of Korhal, and then the other guys. Then Mengsk actually did what you wanted to do—he took over."

Again, Nadaner asked, "What *are* you?"

"You ordered the destruction of the Terra family. You managed to turn Edward Peters against them. But you made one mistake, Cliff. You left one of them alive."

Realization dawned on Nadaner's face. "Oh no. Oh no no no. You're the one who—"

"Yes, Cliff." She had walked to within a meter of him now, and Nadaner was eyeing her assault rifle warily. "I'm the one who killed all your people. I killed Edward and Gustavo and Adam and Tisch and all the other ones you sent to kill my family. Because you did that, I eventually became the very Ghost that the Dominion has assigned to finally put an end to your pathetic existence."

Falling out of his chair, Nadaner got down on his knees and clasped his fists together. Tears were streaming down his cheeks. "Please, no, I'm begging you, don't kill me. I'll do anything, please, I'll do it, just ask, it's yours!"

Nova stared at the man who'd ruined her life. She

had been looking forward to this moment, in many ways, for three years, but now that it was here, she was disgusted. This brilliant mastermind who had plotted the utter destruction of the entire Terra family was just another bully, no better than the people she'd met in the Gutter every day.

She had walked over to him intending to blow Nadaner's head off with the assault rifle, but now she decided he wasn't worth the bullets.

"Can you give me my life back?"

"Huh? No, I mean, I can get you money, or—"

Nova killed him.

Before his bleeding-through-the-eyes body could even hit the floor of this underground bunker, Nova had turned around and walked back to the hatch. Telekinetically lifting herself up to the surface, she then paused to catch her breath. Carrying her own weight was always tricky, and she couldn't do it for very long, as it required a high level of focus. It was certainly nothing she'd try in a fight. . . .

She activated the comm unit that had lain dormant since she got in the drop-pod, and said only two words: "It's finished."

Now, it's really over. Nadaner's dead—and soon, for all intents and purposes, I will be, too.

Six days ago, people claiming to be working with the Korprulu Liberation Front—an organization dedicated to the overthrow of Emperor Mengsk—had taken over a munitions factory on New Sydney. With the deadliest new prototype weapons sitting there for the taking, with the entire staff of the factory their hostages, and with the factory itself a maze of tunnels, catwalks, and twisted corridors, the KLF fully believed that it had the place secured.

Valley Johanssen knew she just had to wait it out. Sooner or later, the rest of her KLF reinforcements would arrive. They were en route now, taking care to follow a circuitous route to avoid Dominion detection. Once they got there, they'd go beyond this lousy factory, and take over all of New Sydney. It would be the KLF's greatest victory.

She had guards at every entry point, each wearing a helmet with state-of-the-art detection equipment. Nobody could get anywhere near them without their knowing it.

That, at least, was what Johanssen believed.

The guard at the north entrance didn't see the lithe form that snuck past him with consummate ease. Neither his incredibly sophisticated equipment nor his rather ordinary eyes were capable of penetrating the baffling fields generated by the white-with-navy-blue-trim suit she wore.

None of the other guards saw the Ghost, either, until and unless she wanted them to.

Her mission was to limit casualties. This takeover indicated a flaw in Dominion intelligence, and so they needed as many alive as possible so they could be questioned.

Of course, she could shut down their brains without killing them. She only did that to a few, though—the ones who weren't due to check in for a little while.

Johanssen was talking to a Dominion negotiator over a screen. The negotiator was pretending to do his job; Johanssen didn't believe that any of his offers were legitimate. And she was right, they weren't, but not because the negotiator was trying to lead her on. He was simply stalling while the Ghost made her move.

The best defense they had was the force field. It didn't stop her—the force field only reacted to something it could detect, and with the suit activated, the Ghost couldn't be detected—but it prevented assault vehicles from attacking the factory. Johanssen was standing right next to the control for the force field, which she had given a new code so that only she could deactivate it.

On a whim, the Ghost went visible. Johanssen whirled around, whipping up a P1000 she'd taken out of this very factory. "How the hell'd you get in here? Who are you?"

"You have two choices, Valley. You can surrender, or I can take down the force field and let in the Grizzly that's standing by over the ridge to rain fire down on you and what's left of your people. I'd take the surrender. It's not like you're ever going to get your brother back anyhow, so there's no point in—"

"Flick you." Johanssen fired the P1000.

The bullets didn't leave the chamber, thanks to the

Ghost's keeping them there telekinetically, so the P1000 exploded in Johanssen's face. She fell to the floor, clutching her burned and bleeding head.

Walking over to the force field control, the Ghost reached down and grabbed one of Johanssen's hands away from her face with her mind. Johanssen fought the Ghost with what willpower she had left after having had a gun blow up in her face, but it was no use.

She typed in the code to lower the force field. It was coded to Johanssen's DNA, so it had to be her hand that did it, which the Ghost had thought to be a nice touch.

"You gonna surrender now?"

Pulling a knife out of her boot with her other hand, Johanssen said, "Long live the KLF!"

Before Johanssen could stab herself in the heart, the Ghost telekinetically removed the knife from her hand. "Sorry, you don't get off that easily. That Grizzly will be here any minute to take you away."

Minutes later, the large metal door to this room—which the Ghost had moved through effortlessly, thanks to her suit—was blown off by a Grizzly, a five-person tank that could take on a small army all by itself.

However, there was no army to take on, and Johanssen finally realized she was defeated, and surrendered.

Major Esmerelda Ndoci of the Annihilators and four of her troops were on the Grizzly. "Why the flick did you even call us in if you took care of it?" she asked angrily.

The Ghost shrugged. "I knew you wanted to break something."

Ndoci shook her head. "You're still a stupid slike, you know that?"

Frowning, the Ghost asked, "Have we met before this mission?"

The major started to say something, then stopped. "Never mind."

Nova Terra shrugged. Nothing mattered prior to when she'd become a Ghost. Maybe in her previous life she and Ndoci had crossed paths. She couldn't imagine it, but she didn't try very hard, either.

Turning on her suit's stealth mode again, she departed the factory without another word. Ndoci could handle the cleanup, and she had to report back to base for her next mission. After all, the enemies of the Terran Dominion were everywhere, and the Ghosts were the best line of defense against them.

It was all Nova ever thought about.

ABOUT THE AUTHOR

KEITH R.A. DeCANDIDO is the author of over two dozen novels, plus whole bunches of novellas, short stories, eBooks, comic books, and nonfiction, all in a wide variety of media universes. This is his second foray into the world of Blizzard Games, following the recent *World of Warcraft* novel *Cycle of Hatred*. He's also written in the milieus of *Star Trek* (in all its incarnations, plus some new ones), Spider-Man, the X-Men, *Resident Evil*, *Buffy the Vampire Slayer*, *Serenity*, *Farscape*, *Andromeda*, *Xena*, and a whole lot more. He is also the author of the high-fantasy police procedural *Dragon Precinct*, and the editor of many anthologies, most recently the award-nominated *Imaginings* and the *Star Trek* anthologies *Tales of the Dominion War* and *Tales from the Captain's Table*. His work has journeyed to several bestseller lists, and has received critical acclaim from *Entertainment Weekly*, *Publishers Weekly*, *TV Zone*, *Starburst*, *Dreamwatch*, *Library Journal*, and *Cinescape*, among others. When he isn't writing or editing, he can be seen playing percussion in a Manhattan club or at a science fiction convention, or practicing *kenshikai* karate. He lives in New York City with his girlfriend and two lunatic cats. Find out too much about Keith at his official Web site at DeCandido.net, keep up with his ramblings on LiveJournal under the rather goofy user name of "kradical," or just send him silly e-mails at keith@decandido.net.